Fawcett Crest Books
by Jeffrey Archer:

KANE & ABEL

SHALL WE TELL THE PRESIDENT?

Shall We Tell the President?

Jeffrey Archer

FAWCETT CREST • NEW YORK

A Fawcett Crest Book
Published by Ballantine Books

Copyright © 1977 by Jeffrey Archer

ISBN 0-449-20806-0

This edition published by arrangement with The Viking Press

Feature Alternate Selection of the Literary Guild

Acknowledgments

Chappel Music Company: from "At Long Last Love" by Cole Porter. Copyright © 1938 by Chappell & Co., Inc. Copyright renewed, assigned to John F. Wharton, Trustee of the Cole Porter Musical and Literary Trusts International Copyright Secured. All Rights Reserved. Used by permission.

Jobete Music Co. Inc.: From "Didn't We" by Jimmy Webb. Copyright © 1967 by Jobete Music Co. Inc. Used by permission.

Printed in Canada

First Fawcett Crest Edition: October 1978
First Ballantine Books Edition: December 1982
Fourth Printing: December 1984

To: ADRIAN AND ANNE

NOTE

Although certain well-known people
have roles in this story,
their portrayals and their actions
beyond the known public record
at the time of writing,
are entirely the work of
the author's imagination.

PERSONAL ACKNOWLEDGMENTS

The author would like to thank all those people
involved in giving advice and
helping with the research for this book.

WASHINGTON:
At The White House
Barry McPherson,
Special Counsel to President Johnson

At the FBI
Clarence Kelley — The Director
Nick Stames — Special Agent in Charge,
Washington Field Office
Bill Gunn — Public-Relations Office

Society of Former FBI Agents
Paul Lamberth
John Flatley

Researchers
Cynthia Farrer of Yale
Natalie Wexler of Harvard
Paul Rowe of Harvard

LONDON:
At the American Embassy
Philip Kaiser — The Minister, 1964-69
Bill Kish — Legal Attaché

The Greek Orthodox Church
His Eminence Archbishop Athenagoras
Bishop Gregory

My personal thanks to
Mr. and Mrs. Robert Opeka for the use of their home
in Barbados.
Clive Exton, Robin Oakley, Tony Townsend,
Henry Togna, Peter Snell, Sonja Jordan, and June Robbins.
My wife, Mary, for the hours spent correcting, editing,
and proofreading.

12:26 PM

"I, Edward Moore Kennedy, do solemnly swear . . ."

"I, Edward Moore Kennedy, do solemnly swear . . ."

". . . that I will faithfully execute the office of the President of the United States . . ."

". . . that I will faithfully execute the office of the President of the United States . . ."

". . . and will to the best of my ability, preserve, protect and defend the Constitution of the United States. So help me God."

". . . and will to the best of my ability, preserve, protect and defend the Constitution of the United States. So help me God."

The United States had for the first time in its history produced two brothers to hold the most coveted position in American political life.

His hand still resting on the Douay Bible, the same book on which the Thirty-fifth President had taken the oath, the book which had belonged to their grandmother, the Fortieth President smiled at the Forty-third First Lady. It was the end of one struggle and the beginning of another. Ted Kennedy knew about struggles. After a

9

fierce primary campaign, he had narrowly managed to defeat President Jimmy Carter on the fifth ballot at the Democratic National Convention in Houston, Texas. In November of 1980, he had survived an even fiercer battle with the Republican candidate, Governor James Thompson of Illinois. Edward Kennedy had become President by 147,000 votes, a mere one per cent, the smallest margin in American history.

The next person to take his hand was ex-President Gerry Ford, who had wanted to stand against Kennedy as the Republican candidate, but his 1980 bandwagon had not got off the ground. Now he would never have another chance.

Former President Nixon was absent.

While the applause died down, the President waited for the twenty-one–gun salute to come to an end. Edward Moore Kennedy cleared his throat and faced fifty thousand attentive citizens on the Capitol Plaza and two hundred million more somewhere out there beyond the television transmitters. There was no need for the blankets and heavy coats which had muffled his brother's moment of glory. The weather was unusually mild for late January, and the crowded grassy area facing the east front of the Capitol, although soggy, was no longer white from the Christmas snow.

"Vice President Bumpers, Mr. Chief Justice, President Carter, Vice President Mondale, Reverend clergy, fellow citizens."

The First Lady looked on, smiling occasionally to herself as she recognized some of the words and phrases she had contributed to her husband's speech.

Their day had begun at about 6:30 that morning. Neither had slept very well after the splendid pre-

Inaugural concert given in their honor the previous evening. Kennedy had gone over his presidential address for the final time, underlining the salient words, making only minor changes. Pierre Salinger had called the night before with a line about allowing the nation's children to write history as well as read it. Kennedy liked rhetoric and he managed to fit it in.

Kennedy rose, washed and shaved in silence, and dressed in a dark suit and tie. He glanced out of the bedroom window at the broad placid expanse of the Potomac River, glinting in the early-morning sunlight. He kissed his sleepy wife on the cheek and walked slowly down the stairs to the drawing room, which on three sides resembled a cathedral hewn from oak. Once again, through the fourth wall, of glass, Kennedy could see the Potomac. Today he was to migrate to the other shore.

Through an arched doorway, Kennedy entered the hall. The butler, who doubled as gardener for the five-and-a-half-acre estate, opened the door without a word. He knew where the President-elect was going. The chauffeur, a stranger provided by the White House, stepped forward to greet his new employer as he emerged from the enclosed court through a pair of wooden gates. He was the first to say: "Good morning, Mr. President." Kennedy consulted his wristwatch; the greeting was premature by over four hours. The Twenty-third Amendment would make him the Fortieth President after he had taken the official oath at 12:30 P.M., although the outgoing President and his staff would vacate the office and all its problems on the stroke of noon.

Kennedy preferred to drive his own car. But not today and perhaps not for the next eight years. He slipped quietly into the back of his Pontiac GTO and gazed with affection at his sprawling modern house, a long low building by John Carl Warnecke, the architect who had designed JFK's grave at Arlington National Cemetery. He looked up at a bedroom window, curtains drawn. The three children would still be asleep.

A mile away, on Chain Bridge Road in McLean, Virginia, Robert Kennedy's widow, Ethel, was leaving her house.

The Pontiac pulled out of the circular driveway at a presidential pace, two cars in front and two behind—Kennedy would never be alone again. Yet in one important way, today would be no different from any other Tuesday in the past sixteen years.

The car made its way along the Potomac on the George Washington Memorial Parkway, and up the hill. The five cars came to a halt. There were no reporters on hand. Kennedy got out of the Pontiac, a private citizen for the last time. He had asked for no coverage of this part of the day, and the world press had honored his request. He stood beside the graves of Jack and Bobby and prayed silently, his head bowed. Ethel Kennedy was already there. They spoke briefly.

Fifteen minutes later, after pausing for a moment to stare down across the river at the glistening monumental whiteness of downtown Washington, Kennedy slipped back into the Pontiac that would return him to McLean for the last time. Steven, the cook, had prepared a light breakfast. Joan, Kara, Patrick, and Ted, Jr., were waiting excitedly for him in the breakfast room. The President-elect ate his meal mechanically as he skimmed *The Washington Post* and *The New York Times*. Both papers wanted to give the new Chief Executive as good a start as possible and they made no mention of past scandals. Kennedy turned as his executive assistant, Richard Burke, came to his side.

"Good morning, Senator."

"Good morning, Rick. Got everything under control?" He smiled up at him.

"I think so, sir."

"Good. Why don't you run the day as usual? Don't worry about me, I'll just follow your instructions. What do you want me to do first?"

"There are 842 telegrams and 2412 letters but they will have to wait, except for the Heads of State. I'll have letters ready for them by twelve o'clock."

"Date them today, they'll like that, and I'll sign every one of them."

"Yes, sir. I have your schedule ready. You start the official day with coffee at the White House at eleven with President Carter and Vice President Mondale, then you will be taken to the Inauguration. In your first hours as President, you'll attend a luncheon at the Senate, then review the Inaugural Parade in front of the White House."

Burke passed him a sheaf of three-by-five index cards, stapled together, as he had done every day for five years. They summarized the Senator's hour-by-hour schedule; there was rather less on them than usual. Kennedy shoved the cards into his inside coat pocket, and thanked his executive assistant. Joan Kennedy rose from the breakfast table; the world didn't realize what a competent First Lady she was going to be. Naturally, she had been in the shadow of Jacqueline for many years, and she now intended to show that this Kennedy had also married a determined lady. In a simply cut suit of pale blue, she stood waiting for her husband's next move.

A crowd of well-wishers had already gathered outside the house.

I wish it would rain, said H. Stuart Knight, the head of the Secret Service, to himself; it was also one of the most important days of his life. I know most of these people are harmless, but these occasions give me the jitters.

The crowd numbered about one hundred and fifty; fifty of them belonged to Mr. Knight. The butler helped the President-elect into his morning coat and Florence Evans, their maid, helped Joan to put on her hat at a flattering angle.

The butler opened the front door, handed Kennedy his high silk hat and the crowds began to cheer. H. Stuart Knight tensed slightly. He only hoped that he and Kennedy would be able to retire peacefully. He had been a junior officer on November 22, 1963, but it was still vivid in his memory.

The President-elect and his wife waved to the smiling eyes and barely noticed that fifty people were not looking at them. The advance car that always goes five minutes ahead of a President was already meticulously checking the route to the White House; Secret Service men were watching small gatherings of people along the way, some waving flags; they were there to witness the Inauguration, and would tell their grandchildren they had seen Edward Kennedy on the day he became President of the United States.

The black limousine came to a noiseless stop at the North Entrance of the White House at 10:59 A.M. The Marine Honor Guard stood at attention and saluted the fifty-six-year-old President Carter, who greeted Kennedy on the Portico, a privilege normally accorded only to visiting heads of state. The President guided his successor through to the library for coffee with Rosalynn Carter and Vice President Mondale and his wife, Joan. President Carter wore a dark suit. His slim shoulders and tan made him look remarkably fit for his years, far fitter than the

14

President-elect. Joan Kennedy chatted with Rosalynn Carter; she had spent the whole of the previous Monday with the First Lady going over the White House as any prospective tenant would, and the two women had ended up genuinely liking each other, despite the nomination battle they had been through six months earlier.

The President was grumbling that he would have to rely on Rosalynn's cooking from now on. "She hasn't dirtied a frying pan in ages, but she used to be good some years ago. To make sure, I've given her a copy of *The New York Times Cook Book;* it's about the only one of their publications that hasn't criticized me." Kennedy was nervous. He wanted to get on with the proceedings, but he was conscious that these were Jimmy Carter's last moments in office, and he pretended to listen attentively, donning a mask that was second nature after nearly twenty years in politics.

The President and the President-elect spent an hour going over problems that they had discussed many times during the previous two months, touching on responsibilities that had to be handled even today, as soon as the ceremony was over.

"Mr. President—" Kennedy had to think quickly to prevent anyone noticing his instinctive response to the words Mr. President. "It's one minute past midday." President Carter looked up at his press secretary, rose from his chair, and led the President-elect and his wife to the steps of the White House. The Marine band struck up "Hail to the Chief" for the last time. At one o'clock they would play it again for the first time.

Carter and Kennedy were escorted to the first car of the motorcade, a black, bubble-topped, bullet-proof limousine. The Speaker of the House, Tip O'Neill, and the Senate Majority Leader, Robert Byrd, representing the

Congress, were already seated in the presidential car. Directly behind the limousine there were two cars filled with Secret Service men. Mrs. Carter and Mrs. Kennedy occupied the fourth car in line. The outgoing and incoming vice presidents, Mondale and Bumpers, rode in the next car, and their wives in the limousine behind them.

H. Stuart Knight was going through one more routine check. His fifty men had now grown to a hundred. By noon, counting the local police and the FBI contingent, there would be five hundred. Not counting the boys from the CIA, Knight thought ruefully. They certainly didn't tell him whether they were going to be there or not, and even he could not always pick them out in a crowd. He listened to the cheering of the onlookers reaching a crescendo as the presidential limousine pulled away, on its way to the Capitol.

The four men in the lead car chatted amicably. Kennedy's thoughts were elsewhere. He waved mechanically at the crowds lining Pennsylvania Avenue, but his mind was on another, earlier motorcade. The renovated Willard Hotel, seven office buildings under construction, the tiered housing units that resembled an Indian cliff-dwelling, the new shops and restaurants and the wide landscaped sidewalks passed by. The J. Edgar Hoover Building, which housed the FBI, still named after its first Director, despite several efforts by certain senators to have the name changed. How this street had been transformed in twenty years. A twenty-year cycle, he mused. A January procession in Washington, a November motorcade in Dallas, a cortège, a January procession in Washington . . .

They approached the Capitol and President Carter interrupted the President-elect's reverie. "God be with you, Ted. Remember, if you ever want any help or just

16

chat, I'll be in Georgia. No need to tell you, it's a lonely job. I'll realize what you're going through, so call on me. Anytime." Ted nodded and smiled warmly, it was a Christian gesture in the circumstances. The six cars came to a stop.

Kennedy entered the Capitol on the ground floor. Jimmy Carter waited for a moment to thank the chauffeur for the last time. The wives, surrounded by Secret Service agents and waving to the crowd, made their way separately to their seats on the platform. "There will come a time," whispered Rosalynn Carter to Joan Kennedy, "one of these years, when a man will do what we're doing. He'll wait to watch his wife being sworn in." Meanwhile the chief usher was taking Kennedy quietly through the tunnel into the reception area, Marines saluting at every ten paces. There he was greeted by the Vice President-elect, Dale Bumpers of Arkansas; they stood talking of nothing, each not listening to the other's reply.

The President of the United States, Jimmy Carter, came through the tunnel smiling, the smile of a man relieved of all his burdens. Once again, he and Kennedy went through the formality of shaking hands with one another; they were to do it seven times that day. The chief usher guided the two men through a small reception room onto the platform. For this, as for all Presidential inaugurations, a temporary platform had been erected on the east steps of the Capitol. The crowds rose and cheered for many seconds as the President and the President-elect waved; finally they sat in silence and waited for the change of government.

"My fellow Americans, as I take office the problems facing the United States across the world are vast and threatening. In South Africa, pitiless civil war rages be-

17

tween black and white; in the Middle East the ravages of last year's war are being repaired, but both sides are rebuilding their armaments rather than their schools and farms. On the borders between China and India, and between China and Russia, there is the potential for war among three of the most powerful and populous nations on earth. South America veers between extreme right and extreme left, but neither extreme seems to be able to improve the living conditions of their peoples. Two of the original signatories of the North Atlantic Treaty Organization, France and Italy, are on the verge of surrendering to communism.

"In 1949, President Harry S. Truman announced that the United States stood ready with all its might and resources to defend the forces of freedom wherever they might be endangered. Today, some thirty-two years later, some would say that this act of magnanimity has resulted in failure, that America was, and is, too weak to assume the full burden of world leadership. In the face of repeated international crises, any American citizen might well ask why he should take an interest in events so far from home, and why he should feel any responsibility for the defense of freedom outside the United States.

"I do not have to answer these doubts in my own words. 'No man is an island,' Donne wrote two and a half centuries ago. 'Every man is a piece of the continent.' The United States stretches from the Atlantic to the Pacific and from the Arctic to the Equator. 'I am involved in mankind; and therefore never send to know for whom the bell tolls; it tolls for thee.' "

Joan liked that part of the speech. It expressed her own feelings. She had wondered, though, whether the audience would respond with the same enthusiasm with which they had greeted flights of Kennedy rhetoric in the sixties. The thunderous applause assaulting her ears in wave after wave reassured her. The magic still worked.

"At home, we will create a medical service that will be the envy of the free world. It will allow all citizens an equal opportunity for the best medical advice and help. No American must be allowed to die because he cannot afford to live."

Many Democrats had voted against Ted Kennedy because of his attitude toward Medicare. As one hoary old G.P. had said to him, "Americans must stand on their own two feet." "How can they if they're already lying on their backs?" retorted Kennedy. "God deliver us from men who were born rich," replied the doctor, and voted Republican.

"And so I say to you, my fellow citizens, let the nineteen-eighties be an era in which the United States leads the world in justice as well as in power, an era in which the United States declares war—war on disease, war on discrimination, war on poverty."

The President sat down; in a single motion, the entire audience rose to its feet.

The sixteen-minute, one-thousand four-hundred-and-ten–word speech had been interrupted by applause on ten occasions. But as the new Chief Executive turned from the microphone, now assured that the crowd was with him, his eyes were not on the cheering mass. He scanned the dignitaries on the platform for the one person he wanted to see. With help, she had managed to get to her feet. Rose Kennedy, at ninety, was nearly half as old as America itself. The whole ceremony would have meant much less to the President if his mother had not been present. But there she was—bent, frail, and triumphant. He walked over and kissed her gently.

He then took the arm of the First Lady. They were

accompanied by a briskly efficient usher. Kennedy motioned him away gently. The scene had changed, for EMK was now President and he didn't want to leave immediately. First, he shook hands with the ex-President of the United States, Jimmy Carter, private citizen, and then with those around him who had helped him attain the office.

H. Stuart Knight hated things that didn't run on schedule, and today nothing was on time. Everybody was going to be at least thirty minutes late for the lunch.

Senator Robert Byrd was there to greet the President. His slight frame and unassuming manner belied the authority he wielded as the man who made things happen within the party machine. Byrd had certainly played that role to perfection inside the Democratic Party, forging the alliances that had brought a Kennedy back to power. "Your last unofficial function for at least four years, Mr. President. From now on you eat for your country."

Seventy-six guests stood as the President entered the room. These were the men and women who now controlled the Democratic party. The Northern Establishment had decided they couldn't take another term of the man from Plains, Georgia, who seemed to have more quarrels with his own party than President Ford had had. The final break came when Carter informed the Democrats in Congress that he would go over their heads and directly to the people. More explicitly, in true Georgia style, he told the majority leaders to fish or cut bait. They cut bait and turned to Edward Kennedy.

All of them were now present, with a few exceptions, those who had stood firmly against EMK as the Democratic candidate. As it turned out, there were only a handful of these, since Carter had had virtually no coattail effect on the makeup of Congress: only four elected representatives in both Houses had done worse than Carter in the 1976 elections. Senior Democrats knew what that meant to a man coming up for re-election. Carter didn't. EMK hadn't wanted to run against Carter but after considerable pressure from the grass roots of the party, he had reluctantly allowed his name to be entered in the New Hampshire primary. Neither Kennedy nor Carter campaigned in New Hampshire, and EMK was genuinely surprised to receive fifty-seven per cent of the votes cast; even then, he seemed reluctant to continue, but as each primary went by and his delegates grew, it became inevitable that a battle was going to take place, like the Ford-Reagan struggle of 1976, on the floor of the Democratic National Convention, a battle with a difference: the challenger won on the fifth ballot when Texas swung behind him. The Atlanta wall was broken and Carter was unable to stop the flood. The Texans had never forgiven Carter for describing President Johnson as "a liar and a cheat" in the now historic *Playboy* interview. They had held out for four ballots but not five. Kennedy was the candidate.

Some of those at the luncheon were already members of his cabinet. Many of them had waited eighteen years for this moment; for others, who were younger, this was the beginning of the Kennedy era.

The President shook hands with Abe Chayes, his new Secretary of State, and Jerome Wiesner, the new Secretary of Health, Education, and Welfare. Senator Byrd took the President by the elbow and guided him from person to person; on this day, everybody wanted to touch the President. Soon, like any Kennedy, he was at home in the sea of flesh.

The President had neither the opportunity nor the inclination to eat his lunch; everyone wanted to talk to him at once. The menu had been specially made up of his favorite dishes, starting with lobster bisque and going on to roast beef. Finally, the chef's *pièce de résistance* was produced, an iced chocolate cake, in the form of the White House. Joan watched her husband ignore the neat wedge of the Oval Office placed in front of him. "If they made him President every day, he'd soon be as thin as a rail," she commented to Marian Edelman, who was the surprise appointment as Attorney General. Marian had been telling Joan about the importance of children's rights. Joan tried to listen; perhaps another day.

By the time the last hand had been pumped and the last wing of the White House demolished, the President and his party were forty-five minutes late for the Inaugural Parade. When they did arrive at the reviewing stand in front of the White House, the most relieved to see them, among the crowd of two hundred thousand, was the Presidential Guard of Honor, who had been standing at attention for just over an hour, awaiting the arrival of the President. He took his seat and the parade began. The State contingent in the military unit marched past, and the United States Marine Band played Sousa and "God Bless America." Floats from each state, some commemorating events from Kennedy's life, added color, and a lighter touch to a serious occasion.

When the three-hour–long parade was finally over and the last uniform had disappeared down the avenue, Kennedy's chief of staff, Eddie Martin, who had served as his administrative assistant in the Senate, leaned over and asked the President what he would like to do between now and the first Inaugural Ball.

"Sign all those cabinet appointments and clear the desk for tomorrow," was the immediate reply. "That should only take four years."

The President went directly into the White House. As he walked through the South Portico, the Marine band struck up "Hail to the Chief." The President had taken off his morning coat even before he reached the Oval Office. He sat himself firmly behind the imposing oak and leather desk. He paused for a moment, looking around the room. Everything had been put where he wanted it; behind him there was the picture of John and Robert playing touch football. In front of him, a paperweight with the quotation from George Bernard Shaw which RFK had used so often in his campaigns: "Some men see things as they are and say, why; I dream things that never were and say, why not." On Kennedy's left was the Presidential flag, on his right the flag of the United States. Dominating the middle of the desk was a replica of the aircraft carrier *John F. Kennedy,* made by Teddy, Jr., out of bottle tops and dime-store balsa wood. Coal was burning in the fireplace. A portrait of Lincoln stared down at the new President, who couldn't help recalling that during the Cuban missile crisis, his brother had looked at the picture and said, "I wish you were with us now, Abe." Outside the bay windows, the green lawns swept up in an unbroken stretch to the Washington Monument. The President smiled. He was at home.

He reached for a pile of official papers and glanced over the names of those who would serve in his cabinet. Les Aspin of Wisconsin, Jerome Wiesner of MIT, Robert Roosa of New York, Richard Lamm of Colorado; there were over thirty appointments. The President signed each one with a flourish. The final one was Abe Chayes. The President ordered that the papers be sent to the Congress immediately. His press secretary picked up the pieces of paper that would dictate the next four years in the history of America and said, "Thank you, Mr. President."

It was the first time Hadley Roth, his long-time Senate press secretary, had ever so addressed him. The President was about to comment on it as Joan came into the room to remind him there was only just over half an hour before they ought to be at the family dinner. The President placed his gold Parker pen back into the leather tray on the desk, together with the eleven other Parker pens. They certainly seemed to play it safe at the White House.

"Right, dear. I'll be with you in a moment."

The President chatted with his press secretary as he walked to the private elevator, which would take him to the Presidential Suite. It was so small that he had to lock the doors himself and press the button to the second floor. He wondered what would happen if the President of the United States got stuck in it between floors and they couldn't get him out. But he arrived safely before he could work out a satisfactory solution.

He strolled across the hall into the President's Bedroom as if he had lived there all his life. The four-poster canopied bed in which Truman, Kennedy, and Johnson had slept dominated everything else. He and Joan had decided to use the First Lady's Bedroom, next door, as a sitting room only.

"Joan, do you remember that painting by Monet in the Gold Room that Jack liked so much?"

"Of course, *Morning on the Seine*."

"That's the one. Let's hang it right in this room. You know, Jimmy Carter just told me that I can transfer paintings from the National Gallery to the White House for my term of office."

"Marvelous," said Joan. "Let's get hold of that Picasso of the family on the beach from his blue period—I think

24

it's called *The Tragedy*—and I've always wanted a Turner, even if it's only for four years."

There was a knock on the door.

"Heavens, can't we be alone even in our own bedroom?"

"It's not our own bedroom, it's a historic site."

The upstairs maid entered the room to check that all was in order. She hesitated. It was the first time she had met the President and all he had on was a towel.

"I don't care for the aroma of President Carter's aftershave, but other than that it's all in great shape."

The maid was not sure whether to laugh or remain impassive, so she took the easy way out and smiled ambiguously. The weak humor of the President's joke was partly nervousness and partly relief at having the first major ceremony behind him. Joan Kennedy took a long time getting dressed for the evening and Teddy, who had taken only twelve minutes, marched around the room saying irritably, "I'm supposed to be governing the United States, I'm supposed to be governing the United States."

"I know, darling," said Joan, "but while you're here, could you just do up my zipper?"

The two walked down the sweeping staircase off the Center Hall and joined the entire Kennedy clan in the family dining room. They all stood as the President entered; they hadn't done that since 1963.

"The first ball is at the D.C. Armory and we should go there immediately, Mr. President; we're still running late," said Hadley Roth. Most of the family hadn't finished the second course. Rose Kennedy smiled from the other end of the table and waved at Ted as he left with Joan. The rest of the evening was a whirl, six balls and twenty thousand people, most of them in no doubt whatever that the

President owed his success to the part they had played in the campaign. The President was patient and charming, and Joan and her new Yves Saint Laurent dress lasted the entire evening. They finally arrived back at their new home, 1600 Pennsylvania Avenue. It was 2:30 the next morning.

Back in the Lincoln Bedroom, the silence was broken only by Joan's comment: "I'm glad we only have to do that once every four years. Thank God it can't happen more than twice in one's lifetime." She couldn't help remembering that no President since Eisenhower had served two terms.

The President climbed into bed. "Not very comfortable, is it?" he said.

"Good enough for Lincoln," Joan replied.

The President was about to turn off the light when he saw the small blue Yale edition of Shakespeare's *Julius Caesar* by his bedside lamp. "That belongs in the Oval Office," he muttered. Joan didn't hear him. He opened it almost naturally at page thirty-six and read the passage he had underlined in red ink and marked with an asterisk:

> Cowards die many times before their deaths;
> The valiant never taste of death but once.
> Of all the wonders that I yet have heard,
> It seems to me most strange that men should fear;
> Seeing that death, a necessary end,
> Will come when it will come.

The President turned off the light.
America slept.

3

5:45 PM

Nick Stames wanted to go home. He had been at work since seven that morning and it was already 5:45 P.M. He couldn't remember if he had eaten lunch or not; his wife, Norma, had been grumbling again that he never got home in time for dinner, or, if he did, it was so late that her dinner was no longer worth eating. Come to think of it, when did he last have a full meal? Norma stayed in bed when he left for the office at 6:30 A.M. Now that the children were away at school, her only real task was to make dinner for him. He couldn't win; if he had been a failure, she would have complained about that, too, and he was, goddamn it, by anybody's standards, a success; the youngest special agent in charge of a Field Office in the FBI and you don't get a job like that at the age of forty-one by being at home for dinner every night. In any case, Nick loved the job. It was his mistress; at least his wife could be thankful for that.

Nick Stames had been head of the Washington Field Office for nine years. The third largest Field Office in America, although it covered the smallest territory—only sixty-one square miles of Washington, D.C.—it had twenty-two squads: twelve criminal, ten security. Hell,

27

he was policing the capital of the world. Of course, he would have to be late sometimes. Still, tonight he intended to make a special effort. When he had the time to do so, he adored his wife. He would try to be home on time this evening. He picked up his internal phone and called his Criminal Coordinator, Grant Nanna.

"Grant."

"Boss."

"I'm going home."

"I didn't know you had one."

"Not you, too."

Nick Stames put the phone down, and pushed his hand through his long dark hair. He would have made a better movie criminal than FBI agent, since everything about him was dark—dark eyes, dark skin, dark hair, even a dark suit and dark shoes, but the last two were true of any special agent. On his lapel he wore a pin depicting the flags of the United States and of Greece.

Once, a few years ago, he had been offered promotion and a chance to cross the street to the Bureau Headquarters and join the Director as one of his thirteen assistants. Being an assistant wasn't his style, so he stayed put. The move would have taken him from a slum to a palace; the Washington Field Office is housed on floors four, five, and eight of the Old Post Office Building on Pennsylvania Avenue, and it should have been demolished twenty-five years before, had not Lady Bird Johnson decided that the building was of national importance. The rooms were a little like railroad coaches and would have been condemned as slums if they had been in the ghetto.

As the sun began to disappear behind the tall buildings, Nick's gloomy office grew darker. He walked over to the light switch. "Don't Be Fuelish," commented a fluorescent label glued to the switch. Just as the constant movement of men and women in dark sober suits in and out of the Old Post Office Building revealed the location of the FBI Washington Field Office, so this government graffito served notice that the czars of the Federal Energy Administration inhabited two floors of the cavernous building on Pennsylvania Avenue.

The National Foundation on the Arts and Humanities had long been planning to renovate the old building and transform it into an arts and office center. Plans were complete, but money had not yet been allocated. The General Services Administration was on the lookout for new office space for the FEA and the FBI. In the meantime, however, Nick Stames ran a sophisticated, modern operation out of an architectural dinosaur.

Nick stared out of his window across the street at the new FBI Headquarters, which had been completed in 1976, a great ugly monster with elevators that were larger than his own office. He didn't let it bother him. He'd reached Grade 18 in the service, and only the Director was paid more than he was. In any case, he was not going to sit behind a desk until they retired him with a pair of gold handcuffs. He wanted to be in constant touch with the agent in the street, feel the pulse of the Bureau. He would stay put at the Washington Field Office and die standing up, not sitting down. Once again, he touched the intercom. "Julie, I'm on my way home."

Julie Bayers looked up and glanced at her watch as if it were lunchtime.

"Yes, sir."

As he passed through the office he grinned at her. "Moussaka, rice pilaf, and the wife; don't tell the Mafia." Nick managed to get one foot out of the door before his private phone rang. One more step and he would have made it, but Nick never could resist just checking. Julie rose and Nick admired, as he always did, the quick flash of leg. She was so proportioned that she was incapable of seeing the keyboard of her typewriter. Could he be arrested for seduction in his own office? He'd have to check the federal regulations.

"No, it's all right, Julie. I'll get it." He strode back into his office and picked up the ringing telephone.

"Stames."

"Good evening, sir. Lieutenant Blake, Metropolitan Police."

"Hey, Dave, congratulations on your promotion. I haven't seen you in . . ." he paused, ". . . it must be five years, when you were only a sergeant. How are you?"

"Thank you, sir, I'm doing just fine."

"Well, Lieutenant, moved into big-time crime, now have you? Picked up a fourteen-year-old stealing a pack of chewing gum and need my best men to find where the suspect has hidden the goods?"

Blake laughed. "Not quite that bad, Mr. Stames. I have a guy in Woodrow Wilson Medical Center who wants to meet the head of the FBI, says he has something vitally important to tell him."

"Do you know whether he's one of our usual informers, Dave?"

"No, sir."

"What's his name?"

"Angelo Casefikis." Blake spelled out the name for Stames.

"Any description?" asked Stames.

"No. I only spoke to him on the phone. All he would say is it will be worse for America if the FBI doesn't listen."

30

"Did he now? Hold on while I check the name. He may be a nut."

Nick Stames pressed a button to connect him with the Duty Officer. "Who's on duty?"

"Paul Fredericks, boss."

"Paul, get out the nut box."

The nut box, as it was affectionately known in the Bureau, was a collection of white three-by-five index cards containing the names of all the people who liked to call up in the middle of the night and claim that the Martians had landed in their back yards, or that they had discovered a CIA plot to take over the world.

Special Agent Fredericks was back on the line, the nut box in front of him.

"Right, boss. What's his name?"

"Angelo Casefikis," said Stames.

"A crazy Greek," said Fredericks. "You never know with these foreigners."

"Greeks aren't foreigners," snapped Stames. His name, before it was shortened, was Nick Stamatakis. He never did forgive his father, God rest his soul, for anglicizing a magnificent Hellenic surname.

"Sorry, sir. No name like that in the nut box or the informants' file. Did this guy mention any agent's name that he knows?"

"No, he just wanted the head of the FBI."

"Don't we all?"

"No more cracks from you, Paul, or you'll be on complaint duty for more than the statutory week."

Each agent in the Field Office did one week a year on the nut box, answering the phone all night, fending off canny Martians, foiling dastardly CIA coups, and, above all, never embarrassing the Bureau. Every agent dreaded it. Paul Fredericks put the phone down quickly. Two weeks on this job and you could write out one of the little white cards with your own name on it.

"Well, what's your opinion, Dave?" said Stames to Blake as he wearily took a cigarette out of his left desk drawer. "How did he sound?"

"Frantic and incoherent. I sent one of my rookies to see him. Couldn't get anything out of him other than America ought to listen to what he's got to say. He seemed genuinely frightened. He's got a gunshot wound in his leg and there may be complications. It's infected; apparently he left it for some days before he went to the hospital."

"How did he get himself shot?"

"Don't know yet. We're trying to locate witnesses, but we haven't come up with any so far, and Casefikis won't give us the time of day."

"Wants the FBI, does he? Only the best, eh?" said Stames. He regretted the remark the moment he had made it, but it was too late. He didn't attempt to cover himself. "Thank you, Lieutenant," he said. "I'll put someone on it immediately and brief you in the morning." Stames put the telephone down. Six o'clock already—why had he turned back? Damn the phone. Grant Nanna would have handled the job just as well and he wouldn't have made that thoughtless remark about wanting the best. There was enough friction between the FBI and the Metropolitan Police without his adding to it. Nick picked up his intercom phone and buzzed the head of the Criminal Section.

"Grant."

"I thought you said you'd gone home."

"Come into my office for a minute, will you?"

"Sure, be right there, boss."

Grant Nanna appeared a few seconds later along with

his trademark cigar. He had put his jacket on, which he only did to see Nick in his office.

Nanna's career had a storybook quality. He was born in El Campo, Texas, and received a B.A. from Baylor. From there, he went on to get a law degree at SMU. As a young agent assigned to the Pittsburgh Field Office, Nanna met his future wife, Betty, an FBI stenographer. They had four sons, all of whom had attended Virginia Polytechnic Institute: two engineers, a doctor, and a dentist. Nanna had been an agent for over thirty years. Twelve more than Nick. In fact, Nick had been a new agent under him. Nanna held no grudge, since he was head of the Criminal Section, loved his job, and greatly respected Nick—as he called him in private.

"What's the problem, boss?"

Stames looked up as Nanna entered the office. He noted that his five-feet-nine, fifty-five-year-old, robust, cigar-chewing Criminal Coordinator was certainly not "desirable," as Bureau weight requirements go. A man of five feet nine was required to keep his weight between a hundred and fifty-four and a hundred and sixty-one pounds. Nanna had always cringed when the quarterly weigh-in of all FBI agents came due. He had many times been forced to purge his body of excess pounds for that most serious transgression of Bureau rules, especially during the Hoover era, when "desirability" meant lean and mean. Like many other well-fed agents, Grant realized the benefits of keeping trim, but felt the weight limits were discriminatory when applied to large-framed men like himself, only one year away from retirement under the 1977 change in regulations.

What the hell, thought Stames. Grant's knowledge and experience were worth a dozen slender, young athletic agents who can be found in the Washington Field

Office halls every day. As he had done a hundred times before, he told himself he would deal with Nanna's weight problem another day.

Nick repeated the story of the strange Greek in Woodrow Wilson Medical Center as it had been relayed to him by Lieutenant Blake. "I want you to send down two men. Any idea who you'll assign, Grant?"

"No. Not really, but if you suspect it might be an informer, boss, I certainly can't send Aspirin."

"Aspirin" was the nickname of the oldest agent still employed in the WFO. After twenty-seven years with Hoover, he played everything by the book, which gave most people a headache. He was due to retire at the end of the year and exasperation was already beginning to be replaced by nostalgia.

"No, don't send Aspirin. Send two youngsters."

"How about Colvert and Andrews?"

"Agreed," replied Stames. "Brief them right away, and I'll still make it home in time for dinner. Call me there if it's anything special."

Grant Nanna left the office, and Nick smiled a second flirtatious good-by to his secretary. Julie looked up and smiled nonchalantly. She was the only attractive thing in the WFO. "I don't mind working for an FBI agent, but there is no way I would ever marry one," she said to the little mirror in her top drawer—not for the first time—once she was sure Nick Stames was out of earshot.

Grant Nanna, back in his office, picked up the extension phone to the Criminal Room.

"Send in Colvert and Andrews."

"Yes, sir."

There was a firm knock on the door. Two special agents entered. Barry Colvert was big by anybody's standards, six-feet-six in his stocking feet and not many people had seen him that way. At thirty-two, he was thought to be one of the most ambitious young men in the Criminal Section. He was wearing a dark green jacket, dark nondescript pants, and clumpy black leather brogues. His brown hair was cut short and parted neatly on the right. His tear-drop aviator glasses had been his only sartorial concession to the seventies. He was always on duty long after the official checkout time of 5:30 and not just because he was fighting his way up the ladder. He loved the job. He didn't love anybody else, so far as his colleagues knew, or at least not on more than a temporary basis. Colvert was a Midwesterner and he had entered the FBI after leaving college with a B.A. in sociology from Indiana University and then took the fifteen-week course at Quantico, the FBI Academy. From every angle, he was the archetype of an FBI man.

By contrast, Marc Andrews had been one of the more unusual FBI entrants. After majoring in history at Yale he finished his education at Yale Law School, and then decided he wanted some adventure for a few years before he joined a law firm. He felt it would be useful to learn about criminals and the police from the inside. He didn't give this as his reason for applying to the Bureau—no one is supposed to regard the Bureau as an academic experiment. In fact, Hoover regarded it so much as a career that he did not allow agents who left the service to return. At six feet Marc Andrews looked small next to Colvert. He had a fresh, handsome face with clear blue eyes and a mop of curly fair hair long enough to skim his shirt collar. At twenty-eight he was one of the youngest agents in the department. His clothes were always smartly fashionable and sometimes not quite regulation. Nick Stames had once caught him in a red sports jacket and brown pants and relieved him from duty so that he could

35

return home and dress properly. Never embarrass the Bureau. Marc's charm got him out of a lot of trouble in the Criminal Section, but he had a steadiness of purpose which more than made up for the Ivy League education and manner. He was self-confident, but never pushy or concerned about his own advancement. He didn't let anyone in on his career plan.

Grant Nanna went over the story of the frightened man waiting for them in Woodrow Wilson.

"Black?" queried Colvert.

"No, Greek."

Colvert's surprise showed in his face. Eighty per cent of the inhabitants of Washington were black, and ninety-eight per cent of those arrested on criminal charges were black. One of the reasons the break-in at the Watergate had been suspicious from the beginning to those who knew Washington well was the fact that no blacks were involved, though no one ever admitted it.

"Okay, Barry, think you can handle it?"

"Sure, you want a report tomorrow morning?"

"No, the boss wants you to contact him direct if there is anything special, otherwise just file a report tonight." Nanna's telephone rang. "Mr. Stames on the radio line from his car for you, sir," said Polly, the night switchboard operator.

"He never stops, does he?" Grant confided to the two junior agents, covering the mouthpiece of the phone with his palm.

"Hi, boss."

"Grant, did I say that the Greek had a bullet wound in his leg, and it was infected?"

"Yes, boss."

"Right, do me a quick favor will you? Call Father

Gregory at my church, Saint Constantine and Saint Helen, and ask him to go over to the hospital and see him."

"Anything you say."

"And get yourself home, Grant. Aspirin can handle the office tonight."

"I was just going, boss."

The line went dead.

"Okay, you two—on your way." The two special agents headed down the dirty gray corridor and into the service elevator. It looked, as always, as if it required a crank to start it. Finally outside on Pennsylvania Avenue, they picked up a Bureau car.

Marc guided the dark-blue Ford sedan down Pennsylvania Avenue past the National Archives and the Mellon Gallery. He circled around the lush Capitol grounds and picked up Independence Avenue going toward the Southeast section of Washington. As the two agents waited for a light to change at First Street, near the Library of Congress, Barry scowled at the rush-hour traffic and looked at his watch.

"Why didn't they put Aspirin on this damn assignment?"

"Who'd send Aspirin to a hospital?" replied Marc.

Marc smiled. The two men had established an immediate rapport when they first met at the FBI Academy at Quantico. On the first day of the fifteen-week training course, every trainee received a telegram confirming his appointment. Each new agent was then asked to check the telegram of the person on his right and his left for authenticity. The maneuver was intended to emphasize the need for extreme caution. Marc had glanced at Barry's telegram and handed it back with a grin. "I guess you're legit," he said, "if FBI regulations allow King Kong in the ranks."

"Listen," Colvert had replied, reading Marc's telegram intently. "You may just need King Kong one day, Mr. Andrews."

The light turned green, but a car ahead of Marc and Barry in the inside lane wanted to make a left turn on First Street. For the moment, the two impatient FBI men were trapped in a line of traffic.

"What do you suppose this guy's gonna tell us?"

"I hope he has something on the big bank job downtown," replied Barry. "I'm still the case agent, and I don't have any leads after three weeks. Stames is beginning to get uptight about it."

"No, can't be that, not with a bullet in his leg. He's more likely to be another candidate for the nut box. Wife probably shot him for not being home on time for his vine leaves. You know, the boss would only send a priest to a fellow Greek. You and I could wallow in hell as far as he's concerned."

They both laughed. They knew if either of them were to land in trouble, Nick Stames would move the Washington Monument if he thought it would help. As the car continued down Independence Avenue into the heart of Southeast Washington, the traffic gradually diminished. A few minutes later, they passed Nineteenth Street and the D.C. Armory and reached Woodrow Wilson Memorial Center. They found the visitors' parking lot and Colvert double-checked the lock on every door. Nothing is more embarrassing for an agent than to have his car stolen and then returned by the Metropolitan Police. It was the quickest way to a month on the nut box.

The entrance to the hospital was old and dingy, and the corridors gray and bleak. The girl on night duty at the reception desk told them that Casefikis was on the fourth floor, in Room 4308. Both agents were surprised by the

38

lack of security. They didn't have to show their credentials, and they were able to wander around the building as if they were a couple of interns. No one gave them a second look. Perhaps, as agents, they were too security conscious.

The elevator took them gradually, grudgingly, to the fourth floor. A man on crutches and a woman in a wheelchair shared the elevator, chatting to one another as though they had a lot of time to spare, oblivious to the slowness of the elevator. When they arrived at the fourth floor, Colvert asked for the doctor on duty.

"I think Dr. Dexter has gone off duty, but I'll check," the staff nurse said and bustled away. She didn't get a visit from the FBI every day and the shorter one with the clear blue eyes was so good-looking. The nurse and the doctor returned together down the corridor. Dr. Dexter surprised both Colvert and Andrews. They introduced themselves. It must have been the legs, Marc decided. The last time he had seen legs like that was when he was fifteen and had been to the movies to see Anne Bancroft in *The Graduate*. It was the first time he had ever really looked at a woman's legs, and he had been looking at them ever since.

Elizabeth Dexter, M.D., was stamped in white on a piece of red plastic that adorned her starched white coat. Underneath it, Marc could see a red silk shirt and a stylish skirt of black crepe that just covered her knees. She was of medium height and slender to the point of fragility. She wore no make-up, so far as Marc could tell; certainly her fine skin and dark eyes were in no need of any help. This trip was going to be worthwhile, after all. Barry showed no interest whatever in the pretty doctor and asked to see the file on Casefikis. Marc thought quickly for an opening gambit.

"Are you related to Senator Dexter?" he asked, slightl[y] emphasizing the word Senator.

"Yes, he's my father," she said flatly, obviously used t[o] the question and rather bored by it—and by those wh[o] imagined it was important.

"I heard him lecture in my final year at Yale Law," said Marc, forging ahead, realizing he was showing off, bu[t] that Colvert would finish that damn report in a matter [of] moments.

"Oh, were you at Yale, too? When did you graduate?[?]

"Seventy-six; Law School, seventy-nine," replied Marc[.]

"We might have met before. I left Yale Med in eighty."

"If I had met you before, Dr. Dexter, I would not hav[e] forgotten it."

"When you two Ivy Leaguers are finished swapping lif[e] histories," Barry Colvert interrupted, "this Midwesterne[r] would like to get on with his job."

Yes, thought Marc, Barry deserves to be the Directo[r] one day.

"What can you tell us about this man, Dr. Dexter?["] asked Colvert.

"Very little, I'm afraid," the doctor said, taking bac[k] the file on Casefikis. "He came in of his own volition an[d] reported a gun wound. The wound was septic and looke[d] as if it had been exposed for about a week; I wish he ha[d] come in earlier. I removed the bullet this morning. As yo[u] know, Mr. Colvert, it is our duty to inform the polic[e] immediately when a patient comes in with a gunsh[ot] wound, and so we phoned your boys at the Metropolita[n] Police."

"Not our boys," corrected Marc.

"I'm sorry," replied Dr. Dexter rather formally. "To [a] doctor, a policeman is a policeman."

"And to a policeman, an M.D. is an M.D., but yo[u]

40

also have specialties—orthopedics, gynecology, neurology —don't you? You don't mean to tell me I look like one of those flatfoots from the Met Police?"

Dr. Dexter was not to be beguiled into a flattering response. She opened the manila folder. "All we know is that he is Greek by origin and his name is Angelo Casefikis. He has never been in this hospital before. He gave his age as thirty-eight. Not much to go on, I'm afraid."

"Fine, it's as much as we usually get. Thank you, Dr. Dexter," said Colvert. "Can we see him now?"

"Of course. Please follow me." Elizabeth Dexter turned and led them down the corridor.

The two men followed her, Barry looking for the door marked 4308, Marc looking at her legs. When they arrived, they peered through the small window and saw two men in the room, Angelo Casefikis and a cheerful-looking black, who was staring at a television set which emitted no sound. Colvert turned to Dr. Dexter.

"Would it be possible to see him alone, Dr. Dexter?"

"Why?" she asked.

"We don't know what he is going to tell us, and he may not wish to be overheard."

"Well, don't worry," said Dr. Dexter, and laughed. "My favorite mailman, Benjamin Reynolds, in the next bed is as deaf as a post, and until we operate on him next week, he won't be able to hear Gabriel's horn on the Day of Judgment, let alone a state secret."

Colvert smiled for the first time. "He'd make a hell of a witness."

The doctor ushered Colvert and Andrews into the room, turned on one slim ankle and left them. See you soon, lovely lady, Marc promised himself. Colvert looked at Benjamin Reynolds suspiciously, but the black mailman merely gave a big happy smile, waved, and continued to

41

watch the soundless "$25,000 Pyramid"; nonetheless, Barry Colvert stood on that side of the bed and blocked his view of Casefikis in case he could lip-read. Barry thought of everything.

"Mr. Casefikis?"

"Yes."

Casefikis was a gray, sick-looking individual of medium build, with a prominent nose, bushy eyebrows, and an anxious expression on his face. His hands seemed particularly large on the white bedspread, and the veins stood out prominently on them. His face was darkened by several days of unshaven beard. His hair was thick, dark, and unkempt. One leg was heavily bandaged and rested on the cover of the bed. His eyes darted nervously from one man to the other.

"I am Special Agent Colvert and this is Special Agent Andrews. We are officers with the Federal Bureau of Investigation."

Both men withdrew their FBI credentials from their right inside coat pockets, and displayed them to Casefikis while holding the credentials in their left hands. Even such a seemingly insignificant maneuver was carefully taught to all new FBI agents so that their "strong hand" would be free to withdraw and fire when necessary.

Casefikis studied their credentials with a puzzled frown, pressing his tongue over his lips, obviously not knowing what to look for. The agent's signature must pass partly over the seal of the Department of Justice to insure authenticity. He looked at Marc's card number, 3302, and his badge number, 1721. He didn't speak, as if wondering where to start, or perhaps whether to change his mind and say nothing at all. He stared at Marc, clearly the more sympathetic, and began his tale.

"I never been in any trouble with police before," he said. "Not with any of police."

Neither agent smiled or spoke.

"But I in big mess now and, by God, I need help."

Colvert stepped in. "How do you need our help?"

"I am illegal immigrant and so is wife. We both Greek nationals, we came in Baltimore on ship and we been working here two years. There's nothing to go back to."

It came out in spurts and dashes.

"I have information to trade if we not deported."

"We can't make that sort—" began Marc.

Barry touched Marc's arm. "If it's important and you are able to help us solve a crime, we will speak to the Immigration authorities. We can promise no more than that."

Marc mused; with six million illegal immigrants in the United States, another couple was not going to sink the boat.

Casefikis looked desperate. "I needed job, I needed money, you understand?"

Both men understood. They faced the same problem a dozen times a week behind a dozen different faces.

"When I offered this job as waiter in restaurant, my wife very pleased. On second week I was given special job to serve lunch in a hotel room for big man. The only trouble that the man wanted waiter who not speak English. My English very bad so bossman tell me I could go, keep my mouth shut, speak only Greek. For twenty dollars I say yes. We go in back of van to hotel—I think in Georgetown. When we arrive I sent to kitchen, join staff in basement. I dress and start taking food to private dining room. There five–six men and I heard big man say I no speak English. So they talk on. I don't listen.

43

Very last cup of coffee, when start talking about Kennedy, I like Kennedy, I listen. I heard say, 'We have do it again.' Another man say: 'The best day would still be March 10, the way we planned it.' And then I heard: 'I agree with Senator, let's get rid of him, same as his brother.' Someone was staring at me, so I left room. When I downstairs washing up, one man came in and shouted, 'Hey, you, catch this.' I looked around put arms up. All at once he start come for me. I run for door and down street. He shoot gun at me, I feel bit pain in leg but I able to get away because he older, big and slower than me. I hear him shout but I knew he couldn't catch me. I scared. I get home pretty damn fast, and wife and I move out that night and hide with friend from Greece out of town. Hoped all would be okay, but my leg got bad after few days so Ariana made me come to hospital and call for you because my friend tell they come around to my place look for me because if they find me they kill me." He stopped, breathed deeply, his unshaven face covered in sweat, and looked at the two men imploringly.

"What's your full name?" said Colvert, sounding about as excited as he would if he were issuing a traffic ticket.

"Angelo Mexis Casefikis."

Colvert made him spell it in full.

"Where do you live?"

"Now at Blue Ridge Manor Apartments, 11501 Elkin Street, Wheaton. Home of my friend, good man, please don't give trouble."

"When did this incident take place?"

"Last Thursday," Casefikis said instantly.

Colvert checked the date. "February twenty-fourth?"

The Greek shrugged. "Last Thursday," he repeated.

"Where is the restaurant you were working in?"

"Down next street from me. It called Golden Duck."

Colvert was taking neat notes. "And where was this otel you were taken to?"

"Don't know, in Georgetown. Maybe could take you ere when out of hospital."

"Now, Mr. Casefikis, please be careful about this, was ere anyone else working at this luncheon who might ave overheard what you say you heard?"

"No, sir. I only waiter attend in room."

"Have you told anyone what you overheard? Your ife? The friend whose house you're staying at? Anyone?"

"No, sir. Only you. No tell wife what I hear. No tell no ne, too scared."

Colvert continued the interview, asking for descriptions f the other men in the room and making the Greek repeat verything to see if the story remained the same. It did. Marc looked on silently.

"Okay, Mr. Casefikis, that's all we can do for this vening. We'll come and see you in the morning and have ou sign a written statement."

"But they going to kill me. They going to kill me."

"Please don't worry, Mr. Casefikis. We'll put a police uard on your room as soon as possible; no one is going kill you."

Casefikis dropped his eyes, unassured.

"We'll see you again in the morning," said Colvert, losing his notebook. "You just get some rest. Good night, Mr. Casefikis."

Colvert glanced at a happy Benjamin, still deeply ab- orbed in "$25,000 Pyramid" with no words, just money. Ie waved again at them and smiled, showing all three of is teeth, two black and one gold. Colvert and Andrews eturned to the corridor.

"I don't believe a word of it," Barry said immediately. With his English, he could easily have gotten hold of the

wrong end of the bat. It was probably quite innocen[t]
People are cursing Kennedy all the time. My father doe[s]
but that doesn't mean he would kill him."

"Maybe, but what about that gunshot wound? That['s]
for real," said Marc.

"I know. I guess that's the one thing that worries me,["]
Barry said. "It may just be a cover for something com[-]
pletely different. I think I'll speak to the boss to be o[n]
the safe side."

Colvert headed for the pay phone by the side of th[e]
elevator and took out two dimes. All agents carry [a]
pocketful of dimes; there are no special telephone priv[-]
ileges for members of the Bureau, a regulation that be[-]
came more costly after the rate rose to twenty cents i[n]
1981.

"Well, has he robbed Fort Knox?" Elizabeth Dexter['s]
voice startled Marc, although he had half-expected her t[o]
return. She was obviously on her way home: the whit[e]
coat had been replaced by a red jacket.

"Not exactly," replied Marc. "We'll have to com[e]
around tomorrow morning to tidy things up; probabl[y]
get him to sign a written statement and take his finger[-]
prints."

"Fine," she said. "Dr. Delgado will be here to hel[p]
you. I'm off duty tomorrow." She smiled sweetly. "You'[ll]
like her, too."

"Is this hospital entirely staffed by beautiful lady doc[-]
tors?" said Marc. "Tell me, how do I get sick?"

"Well," she said, "the flu is the fashionable diseas[e]
this month. Even President Kennedy has had it."

Colvert looked around sharply at the mention of th[e]
name. Elizabeth Dexter glanced at her watch.

"I just did two hours unpaid overtime," she said. "[If]
you don't have any more questions, Mr. Andrews, I ough[t]

get home now." She smiled and turned to go, her heels pping sharply against the tiled floor.

"Just one more question, Dr. Dexter," said Marc, fol- wing her around the corner beyond the range of Barry olvert's disapproving eyes and ears. "What would you y to having dinner with me tonight?"

"What would I say?" she said teasingly. "Let me see, think I'd accept gracefully and not too eagerly. It might fun to find out what G-men are really like."

"We bite," said Marc. They smiled at each other. Okay, it's seven-fifteen now. If you're willing to take a ance on it, I could probably pick you up by eight- irty, if you'll reveal where you live."

She jotted her address and phone number on a page of s diary.

"So you're a left-hander, are you, Liz?"

The dark eyes flashed momentarily up to meet his. Only my lovers call me Liz," she said, and was gone.

"It's Colvert, boss. I can't make my mind up about is one. I don't know if he's a jerk or for real but I'd e to run it past you."

"Okay, Barry. Shoot."

"Well, it could be serious, or just a hoax. He may just a small-time thief trying to get off the hook for some- ing bigger. But I'm just not sure. If every word he said rned out to be true, I figured you ought to know im- ediately." Barry relayed the salient parts of the inter- ew without mentioning the Senator, stressing that there as a factor he did not want to discuss over the phone.

"What are you trying to do, get me in the divorce urts—I suppose I'll have to go back to the office," said ick Stames, avoiding his wife's expression of annoy-

ance. "Okay, okay. Thank God I got to eat at least som
of the moussaka. See you in thirty minutes, Barry."

"Right, boss."

Colvert depressed the telephone cradle with his han
momentarily and then dialed the Metropolitan Polic
Two more dimes, leaving sixteen in his pockets. He ofte
thought the quickest way to check out an FBI age
would be to make him turn his pockets inside out; if h
produced twenty dimes, he was a genuine member of th
Bureau.

"Lieutenant Blake is on the front desk now. I'll p
you right through."

"Lieutenant Blake."

"Special Agent Colvert. We've seen your Greek an
we'd like a guard put on his room. He's scared to he
about something and we don't want to take any chances.

"He's not my Greek, damn it," said Blake. "Can't yo
use one of your own fancy guys?"

"There's no one we can spare at the moment, Lieu
tenant."

"I'm not exactly overstaffed myself, for God's sak
What do you think we're running, the Shoreham Hote
Oh hell, I'll do what I can. They may not be able to g
there for a couple of hours."

"Fine. Thanks for your help, Lieutenant. I'll brief m
office." Barry replaced the receiver.

Marc Andrews and Barry Colvert waited for the ele
vator, which was just as slow and reluctant to take the
down as it had been to take them up. Neither of the
spoke until they were inside the dark-blue Ford.

"Stames is coming down to listen to the story," sai
Colvert. "I can't imagine he'll want to take it any furthe
but we'd better keep him informed. Then maybe we ca
call it a day."

Marc glanced at his watch; another hour and forty-five minutes overtime, technically the maximum allowed an agent on any one day.

"I hope so," said Marc. "I just got myself a date."

"Anyone we know?"

"The beautiful Dr. Dexter."

Barry raised his eyebrows. "Don't let the boss know. If he thought you picked up someone while you were on duty, he'd send you to the salt mines in Butte, Montana."

"I didn't know there were salt mines in Butte, Montana."

"Only FBI agents who really screw it up know there are salt mines in Butte."

Marc drove back to downtown Washington while Barry wrote up his report of the interview. It was 7:40 when they reached the Old Post Office Building, and Marc had the whole parking lot almost to himself. By this time, civilized people were at home doing civilized things, like eating moussaka. Stames's car was already there. Goddamn him. They took the elevator to the fifth floor and went into Stames's reception room. It looked empty without Julie. Colvert knocked quietly on the chief's door and the two agents walked in. Stames looked up. He had already found a hundred and one things to do since he'd been back, almost as if he had forgotten that he had specifically come down to see them.

"Right, Barry. Let's have it from the top, slowly and accurately."

Colvert recounted exactly what had happened from the moment they had arrived at Woodrow Wilson to the moment he had asked the Metropolitan Police to put a guard on the room to protect the Greek. Marc was impressed by Barry's total recall. At no point was it exaggerated. At no point was it prejudiced, and it didn't reveal

Barry's own conclusions. The boss hadn't asked for an opinion. Stames thought silently for a few moments and then suddenly turned to Marc.

"What do you think, Marc?"

"I don't know, sir. It was all a bit melodramatic. But he didn't seem to be the type of person who normally lied, and he was certainly frightened and there's no trace of him in any of our files. I radioed the Night Super for a name check. Negative on Casefikis."

Nick picked up the phone and asked to be put through to Bureau Headquarters. "Give me the National Computer Information Center, Polly." He was put through. A young woman answered the phone.

"Stames, Washington Field Office. Would you please have the following person checked out on the computer immediately?—Angelo Casefikis: Caucasian; male; Greek ancestry; height, five feet nine inches; weight, about a hundred and sixty-five pounds; hair, dark brown; eyes, brown; age, thirty-eight; no distinguishing marks or scars known; no identifying numbers known." He was reading from the report Colvert had placed in front of him. He waited silently.

"If his story is true," Marc said, "we should have no listing for him at all."

"If it's true," said Colvert.

Stames continued to wait. The days of waiting a long time to find out who was in the FBI files and who wasn't had long gone. The new computer that had come into service in 1979 could search through the one million profiles stored in its data bank and produce a print-out in a few seconds. The girl came back on the line.

"We have nothing on a Casefikis, Angelo. We don't even have a Casefikis. The best the computer can offer is a Casegikis who was born in 1901. Sorry I can't help, Mr. Stames."

"Thanks very much." Stames put the phone down. "Okay boys, for the moment let's give Casefikis the benefit of the doubt. Let's assume he is telling the truth and that this is a serious investigation. We have no trace of him in any of our files, so we'd better start believing his story until it's disproved; he just might be onto something, and if he is, then it goes way above us. Tomorrow morning, Barry, I want you back at the hospital with a fingerprint expert; take his prints in case he is giving a false name, put them through the identification computer right away and make sure you get a full written statement, signed. Then check the MPD files for any shooting incidents on February twenty-fourth he could have been involved in. As soon as we can get him out, I want him in an ambulance showing us where that luncheon was. Push the hospital into agreeing to that tomorrow morning, if possible. To date, he's not under arrest or wanted for any crime we know about, so don't go too far, not that he strikes me as a man who would know much about his rights. Marc, I want you to go back to the hospital immediately and make sure the Met are there. If not, stay with him until they do arrive. In the morning, go around to the Golden Duck and check it out. I'm going to make a provisional appointment for us to see the Director tomorrow morning, say at ten, which will give you time to report back to me. And if, when we check the fingerprints through the identification computer, nothing comes up at all, and the hotel and the restaurant exist, we may be in a whole lot of trouble. I'm not taking it one hour further without the Director knowing. For the moment, I want nothing in writing. Don't hand in the official memorandum until tomorrow morning. Above all, don't mention that a senator might be involved to anybody—and that includes Grant Nanna. It's possible tomorrow, after we have seen the Director, that we will do no more than make a full report and hand the whole thing over to the Secret Service. Don't forget the division of responsibility —the Secret Service guards the President, we cover federal crime. If a senator is involved, it's us; if the President's involved, it's them. We'll let the Director decide the finer points—I'm not getting involved in Capitol Hill, that's the Director's baby, and with only seven days to play with, we can't sit and discuss the academic niceties here."

Stames picked up the red phone which put him straight through to the Director's office.

"Nick Stames, WFO."

"Good evening," said a low, quiet voice. Mrs. McGregor, a dedicated servant of the Director of the Federal Bureau of Investigation, was still on duty. It was said that even Hoover had been slightly frightened of her.

"Mrs. McGregor, I'd like to make a provisional appointment for myself and Special Agents Colvert and Andrews to see the Director for fifteen minutes, if it's not inconvenient. Anytime between nine and eleven tomorrow morning. It's possible that after further investigation tonight and early tomorrow, I won't have to bother him."

Mrs. McGregor consulted the Director's desk diary. "The Director is going to a meeting of police chiefs at eleven but he is expected in the office at eight-thirty and he has nothing on his diary before eleven. I'll pencil you in for ten-thirty, Mr. Stames. Do you want me to tell the Director what the outline of the subject would be?"

"I'd prefer not to."

Mrs. McGregor never pressed or asked a second question. She knew if Stames called, it was important. He

aw the Director ten times a year on a social basis, but
nly three or four times a year on a professional basis,
nd he was not in the habit of wasting the Director's time.

"Thank you, Mr. Stames. Ten-thirty tomorrow morn-
ng, unless you cancel beforehand."

Nick put the phone down and looked at his two men.

"Okay, we're fixed to see the Director at ten-thirty.
Barry, why don't you give me a lift home, then you can
ake yourself on home afterward, and pick me up again
irst thing in the morning. That'll give us more time to go
ver the details again." Barry nodded. "Marc, you get
traight back to the hospital."

Marc had let his mind slip away to visualize Elizabeth
Dexter walking down the corridor of Woodrow Wilson
oward him, red silk collar over the white medical coat,
lack skirt swinging. He was doing this with his eyes
pen and the result was quite pleasant. He smiled.

"Andrews, what the hell is so amusing about a reported
hreat on the President's life?" Stames demanded.

"Sorry, sir. You just shot my social life down in flames.
Would it be okay if I use my own car? I want to go
irectly from the hospital to dinner."

"Yes, that's fine. We'll use the duty car and see you
irst thing in the morning. Get your tail in gear, Marc.
Hope the Met makes it before breakfast." He looked at
is watch. "Christ, it's already eight o'clock."

Marc left the office slightly annoyed. Even if the Met
were there when he arrived, he was sure to be late for
Elizabeth Dexter. Still, he could call her from the hos-
ital.

"Like a plate of warmed-up moussaka, Barry, and a
ottle of retsina?"

"That sounds great, boss. Sure."

The two men left the office. Stames mentally checked off the items on his nightly routine.

"Barry, will you double-check that Aspirin is on duty, as you go out, and tell him we won't be back again tonight."

Colvert made a detour to the Criminal Room and delivered the message to Aspirin. He was doing the crossword from *The Washington Star*. He had finished three clues; it was going to be a long night. Barry caught up with Nick Stames by the blue Ford.

"Yes, boss, he's working away."

They looked at each other, a night of headaches. Barry got in the driver's seat, slid it back as far as it would go, and adjusted the seat belt. They moved quietly up Constitution Avenue, then past the White House onto the E Street Expressway, and on toward Memorial Bridge.

"If Casefikis is onto something, we've got a hell of a week ahead of us," said Nick Stames. "Did he seem sure of the date for the assassination attempt?"

"When I questioned him a second time about the details, he repeated March tenth, in Washington."

"Hum-uh, seven days, not very long. Wonder what the Director will want to do," said Stames.

"Hand it over to the Secret Service, if he has any sense," Barry said.

"Ah, let's forget it for the moment. Let's think about warmed-over moussaka and deal with tomorrow when tomorrow comes."

The car stopped at a traffic light, just beyond the White House, where a bearded, long-haired, dirty youth, who had been picketing the home of the President, stood with a large poster advising the world: BEWARE THE END IS NIGH. Stames glanced at it and nodded to Barry.

"That's all we need tonight."

They passed under Virginia Avenue on the Expressway and sped across Memorial Bridge. A black 3.5 Lincoln passed them at about seventy miles an hour.

"Bet the cops pick him up," said Stames.

"Probably late for Dulles Airport," replied Barry.

The traffic was light, the rush hour well behind them and when they turned onto George Washington Parkway they managed to pick up more speed. The parkway, which follows the Potomac along the wooded Virginia shore, was dark and winding. Barry's reflexes were as fast as any man's in the service and Stames, although older, saw exactly what happened at the same time. A Buick, large and black, started to overtake them on the left. Colvert glanced toward it and when he looked forward again an instant later, another car, a black Lincoln, had swung in front of them on the wrong side of the highway. He thought he heard a rifle shot. Barry wrenched the wheel around, but there was no time to get clear. Both cars hit him at once, but he managed to take one of them with him down the rocky slope. They gathered speed until they hit the surface of the river with a thud. Nick thought as he struggled in vain to open the door that the sinking seemed grotesquely slow, but inevitable.

The black Buick continued down the highway as if nothing had happened, past a car skidding to a halt, carrying a young couple, two terrified witnesses to the accident. They leapt out of their car and ran to the edge of the slope. There was nothing they could do but watch helplessly for the few seconds it took the blue Ford sedan and the Lincoln to sink out of sight.

"Jee-sus, what the hell happened?" said the young man.

"I don't know. I just saw the two cars go over the top. What do we do now, Jim?"

"Get the police fast."

Man and wife ran back to their car.

8:15 PM

"Hello, Liz."

There was a second's pause at the other end of the phone.

"Hello, G-man. Aren't you getting a little ahead of yourself?"

"Just wishful thinking. Listen, Elizabeth, I've had to come back to the hospital to keep an eye on your Mr. Casefikis until the police arrive. It's just possible that he could be in some danger, so we're having to put a guard on him which means I'm going to be late for our date. Do you mind waiting?"

"No, I won't starve. I always have lunch with my father on Thursdays, and he's a big eater. Still, I'll try to be hungry by the time you arrive."

"That's good. You need to be fed. You look as though you'd be hard to find in the dark. I'm still trying to get the flu, incidentally."

"Keep away from me, then. I don't have immunity just because I heal the sick, you know."

"Hell, what kind of a doctor are you? The next time I get the urge to call you up, I'll take a cold shower instead."

"It may be safer than wishful thinking."

"Safer for who, lovely lady? See you as soon as I can."

"Perhaps, perhaps."

Marc put the telephone back on the hook and walked

over to the elevator, and pressed the arrow on the Up-button.

He only hoped the Met policeman had arrived and was on duty. Christ. How long was the elevator going to take to get to him? Patients must have died just waiting for it. Eventually the doors slid open and a burly Greek Orthodox priest hurried past him. He could have sworn it was a Greek Orthodox priest, from the high dark hat and long trailing veil and the Orthodox Cross around his neck. Something about the priest struck Marc as strange, but he couldn't put his finger on it. He stood, puzzling for a moment, staring at his retreating back and just managing to get into the elevator in time. He pressed the fourth-floor button several times. Come on, come on. Get going, you bastard, but it had no ears for Marc, and proceeded upward at the same stately pace as it had earlier in the afternoon. It knew nothing of his date with Elizabeth Dexter. The door opened slowly, and he went through the widening gap sideways and ran down the corridor to Room 4308 but no cop was on duty. In fact, the corridor was deserted. It looked as if he was going to be stuck here for some time. He peered through the little window in the door at the two men, asleep in their beds, the voiceless television set was still on. Marc went looking for the staff nurse and eventually found her reading in the head nurse's office. She was pleased to see that it was the better-looking FBI man who had returned.

"Has anyone come from the Metropolitan Police to keep an eye on Room 4308?"

"No, no one's been anywhere near the place tonight. Silent as the grave. Were you expecting someone?"

"Yes, damn it. Guess I'll have to wait. Do you think you could find me a chair? I'm going to have to stick around till an officer from the Metropolitan Police comes. I hope I won't be in your way."

"You won't be in my way. You can stay as long as you like. I'll see if I can find you a nice comfortable chair." She put her book down. "Would you like a cup of coffee?"

"I certainly would." Marc looked at her more carefully. It might be an evening with the nurse rather than the doctor, a pity, since the doctor won the competition hands down. Marc decided he would go back and check the room first, reassure Casefikis, if he was still awake, and then call the Met and ask where the hell their man was. He walked slowly to the door a second time; there was no need to hurry now. He opened the door quietly. It was pitch black except for the light from the TV, and his eyes were not yet focused. He glanced at the two. They were very still. He wouldn't have bothered to look any farther if it hadn't been for the dripping.

Drip, drip, drip.

It sounded like tap water but he couldn't remember a tap.

Drip, drip.

He moved quietly to the bedside of Angelo Casefikis, and glanced down.

Drip.

Warm fresh blood was flowing over the bottom sheet, trickling from his mouth, his dark eyes bulged from their sockets, his tongue was hanging loose and swollen. His throat had been cut, ear to ear, just below the chin line. Blood was starting to make a pool on the floor. Marc was standing in it. He felt his legs give, and he was barely able to catch hold of the side of the bed. He lurched over to the deaf man. Marc's eyes were now focused, and he retched loudly. The postman's head was hanging loose from the rest of his body; only the color of his skin showed

58

that they were once connected. Marc managed to get out of the door and to the pay phone, his heartbeat thudding madly in his ears. He could feel his shirt clinging to his body. His hands were covered with blood. He fumbled ineffectually for a couple of dimes. He dialed Homicide and gave the bare outline of what had happened. This time they wouldn't be casual about sending someone. The nurse on duty returned with a cup of coffee.

"Are you okay? You look a bit pale," she said, and then she saw his hands and screamed.

"Don't go into Room 4308 whatever you do. Don't let anyone into that room unless I say so. Send me a doctor immediately."

The nurse thrust the cup of coffee at him, forcing him to take it, and ran down the corridor. Marc made himself go back into Room 4308, although his presence was irrelevant. There was nothing he could do except wait. He switched on the lights and went over to the bathroom; he tried to remove the worst of the blood and vomit from himself and his clothes. Marc heard the swinging door and rushed back into the room. Another young, white-coated female doctor . . . Alicia Delgado, M.D., said her plastic label.

"Don't touch anything," said Marc.

Dr. Delgado stared at him and then the bodies and groaned.

"Don't touch anything," repeated Marc, "until Homicide arrive; they will be here shortly."

"Who are you?" she asked.

"Special Agent Marc Andrews, FBI." He instinctively took out his wallet and showed his credentials.

"Do we just stand here staring at each other or are you going to allow me to do something about this mess?"

"Nothing until Homicide has completed their investigation and given clearance. Let's get out of here." He passed her and pushed the door with his shoulder, not touching anything.

They were back in the corridor.

Marc instructed Dr. Delgado to wait outside the door and to allow no one else inside while he phoned the Metropolitan Police.

She nodded reluctantly.

He went over to the pay phone, two dimes; he dialed the Metropolitan Police and asked for Lieutenant Blake.

"Lieutenant Blake went home about an hour ago. Can I help you?"

"When are you sending someone over to guard Room 4308 at Woodrow Wilson Medical Center?"

"Who's speaking?"

"Andrews, FBI, Washington Field Office." Marc repeated the details of the double murder.

"Well, our man should be there by now. He left the office over half an hour ago. I'll inform Homicide immediately."

"I've already done that," snapped Marc.

He put the phone down and collapsed into a nearby chair. The corridor was now full of white coats. Two gurneys were being wheeled up to Room 4308. They were all waiting. What was the right thing to do?

Two more dimes, he dialed Nick Stames's home. The phone seemed to ring for a long time. Why didn't he answer? Eventually a female voice came on.

Mustn't show panic, he thought, holding on to the phone box. "Good evening, Mrs. Stames. It's Marc Andrews. Can I speak to your husband?" An even tone, no sign of stress.

"I'm afraid Nick is not home, Marc. He went back to

60

the office about two hours ago. Funny, he said he was going to see you and Barry Colvert."

"Yes, we saw him, but he left the office to go back home about forty minutes ago."

"Well, he hasn't arrived yet. He only finished the first course of his dinner and said he would be right back. No sign of him. Maybe he went back to the office. Why don't you try him there?"

"Yes, of course. Sorry to have bothered you." Marc hung up, looked over to check that no one had gone into Room 4308. No one had. He put two more dimes in and phoned the office. Polly was on duty.

"Marc Andrews. Put me through to Mr. Stames, quickly, please."

"Mr. Stames and Special Agent Colvert left about forty-five minutes ago—on their way home, I think, Mr. Andrews."

"That can't be right. It can't be right."

"Yes they did, sir. I saw them go."

"Could you double-check that?"

"If you say so, Mr. Andrews."

Marc waited, it seemed to him, for an interminable time. What should he be doing? He was only one man, where was everyone else? What was he supposed to do? Christ, nothing in his training covered this—the FBI are meant to arrive twenty-four hours after a crime, not during it.

"There's no answer, Mr. Andrews."

"Thanks, Polly."

Marc looked desperately at the ceiling for inspiration. He had been briefed not to tell anybody about the earlier events of the evening, not to say a word whatever the circumstances until after Stames's meeting with the Director. He must find Stames; he must find Colvert. He must find somebody he could talk to. Two more dimes. He tried Barry Colvert. The phone rang and rang. No reply from the bachelor apartment. Same two dimes. He called Norma Stames again. "Mrs. Stames, Marc Andrews. Sorry to trouble you again. The moment your husband and Mr. Colvert arrive, please have them call me at Woodrow Wilson."

"Yes, I'll tell Nick as soon as they come in. They probably stopped off on the way."

"Yes, of course, I hadn't thought of that. Maybe the best thing will be for me to go back downtown as soon as the relief arrives. So perhaps they could contact me there. Thank you, Mrs. Stames." He hung up the receiver.

At exactly that moment the Met policeman arrived, walking jauntily down the middle of the now crowded corridor, an Ed McBain novel under his arm. Marc thought of bawling him out for his late arrival, but what was the point. No use crying over spilt blood he thought, morbidly, and began to feel sick again. He took the young officer aside, and briefed him on the killings, giving no details of why the two men were important, only of what had happened. He asked him to inform his chief and added that the Homicide Squad were on their way, again adding no details. The policeman called his own duty officer, and reported all he had been told, matter-of-factly. The Washington Metropolitan Police handled over six hundred murders a year.

The medical personnel were all waiting impatiently; it was going to be a long wait. Professional bustle seemed to have replaced the early panic. Marc still wasn't sure where to turn, what to do. Where was Stames? Where was Colvert? Where the hell was anybody?

He went over to the policeman again, who was explain-

ng in detail why no one must enter the room . . . they
were not convinced but waited; Marc told him he was
leaving for the Field Office. He still gave him no clue
why Casefikis had been important. The Metropolitan
policeman felt he had things under control. Homicide
would be there at any moment. He told Marc they'd
want to talk to him later that night. Marc left him.

When he arrived back at his car, he took the flashing
red light out of the side compartment and fixed it to the
roof, placing the switch into its special slot. He was going
to get back to the office, at top speed, to people he knew,
to reality, to men who would make some sense out of this
nightmare.

Marc flicked on the car radio. "WFO 180 in service.
Please try and locate Mr. Stames and Mr. Colvert. Urgent. I am returning to Field Office immediately."

"Yes, Mr. Andrews."

"WFO 180 out of service."

Twelve minutes later, he arrived at the Washington
Field Office and parked his car. He ran to the elevator.
The operator took him up. He rushed out.

"Aspirin, Aspirin. Who the hell's on duty tonight?"

"I'm the only one, I'm here on my own," said Aspirin,
looking over his glasses, rather bored. "What's the matter?"

"Where's Stames? Where's Colvert?" Marc demanded.

"They went home just over an hour ago."

Sweet Jesus, what should he do now? Aspirin was not
a man to confide in, but he was the only person Marc
could seek any advice from. And although Stames had
carefully instructed him not to speak to anyone about
anything until they had seen the Director, this was an
emergency. He wouldn't give away any details, he would
just find out what a Hoover man would have done.

"I have to find Stames and Colvert, wherever they are. Any suggestions?"

"Well, first of all, have you tried the car radio stations?" asked Aspirin.

"I asked Polly to check. I'll try her again."

Marc quickly got through to her. "Polly, did you locate Mr. Stames or Mr. Colvert on the car radio?"

"Still trying, sir."

He seemed to wait endlessly, endlessly; and nothing happened. "What's going on, Polly, what's going on?"

"I'm trying as hard as I can, sir. All I can get is a buzzing sound."

"Try One, Two, Three, or Four. Doesn't matter what you try. Try every station."

"Yes, sir. I can only do one at a time. There are four stations and I can only do one at a time."

Marc realized he was panicking. It was time to sit down and be calm. The end of the world hadn't come—or had it?

"They're not on One, sir. Not on Two. Why would they be on Three or Four at this time of night? They're only on their way home."

"I don't care where they're going. Just find them. Try again."

"Okay, okay." She tried Three. She tried Four. She had to have authorization to break the code for Five and Six. Marc looked at Aspirin. The duty officer was authorized to break the code.

"This is an emergency—I swear to you it's an emergency."

Aspirin told Polly to try Five and Six. Five and Six are Federal Communications Commission to the FBI. They are known by the initials KGB: it always amused FBI men to have KGB as their network call code. But at

64

at moment it didn't seem particularly funny. There was o reply to be had on KGB 5. Then KGB 6 was raised; kewise nothing. Now what, dear God, now what? Where id he turn next? Aspirin looked at him inquiringly, not eally wanting to get involved.

"Just remember, boy, C-Y-A. That's the ticket. C-Y-A."

"Covering your ass will not help me to locate Mr. tames," said Marc, forcing himself to speak calmly. "It oesn't matter, Aspirin, you get back to your crossword uzzle."

Marc left him and went into the men's room, cupped is hands under the faucet and washed his mouth out; he ill smelled of vomit and blood. He cleaned up as best e could. He returned to the Criminal Room, sat down, nd counted to ten very slowly. He had to make up his lind what to do, and then do it, come what may. Some- ing had probably happened to Stames and Colvert, he new something had happened to the black postman and le Greek. Perhaps he should try to contact the Director, lthough it was an extreme course. A man of his rank, wo years out of training didn't just call the Director. In ny case he could keep Stames's appointment with the lirector at 10:30 the next morning. Ten-thirty the next lorning. That was half a day away. More than twelve ours of not knowing what to do. Nursing a secret that e had been told not to discuss with anyone. Holding aformation he couldn't impart to anybody else.

The phone rang and he heard Polly's voice. He prayed would be Stames, but his prayer was not answered.

"Hey, Marc, are you still there? I've got Homicide on le line. Captain Hogan wants to talk to you."

"Andrews?"

"Yes, Captain."

"What can you tell me?"

65

Marc reported truthfully that Casefikis was an illegal immigrant who had delayed seeking treatment for his leg and untruthfully that he alleged he had been shot by a crook who had subjected him to blackmail, threatening exposure of his illegal entry into the States. A full written report would be sent around tomorrow morning.

The detective was suspicious.

"Are you holding out on me, son? What was the FBI doing there in the first place? There's going to be one hell of a scene if I find out you're withholding information. I wouldn't hesitate to roast your ass over the hottest coals in Washington."

Marc thought of Stames's repeated injunctions about secrecy.

"No, I am not holding out," he said in a raised voice; he knew he was trembling and could hardly have sounded less convincing. The Homicide detective grumbled to himself, asked a few more questions, and hung up. Marc put the phone down. The receiver was clammy with sweat, his clothes stuck to him. He tried Norma Stames again; still the boss wasn't home. He tried Colvert; still no reply from the bachelor apartment. He called Polly again, and asked her to go through the whole routine with the radio channels again; still nothing except a buzzing sound on Channel One. Finally, Marc abandoned the telephone and told Aspirin he was leaving. Aspirin didn't seem interested.

Marc headed for the elevator and made his way to his car. Must get onto home ground. Call the Director. Once again he was speeding through the streets.

When he reached his apartment in the Southwest section of Washington, he burst through the door and picked up the phone. After several rings, the Bureau answered. "Director's office. Duty officer speaking."

Marc counted to ten again.

"My name is Special Agent Andrews, Washington Field Office," Marc began slowly. "I want to speak to the Director, urgent and immediate."

The Director, it seemed, was dining with the Attorney General at her home. Marc asked for the telephone number. Did he have special authority to contact the Director at this time of night? He had special authority, he had an appointment with him at 10:30 tomorrow morning and, for God's sake, he had special authority.

The man must have sensed Andrews was desperate.

"I'll call you right back, if you'll give me your number."

Andrews knew that this was simply to check that he was an FBI agent and that he was scheduled to see the Director in the morning. The phone rang after one minute and the duty officer was back.

"The Director will still be with the Attorney General. Her private number is 761-4386."

Marc dialed the number.

"Mrs. Edelman's residence," said a deferential voice.

"This is Special Agent Marc Andrews," he began. "I need to speak to the Director of the Federal Bureau of Investigation."

He said it slowly, he said it clearly, although he was still trembling. The reply came back from a man whose biggest worry that night had been that the potatoes had taken longer than expected.

"Will you hold the line one moment please, sir."

He waited, he waited, he waited.

A new voice said: "Tyson here."

Marc drew a deep breath and plunged in.

"My name is Special Agent Marc Andrews. I have an appointment to see you with SAC Stames and Special Agent Colvert at ten-thirty tomorrow morning. You don't

know about it, sir, because it was made through Mr
McGregor after you had left your office. I have to se
you immediately, you may wish to call me back. I'm a
home."

"Yes, Andrews," said Tyson, "I'll call you back. Wha
is your number?"

Marc gave it.

"Young man," Tyson said, "this had better be serious.

"It is, sir, very serious."

Marc waited again. One minute passed, and then an
other. Had Tyson dismissed him as a fool? What wa
going on? Three minutes passed. Four minutes passed
he was obviously checking more thoroughly than his dut
officer had done.

The phone rang. Marc jumped.

"Hi, Marc, it's Roger. Want to go out for a beer?"

"Not now, Roger, not now." He slammed the phon
down.

It rang again immediately.

"Right, Andrews, what do you want to tell me? Mak
it quick and to the point."

"I want to see you now, sir. I need fifteen minutes o
your time and I need you to tell me what the hell to do."

He regretted "hell" the moment he had said it.

"Very well, if it's that urgent. Do you know where th
Attorney General lives?"

"No, sir."

"Take this down: 2942 Edgewood Street, Arlington."

Marc put the phone down, wrote the address carefull
in block capitals of the inside of a matchbook advertisin
life insurance, and called Aspirin, who just couldn't ge
7-across.

"If anything happens, I'll be on my car radio; you ca
get me there, I'll leave the line open on Channel Two th

whole time. Something's wrong with Channel One."

Aspirin sniffed: the young agents took themselves far too seriously nowadays. It wouldn't have happened under J. Edgar Hoover, shouldn't be allowed to happen now. Still, he only had one more year and then retirement. He returned to the crossword. 7-across, ten letters: gathering of those in favor of buccaneering. Aspirin started to think.

Marc Andrews was thinking too as he rushed into the elevator, into the street, into his car, and moved off at full speed to Arlington. He raced up East Basin Drive to Independence Avenue, past the Lincoln Memorial to get onto Memorial Bridge. He drove as fast as possible through the early night, cursing the people calmly strolling across the road on this mild, pleasant evening, casually on their way to nowhere in particular, cursing the people who took no notice of the flashing red light he had affixed to the car roof, cursing all the way. Where was Stames? Where was Barry? What the hell was going on? Would the Director think he was crazy?

He crossed Memorial Bridge and took the G.W. Parkway exit. A tie-up. He couldn't move an inch. Probably an accident. A goddamn accident right now. That was all he needed. He pulled into the center lane and leaned on his horn. Most people assumed he was connected with the police rescue team: most people let him by. Eventually he made it to the group of police cars and rescue-squad ambulances. A young Metropolitan policeman approached the car. "Are you on this detail?"

"No. FBI. I've got to get to Arlington. Emergency."

He flashed his credentials. The policeman ushered him through. He raced away from the accident. Goddamn accident. Once he was clear of it, the traffic became light. Fifteen minutes later, he arrived at 2942 Edgewood Street, Arlington. One last check with Polly at the Washington

Field Office, on the car phone. No, neither Stames no Colvert had called in.

Marc jumped out of the car. Before he had taken step, a Secret Service man stopped him. Marc showe his credentials and said that he had an appointment wit the Director. The Secret Service man courteously aske him to wait by his car. After consultation at the doo Marc was shown into a small room just on the right of th hall which was obviously used as a study. The Directo came in. Marc stood up.

"Good evening, Director."

"Good evening, Andrews. You've interrupted a ver important dinner. I hope you know what you are doing.

The Director was cold and abrupt, clearly displease at being summoned to a meeting by an unknown junio agent.

Marc went through the whole story from the first meet ing with Stames through to his decision to go over every body's head. The Director's face remained impassiv throughout the long recital. It was still impassive whe Marc had finished. Marc's only thought was: I've don the wrong thing. He should have gone on trying to reacl Stames and Colvert. They were probably home by now He waited, a little sweat appearing on his forehead. Per haps this was his last day in the FBI. The Director's firs words took him by surprise.

"You did exactly the right thing, Andrews. I'd hav made the same decision in your place. It must have take guts to bring the whole thing to me." He looked hard a Marc. "You're absolutely certain only Stames, Colvert you, and I know all the details of what happened thi evening? No one from the Secret Service, and no from the Metropolitan Police Department?"

"That's correct, sir, just the four of us."

"And the three of you already have an appointment with me at ten-thirty tomorrow morning?"

"Yes, sir."

"Good. Take this down on your pad."

The pad, as it was commonly known in the FBI, was a small four-by-two card on which everything could be kept and which could be held in the palm of one's hand. Marc took one out of his inside coat pocket.

"You have the Attorney General's number here?"

"Yes, sir."

"And my number at home is 721-4069. Learn them and then destroy them. Now I'll tell you exactly what you will do. Go back to the Washington Field office. Check on Stames and Colvert again. Call the morgue, call the hospitals, call the highway police. If they don't turn up, I'll see you in my office at eight-thirty tomorrow morning, not ten-thirty. That's your first job. Second, get me the names of the Homicide officers working on this detail with the Metropolitan Police. Now tell me if I have this right—you told them nothing about the reason you went to see Casefikis."

"Nothing, sir."

"Good."

The Attorney General put her head around the door.

"Everything under control, Halt?"

"Fine, thanks, Marian. I don't think you've met Special Agent Andrews of the Washington Field Office."

"No. Nice to meet you, Mr. Andrews."

"Good evening, ma'am."

"Will you be long, Halt?"

"No, I'll be back as soon as I've finished briefing Andrews."

"Anything special?"

"No, nothing to worry about."

71

The Director had obviously decided nobody would hear the story until he got to the bottom of it himself.

"Where was I?"

"You told me to go to the Washington Field Office, sir, and check on Stames and Colvert."

"Yes."

"And then to call the morgue, the hospitals, and the highway police."

"Right."

"And you told me to check on the Homicide officers, get their names."

"Right. Take down the following: check the names of all hospital employees and visitors, as well as any other persons who can be identified as having been in the vicinity of Room 4308 between the time the two occupants were known to be alive and the time you found them dead. Check the names of the two dead men through NCIC and Bureau indexes for any background information we may have. Get fingerprints of all persons on duty and all visitors and all others who can be identified as having been near Room 4308, as well as fingerprints of the two dead men. We will need all these prints both for elimination purposes and possible suspect identification. If you don't find Stames and Colvert, as I said, see me at eight-thirty in my office tomorrow morning. If anything else arises tonight, you call me here or at home. Don't hesitate. If it's after eleven-thirty, I'll be home. If you call me on the phone, use a code name—now let me think—Julius—let's hope it's not prophetic, and give me your number. Make sure you use a pay phone and I'll call you back immediately. Don't bother me before seven-fifteen in the morning, unless it's really important. Got all that?"

"Yes, sir."

"Right. I think I'll get back to dinner."

Marc stood up, ready to leave. The Director put a hand on his shoulder.

"Don't worry, young man. These things happen from time to time and you made the right decision. You showed a lot of self-possession in a lousy situation. Now get back to work."

"Yes, sir."

Marc was relieved that someone else knew what he was going through; someone else with far bigger shoulders was there to share it.

On his way back to the FBI office, he picked up the car microphone. "WFO 180 in service. Any word from Mr. Stames?"

"Nothing yet, WFO 180, but I'll keep trying."

Aspirin was still there when he arrived, unaware that Marc had just been talking with the Director of the FBI. Aspirin had met all four directors at cocktail parties, though none of them would have remembered his name.

"Emergency over, son?"

"Yes," Marc said, lying. "Have we heard from Stames or Colvert?" He tried not to sound anxious.

"No, must have goofed off somewhere. Never you worry. The little sheep will find their way home without you to hold their tails."

Marc did worry. He went to his office and picked up the phone. Polly had still heard nothing. Just a buzz on Channel One. He called Norma Stames, still no news. Mrs. Stames asked if there might be anything to worry about.

"Nothing at all." Another lie. Was he sounding too unconcerned? "We just can't find out which bar he's in."

She laughed, but she knew Nick didn't frequent bars.

Marc tried Colvert; still no reply from the bachelor apartment. He knew in his bones something was wrong.

He just didn't know what. At least the Director was there, and the Director knew everything now. He glanced at his watch: 11:15. Where had the night gone? And where was it going? 11:15. What was he supposed to have done tonight? Hell. He had persuaded a beautiful girl to have dinner with him. Yet again, he picked up the telephone. At least she would be safely at home, where she ought to be.

"Hello."

"Hello, Elizabeth, it's Marc Andrews. I'm really sorry about not making it tonight. Something happened that got way out of my control."

The tension in his voice was apparent.

"Don't worry," she said lightly. "You warned me you were unreliable."

"I hope you'll let me take a rain check. Hopefully, in the morning, I can sort things out. I'll probably see you then."

"In the morning?" she said. "If you're thinking of the hospital, I'm off duty tomorrow."

Marc hesitated, thinking quickly of what he could prudently say. "Well, that may be best. I am afraid it's not good news. Casefikis and the other man in his room were murdered tonight. The Met is following it up, but we have nothing to go on."

"Murdered? Both of them? Why? Who? Casefikis wasn't killed without reason, was he?" The words came out in a torrent. "What's going on, for heaven's sake? No, don't answer that. You wouldn't tell me the truth in any case."

"I wouldn't waste my time lying to you, Elizabeth. Look, I've had it for tonight, and I owe you a big steak for messing your evening up. Can I call you some time soon?"

"I'd like that. Murder isn't food for the appetite, though. I hope you catch the men responsible. We see the results of a great deal of violence at Woodrow Wilson, but it isn't usually inflicted within our walls."

"I know. I'm sorry it involves you. Good night, lovely lady. Sleep well."

"And you, Marc. If you can."

Marc put the phone down, and immediately the burden of the day's events returned. What now? There was nothing he could do before 8:30, except keep in touch on the radio phone until he was home. There was no point just sitting there looking out of the window, feeling helpless, sick, and alone. He went in to Aspirin, told him he was going home, and that he'd call in every fifteen minutes because he was still anxious to speak to Stames and Colvert. Aspirin didn't even look up.

"Fine," he said, his mind fully occupied by the crossword puzzle. He had completed eleven clues, a sure sign it was a quiet evening.

Marc drove down Pennsylvania Avenue toward his apartment. At the first traffic circle, a tourist who didn't know he had the right of way was holding up traffic. Damn him, thought Marc. Washington was full of traffic circles, and they were a nuisance. When Major Pierre L'Enfant had laid out the symmetrical city in a grid pattern of streets and avenues that fan out from the center of town, the automobile had not been invented. Later, city planners had reconciled geometry with geography by putting traffic circles at most of the intersections. Newcomers to Washington who hadn't mastered the knack of cutting out at the right turnoff could end up circling round and round many more times than originally planned. Eventually, Marc managed to get around the circle and back on Pennsylvania Avenue. He continued to drive slowly toward his home, at the Tiber Island Apartments, his thoughts heavy and anxious. He turned on the car radio for the midnight news; must take his mind off it somehow. There were no big stories that night and the newscaster sounded rather bored; the President had held a press conference about the Gun-Control Bill, and the situation in South Africa seemed to be getting worse. Then the local news; there had been an automobile accident on the G.W. Parkway and it involved two cars, both of which were being hauled out of the river by cranes, under floodlights. One of the cars was a black Lincoln, the other, a blue Ford sedan, according to eyewitnesses, a married couple from Jacksonville vacationing in Washington. No other details as yet.

A blue Ford sedan. Although he had not really been concentrating, it came through to him—a blue Ford sedan? Oh no, God, please no. He veered right off 9th Street onto Maine Avenue, narrowly missing a fire hydrant, and raced toward Memorial Bridge, where he had been two hours before. At the scene of the accident the Metropolitan Police were still thick on the ground and one lane of the G.W. was closed off by barriers. Marc was stopped at the barrier as he came running. He showed his FBI credentials and found the officer in charge; he explained that he feared one of the cars involved might have been driven by an agent from the FBI. Any details yet?

"Still haven't got them out," the inspector replied. "We only have two witnesses to the accident, if it was an accident. Apparently there was some very funny driving going on. They'll be up in about thirty minutes. Let me know if we can help in any way."

Marc went over to the side of the road to watch the vast cranes and tiny frogmen groping around in the river under klieg lights. The thirty minutes wasn't thirty minutes; he shivered in the cold, waiting and watching. It was forty minutes, it was fifty minutes, it was sixty minutes when the black Lincoln came out. Inside the car was one body. Cautious man, he was wearing a seat belt. The police moved in immediately. Marc went back to the officer in charge and asked how long before the second car.

"Not long. That Lincoln wasn't your car, then?"

"No," said Marc.

Ten minutes, twenty minutes, he saw the top of the second car, a dark-blue car; he saw the side of the car, one of the windows fractionally opened; he saw the whole of the car. Two men were in it. He saw the license plate. For a second time that night, Marc felt sick. Almost crying, he ran back to the officer in charge and gave the names of the two men in the car, and ran to a pay phone at the side of the road. It was a long way. He dialed the number, checking his watch as he did so; it was nearly one o'clock. After one ring he heard a tired voice say "Yes."

Marc said, "Julius."

The voice said, "What is your number?"

He gave it. Thirty seconds later, the telephone rang.

"Well, Andrews. It's one o'clock in the morning."

"I know, sir, it's Stames and Colvert, they're dead."

There was a moment's hesitation, the voice was awake now.

"Are you certain?"

"Yes, sir."

Marc gave the details of the car crash, trying to keep the weariness and emotion out of his voice.

"Call your office immediately, Andrews," Tyson said, "without giving any of the details that you gave me this evening. Only tell me about the car crash—nothing more. In the morning, get any further information about it you can from the police. See me in my office at seven-thirty, not eight-thirty; come through the wide entrance on the far side of the building; there will be a man waiting there for you. He'll know you; don't be late. Go home now and try to get some sleep and keep yourself out of contact until tomorrow. Don't worry, Andrews. Two of us know, and I'll have a lot of agents working on the routine checks that I gave you to do earlier."

The phone clicked. Marc called Aspirin, what a night for him to have to be on duty, told him about Stames and Colvert, hanging up abruptly before Aspirin could ask questions. He returned to his car and drove home slow through the night. There was hardly another car on the streets and the early-morning mist gave everything an unearthly look.

At the entrance to his apartment garage, he saw Simon, the young black attendant, who liked Marc and, even more, Marc's Mercedes. Marc had blown a small legacy from his aunt on the car just after graduating from college, but never regretted his extravagance. Simon knew Marc had no assigned spot in the garage and always offered to park his car for him—anything for a chance to drive the magnificent silver Mercedes SLC 580. Marc usually exchanged a few bantering words with Simon; tonight he passed him the keys without even looking at him.

"I'll need it at seven in the morning," he said, already walking away. "Christ, I need some rest."

Marc heard Simon restart the car with a soft whoosh before the elevator door closed behind him. He arrived at his apartment; three rooms, all empty. He locked the door, and then bolted it, something he had never done before. He walked around the room slowly, undressed, throwing his sour-smelling shirt into the laundry hamper. He washed for the third time that night and then went to bed, to stare up at the white ceiling. He tried to make some sense out of the night's events; he tried to sleep. Six hours passed, he couldn't say where.

4

7:00 AM

Eventually Marc could stand it no longer and at 7:00 A.M.
he rose, showered, and put on a clean shirt and a fresh
suit. From his apartment window, he looked out across
the Washington Channel to East Potomac Park. In a few
weeks the cherry trees would bloom. In a few weeks . . .

He closed the apartment door behind him, glad simply
to be on the move again. Simon gave him the car keys; he
had managed to find a space for the Mercedes in one of
the private parking lots.

Marc drove the car slowly up 6th Street, turned left
on G and right on 7th. No traffic at this time of morning
except trucks. He passed the Hirshhorn Museum, locally
known as the concrete doughnut, and the National Air
and Space Museum, as he moved into Independence Avenue. At the intersection of 7th and Pennsylvania, next to
the National Archives, Marc came to a halt at a red light.
He felt an eerie sense of nothing being out of the ordinary, as though the previous day had been a bad dream.
He would arrive at the office and Nick Stames and Barry
Colvert would be there as usual. The vision evaporated as
he looked to his left. At one end of the deserted avenue,
he could see the White House grounds and patches of

he white building through the trees. To his right, at the other end of the avenue, stood the Capitol, gleaming in the early morning sunshine. And between the two, between Caesar and Cassius, thought Marc, stood the FBI building. Alone in the middle, he mused, the Director and himself, playing with destiny.

Marc drove the car down the ramp at the back of FBI Headquarters and parked. A young man in a dark-blue blazer, gray flannels, dark shoes, and a smart blue tie, the regulation uniform of the Bureau, awaited him. An anonymous man, thought Marc, who looked far too neat to have just got up. Marc Andrews showed him his identification. The young man led him toward the elevator without saying a word; it took them to the seventh floor, where Marc was noiselessly escorted to a reception room and asked to wait.

He sat in the reception room, next to the Director's office, with the inevitable out-of-date copies of *Time* and *Newsweek;* he might have been at his dentist's. It was the first time he'd rather have been at his dentist's. He pondered the events of the last fourteen hours. He'd gone from being a man with no responsibility enjoying the second of five eventful years in the FBI to one who was staring into the jaws of a tiger. His only previous trip to the Bureau itself had been for his interview; they hadn't told him that this might happen. They had talked of salaries, bonuses, holidays, a worthwhile and fulfilling job, serving the nation, nothing about immigrant Greeks and black postmen with their throats cut, nothing about friends being drowned in the Potomac. He paced around the room trying to compose his thoughts; yesterday should have been his day off, but he had decided he could do with the overtime pay. Perhaps another agent would have gotten back to the hospital quicker and forestalled the double murder. Perhaps if he had driven the Ford sedan last night, it would have been he, not Stames and Colvert in the Potomac. Perhaps. . . . Marc closed his eyes and felt an involuntary shiver run down his spine. He made an effort to disregard the panicky fear that perhaps it would be his turn next.

His eyes came to rest on a plaque on the wall, which stated that, in the almost sixty years of the FBI's history, only thirty-four people had been killed while on duty; on only one occasion had two officers died on the same day. Yesterday made that out-of-date, Marc thought grimly. His eyes continued moving around the wall and settled on a large picture of the Capitol hanging next to an equally large picture of the Supreme Court; government and the law hand-in-hand. On his left were the five directors, Hoover, Gray, Ruckelshaus, Kelley, and now the redoubtable H. A. L. Tyson, known by everyone in the Bureau by the acronym Halt. Apparently, no one except his secretary, Mrs. McGregor, knew his first name. It was a long-standing joke in the Bureau. When you joined, you paid one dollar and went to see Mrs. McGregor, who had served him for twenty-seven years, and told her what the Director's first name was. If you got it right, you won the pool. Right now, it stood at $3516. Marc had guessed Hector. Mrs. McGregor had laughed and the pool was one dollar the richer. If you wanted a second guess, that cost you another dollar, but if you got it wrong, you paid a ten-dollar fine. Quite a few people tried the second time and the kitty grew larger as each new victim arrived. Marc had had what he thought was the bright idea of checking the Criminal Fingerprints File. The FBI fingerprint records fall into three categories—military, civil, and criminal, and all FBI agents have their prints in the criminal file. This insures that they are able to trace any

BI agent who turns criminal, or to eliminate an agent's rints at the scene of a crime; these records are very rarely sed. Marc had considered himself very clever as he sked to see Tyson's card. The Director's card was handed o him by an assistant from the Fingerprints Department. t read—"Height: 6′1″; Weight: 180 lbs.; Hair: brown;)ccupation: Director of FBI; Name: Tyson, H. A. L." Vo forename given. The assistant, another anonymous nan in a blue suit, had smiled sourly at Marc and had aid, loud enough for Marc to hear, as he returned the ard to its file, "One more sucker who thought he was oing to make a quick three thousand bucks."

Tyson had been a Kennedy nominee and although the 3ureau had become more political under the last two 'residents of the United States, Halt was a man whom Congress found very easy to endorse. Law enforcement vas in his blood. His great-grandfather had been a Wells 'argo man, riding shotgun on the stage between San 'rancisco and Seattle in the other Washington. His grandather had been mayor of Boston and its chief of police, rare combination, and his father before his retirement ad been a distinguished Massachusetts attorney. That he great-grandson had followed family tradition, and nded up as Director of the Federal Bureau of Investigaion, surprised no one. The anecdotes about him were egion and Marc wondered just how many of them were pocryphal.

There was no doubt that Tyson had scored the winning ouchdown in his final Harvard-Yale game because it was here on record, as indeed was the fact that he was the nly white man to box on the 1948 American Olympic eam in London. Whether he had actually said to President Vixon that he would rather serve the devil than direct the FBI under his presidency, no one other than Richard

Nixon could be quite sure, but it was certainly a story th Kennedy camp made no effort to suppress.

His wife had died five years earlier of multiple sclerosis He had nursed her for twenty years with a fierce loyalty.

He feared no man and his reputation for honesty and straightforwardness had raised him above most govern ment employees in the eyes of the nation. After a perio of malaise, following Hoover's death, Kelley and Hal Tyson had restored the Bureau to the prestige it had enjoyed in the thirties and forties. Tyson was one of th reasons Marc had been happy to commit five years of hi life to the FBI.

Marc began to fidget with the middle button of hi jacket, as all FBI agents tend to do. It had been drumme into him in the fifteen-week course at Quantico tha jacket buttons should always be undone, allowing acces to the gun, on the hip holster, never on a shoulder strap It annoyed Marc that the television series about the FB always got that wrong. Whenever an FBI man sensed danger, he would fiddle with that middle button to mak sure his coat was open. Marc sensed fear, fear of the un known, fear of H. A. L. Tyson, fear which an accessibl Smith and Wesson could not cure.

The anonymous young man with the vigilant look and the dark-blue blazer returned.

"The Director will see you now."

Marc rose, felt unsteady, braced himself, rubbed hi hands against his pants to remove the sweat from hi palms and followed the anonymous man through the oute office and into the Director's inner sanctum. The Directo glanced up, waved him to a chair, and waited for th anonymous man to leave the room and close the door Even seated, the Director was a bull of a man with a larg head placed squarely on massive shoulders. Bushy eye brows matched his care-less, wiry brown hair; it was so curly you might have thought it was a wig if it hadn't been H. A. L. Tyson. His big hands rested splayed on the desk as though the desk might try to get away. The delicate Queen Anne desk was quite subdued by the grip of the Director. His cheeks were red, not the red of alcohol, but the red of good and bad weather. Slightly back from Marc's chair sat another man, muscular, clean-shaven, and silent, a policeman's policeman.

The Director spoke. "Andrews, this is Assistant Director Matthew Rogers. I have briefed him on the events following Casefikis's death; we will be putting a couple of men on the investigation with you." The Director's gray eyes were piercing—piercing Marc. "I lost two of my best men yesterday, Andrews, and nothing—I repeat, nothing—will stop me from finding out who was responsible, even if it was the President himself, you understand."

"Yes, sir," Marc said very quietly.

"You will have gathered from the press releases we gave to *The New York Times* and *The Washington Post* that the public is under the impression that what happened yesterday evening was just another automobile accident. No journalist has connected the murders in Woodrow Wilson Medical Center with the deaths of my agents. Why should they, with a murder every twenty-six minutes in America?"

A Metropolitan Police file marked "Chief of Metropolitan Police" was by his side; even they were under control.

"We, Mr. Andrews . . ."

It made Marc feel slightly royal.

". . . we are not going to disillusion them. I have been going over carefully what you told me last night. I'll summarize the situation as I see it. Please feel free to interrupt me whenever you want to."

Under normal circumstances, Marc would have laughed.

The Director was looking at the file.

"So the Greek wanted to see the head of the FBI," he went on. "Perhaps I should have granted his request, had I known about it." He looked up. "Still, the facts: Casefikis made an oral statement to you at Woodrow Wilson, and the gist of it was that he thought there was a plot in motion to assassinate the President of the United States on March 10; that he overheard this information while waiting on a private lunch in a Georgetown hotel, at which he believed a U.S. senator was present. Is that correct so far, Andrews?"

"Yes, sir."

Once more the Director looked down at the file.

"The police took prints off the dead man, and he hasn't shown up in the NCIC files or in the Metropolitan Police files. So for the moment we must act on the assumption, after last night's four killings, that everything the Greek immigrant told us was the truth. He may not have gotten the story entirely accurately, but he really was onto something big enough to cause four murders in one night. I think we may also assume that whoever the people behind these diabolical events, they believe they are now in the clear and that they have killed anyone who might have known of their plans. You may consider yourself lucky, young man."

"Yes, sir."

"I suppose it had crossed your mind that they thought it was you in the blue Ford sedan?"

Marc nodded. He had thought of little else for the past ten hours; he hoped Norma Stames would never think of it.

"I want these conspirators to think they are now in the

86

clear and for that reason, I am going to allow the President's schedule for March 10 to continue as planned, at least for the moment."

Marc ventured a question. "But, sir, won't that put the President in grave danger?"

"Andrews, somebody, somewhere, and it may be a United States senator, is planning to assassinate the President; so far, he has been prepared to murder two of my best agents, a Greek who might have recognized him, and a deaf postman whose only connection with the matter was that he may have been able to identify Casefikis's killer. If we rush in now with the heavy artillery, then we will scare them off. We have almost nothing to go on; we would be unlikely to discover their identities. And if we did, we certainly wouldn't be able to nail them. Our only hope of catching them is to let the bastards think they are in the clear—right up to the last moment. That way, we just might get them. It's possible they have already been frightened off, but I think not. They have used such violent means to keep their intentions secret they must have some overriding reason for wanting the President out of the way on March 10. We must find out what the reason is."

"Shall we tell the President?"

"No, no, not yet. God knows, he has enough problems without having to look over his shoulder trying to figure out which senator is Mark Antony and which is Brutus."

"So what do we do for the next six days?"

"You and I have to find Cassius. And he may not be the one with the lean and hungry look."

"What if we don't find him?" asked Marc.

"God help America."

"And if we do?"

"You may have to kill him."

87

Marc thought for a moment. He'd never killed anybody in his life; come to think of it, he hadn't knowingly killed anything at all. He didn't like stepping on insects. And the thought that the first person he might kill could be a U.S. senator was, to say the least, daunting.

"Don't look so worried, Andrews. It probably won't come to that. Now let me tell you exactly what I intend to do. I'm going to brief Stuart Knight, the head of the Secret Service, that two of my officers were investigating a man claiming that the President of the United States was going to be assassinated some time within the next month. However, I have no intention of telling him that a senator may be involved; and I won't tell him that two of our men died on the job; that's not his problem. It may actually have nothing to do with a senator, and I'm not having a whole bunch of people staring at their elected representatives wondering which one of them is a criminal."

The Assistant Director cleared his throat and spoke for the first time. "Some of us think that anyway."

The Director continued unswervingly. "This morning, Andrews, you will write a report on Casefikis's information and the circumstances of his murder, and you will hand it in to Grant Nanna. Do not include the subsequent murders of Stames and Colvert: no one must connect these two events. Report the threat on the President's life but not the possibility that a senator is involved. Don't you think that's wise, Matt?"

"Yes, I do," said Rogers. "If we voice our suspicions to people who don't need to know them, we will run the risk of provoking a security operation that will make the assassins run a mile; then we would simply have to pick up our marbles and start over—if we were lucky enough to get a second chance."

"Right," said the Director. "Here's how we'll play it. Andrews, there are one hundred senators. One of them provides our only link with the conspirators. It's going to be your task to pinpoint that one man. The Assistant Director will have a couple of junior men follow up the few other leads that we have. No need for them to know the details. Matt, to start with, check out the Golden Duck Restaurant."

"And every hotel in Georgetown, to see which one put on a private luncheon party on February 24," said Rogers. "And the hospital. Maybe someone saw some suspicious characters hanging around the parking lot or the corridors; the assassins must have seen our Ford there while Colvert and you, Andrews, were interviewing Casefikis. I think that's about all we can do for the moment."

"I agree," said the Director. "Okay, thanks, Matt, I won't take up any more of your time. Please let me have anything you turn up immediately."

"Sure," said the Assistant Director. He rose and left the room.

Marc had sat silently, impressed by the clarity with which the Director had grasped the details of the case; his mind must be like a filing cabinet.

The Director pressed a button on his intercom.

"Coffee for two, please, Mrs. McGregor."

"Yes, sir."

"Now, Andrews, you come in to the Bureau at seven o'clock every morning and report to me. Should any emergency arise, call me, using the code name Julius. I will use the same code name when calling you. When you hear the word 'Julius,' break off whatever you are doing. Do you have that straight?"

"Yes, sir."

"Now, a most important point. If, in any circumstances

I die or disappear, you brief only the Attorney General, and Rogers will take care of the rest. If you die, young man, you can leave the decision to me." He smiled for the first time—it was not Marc's idea of a joke. "I see from the files that you're entitled to two weeks' leave. You'll take it, starting at noon today. I don't want you to exist officially for at least a week. Grant Nanna has already been briefed that you have been seconded to me," continued the Director. "You may have to tolerate me night and day for six days, young man, and no one other than my late wife has had to do that before."

"And you me, sir," was Marc's quick and unthinking reply.

He waited for his head to be bitten off; instead the Director smiled again.

Mrs. McGregor appeared with the coffee, served them, and left. The Director drank his coffee in one swallow and began to pace around the room as if it were a cage; Marc did not move, though his eyes never left Tyson. His massive frame and great shoulders heaved up and down, his large head with its bushy hair rocking from side to side. He was going through what the boys called the thought process.

"The first thing you're to do, Andrews, is find out which senators were in Washington on February 24. As it was near the weekend, most of those dummies would have been floating all over the country, making speeches or vacationing with their pampered children."

What endeared the Director to everyone was not that he said it behind their backs but that he said it even more explicitly to their faces. Marc smiled and began to relax.

"When we have that list, we'll try and figure out what they have in common. Separate the Republicans from the Democrats, and then put them under party headings as to interests, public and private. After that, we have to find out which ones have any connection with President Kennedy, past or present, friendly or unfriendly. Your report will cover all these details and be ready for our meeting tomorrow morning. Understood?"

"Yes, sir."

"Now there's something else I want you to understand, Andrews. As I am sure you know, for the past decade, the FBI has been in a very sensitive political position. Those watchdogs in Congress are just waiting for us to exceed our legitimate authority. If we in any way cast suspicion upon a member of Congress, without indisputable evidence of his guilt, they will draw and quarter the Bureau. And rightly so, in my opinion. Police agencies in a democracy must prove that they can be trusted not to subvert the political process. Purer than Caesar's wife. Understood?"

"Yes, sir."

"From today we have six days, from tomorrow five, and I want to catch this man and his friends red-handed. So neither of us will be on statutory overtime."

"No, sir."

The Director returned to his desk and summoned Mrs. McGregor.

"Mrs. McGregor, this is Special Agent Andrews, who'll be working closely with me on an extremely sensitive investigation for the next six days. Whenever he wants to see me, let him come right in; if I'm with anybody but Mr. Rogers, notify me immediately—no red tape, no waiting."

"Yes, sir."

"And I'd appreciate it if you didn't mention this to anybody else."

"Of course not, Mr. Tyson."

The Director turned to Marc. "Now you go back to the WFO and start working. I'll see you in this office at seven o'clock tomorrow morning."

Marc stood up. He hadn't finished his coffee; perhaps by the sixth day he would feel free to say so. He shook hands with the Director and headed toward the door. Just as he reached it, the Director added: "Andrews, I hope you'll be very careful. Keep looking over both shoulders at once."

Marc shivered and moved quickly out of the room, down the corridor, keeping his back firmly to the wall when he reached the elevator, and walking along the sides of the passage on the ground floor, where he ran into a group of tourists who were studying pictures of the Ten Most Wanted Criminals in America. Next week, would one of them be a senator?

When he reached the street, he dodged the traffic until he arrived at the Washington Field Office, on the other side of Pennsylvania Avenue. It wouldn't quite be like home this morning. Two men were missing, and they weren't going to be able to replace them with a training manual. The flag on top of the FBI Building and the flag on top of the Old Post Office Building were at half-mast; two of their agents were dead.

Marc went straight into Grant Nanna's office; he had aged ten years overnight. For him, two friends had died, one who worked under him and one who worked above him.

"Sit down, Marc."

"Thank you, sir."

"The Director has already spoken to me this morning. I didn't ask any questions. I understand you're taking a two-week leave as of noon today, and that you are writing me a memorandum on what happened at the hospital. I have to pass it on to higher authorities and that will be the end of it as far as the WFO is concerned, because Homicide will take over. They are also trying to tell me Nick and Barry died in a car accident."

"Yes, sir," said Marc.

"I don't believe a goddamn word of it," said Nanna. "Now you're in the middle of this, somehow, and maybe you can nail the bastards who did it. When you find them, grind their balls into powder and then call me so that I can come help you, because if I lay my hands on those bastards—"

Marc looked at Grant Nanna, and then tactfully away again, waiting until his superior had regained control of his face and voice.

"Now, you're not allowed to contact me once you leave this office, but if I can help at any time, just call me. Don't let the Director know, he'd kill us both if he found out. Get going, Marc."

Marc left quickly and went to his own office. He sat down and wrote out his report exactly as the Director had instructed, bland and brief. He took it back to Nanna, who flicked through it and tossed it into the out-box. "Neat little whitewash job you've done there, Marc."

Marc didn't speak. He signed out of the Washington Field Office, the one place in which he felt secure. He'd be on his own for six days. Ambitious men wanted to see a few years ahead, to know the shape of their careers; Marc would have settled for a week.

The Director pressed a button. The anonymous man in the dark-blue blazer and light-gray trousers entered the room.

"Yes, sir."

"I want full surveillance on Andrews, night and day;

six men on three shifts reporting to me every morning. I want detailed background on him, his education, girl friends, associates, habits, hobbies, religious background, organizational affiliations, everything by tomorrow morning, six-forty-five. Understood?"

"Yes, sir."

Aware that Senate staff members would be suspicious of an FBI agent who asked for information about their employers, Marc began his research at the Library of Congress. As he climbed the long flight of steps, he remembered a scene from *All the President's Men,* in which Woodward and Bernstein had spent innumerable fruitless hours searching for a few slips of paper in the bowels of the building. They were trying to find proof that E. Howard Hunt had checked out materials on none other than the man Marc was trying to protect, Edward M. Kennedy. And for an FBI agent on the trail of a killer, just as for the investigative reporters, it would be tedious research, not glamorous assignments, that would make the difference between success and failure.

Marc opened the door marked "Readers Only" and strolled into the Main Reading Room, a huge, circular, domed room decorated in muted tones of gold, beige, rust, and bronze. The ground floor was filled with rows of dark, curved wooden desks, arranged in concentric circles around the reference area in the center of the room. On the second floor, visible from the reading area through graceful arches, were thousands of books. Marc approached the reference desk and, in the hushed tones appropriate to all libraries, asked the clerk where he could find current issues of the *Congressional Record.*

"Room 244. Law Library Reading Room."

"How do I get there?"

"Go back past the card catalogue to the other side of the building and take an elevator to the second floor."

Marc managed to find the Law Library, a white, rectangular room with three tiers of bookshelves on the left-hand side. After questioning another clerk, he located the *Congressional Record* on one of the dark-brown reference shelves along the right-hand wall. He carried the unbound volume marked February 24, 1983, to a long, deserted table and began the tedious weeding-out process.

After leafing through the digest of Senate business for half an hour, Marc realized that he was in luck. Many senators had apparently left Washington for the weekend, because a check of the roll calls on February 24 revealed that the number of senators present on the floor never exceeded sixty. And the bills which were voted on were sufficiently important to command the presence of those senators who might have been hiding in the nooks and crannies of the Senate or the city. When he had eliminated those senators who were listed by the Whips of each party as "absent because of illness" or "necessarily absent," and added those who were merely "detained on official business," Marc was left with sixty-two senators who were definitely in Washington on February 24. He then double-checked the other thirty-eight senators, one by one, a long and tiresome task. All of them had for some reason been out of Washington that day. He glanced at his watch: 12:15. He couldn't afford to take time off for lunch.

12:30 PM

Three men had arrived. None of them liked one another; only the common bond of financial reward could have got them into one room. The first went by the name of Tony; he'd had so many names that nobody could be sure what his real name was, except perhaps his mother, and she hadn't seen him in the twenty years since he had left Sicily to join his father, her husband, in the States. Her husband had left twenty years before that; the cycle repeated itself.

Tony's FBI criminal file described him as five feet eight, a hundred and forty-six pounds, medium build, black hair, straight nose, brown eyes, no distinguishing features, arrested and charged once in connection with a bank robbery; first offense, two-year jail sentence. What the rap sheet did not reveal was that Tony was a brilliant driver; he had proved that yesterday and if that fool of a German had kept his head, there would have been four people in the room now instead of three. He had told the boss, "If you're going to employ a German, have him build the damn car, never let him drive it." The boss hadn't listened and the German had been dragged out of the bottom of the Potomac. Next time they'd use Tony's cousin Mario. At least then there would be another human on the team; you couldn't count the ex-cop and the little Jap who never said a word.

Tony glanced at Xan Tho Huc, who never spoke unless asked a direct question. He was actually Vietnamese, but he had escaped to Japan in 1973. Everyone would have known his name if he had entered the Montreal Olympics, because nobody could have stopped him from getting the gold medal for rifle shooting, but Xan had decided, with his chosen career in mind, he had better keep a low profile and withdraw from the Japanese Olympic trials. His coach tried to get an explanation, but without success. To Tony, Xan remained a goddamn Jap, though he grudgingly admitted to himself he knew no other man who could fire

en shots into a three-inch square at eight hundred yards.
The size of Kennedy's forehead.

The Nip sat staring at him, motionless. Xan's appearance helped him in his work. No one expected that the light frame, only about five feet two and a hundred and ten pounds, was that of a superlative marksman. Most people still associated marksmanship with hulking cowboys and lantern-jawed Caucasians. If you had been told this man was a ruthless killer, you would have assumed he worked with his hands, with a garrote or nunchaki, or even with poison. Among the three, Xan was the only one who had been married—to a good, quiet woman who was bringing up twin daughters in the traditional Vietnamese way, until the American bastards had killed all three of them. Xan had stood by the pathetic rumpled body of his wife and the unbearably mutilated bodies of his two beautiful little daughters and had shed not a tear. He had been a supporter of the Americans in Vietnam, but no longer; he had vowed in silent torment to avenge his loss. He escaped to Japan and there, for two years after the fall of Saigon, he had lain low, getting a job in a Chinese restaurant, and participating in the U.S. government program for Vietnamese refugees. Then he had gone with the offer of practical assistance to some of his old contacts in the Vietnamese intelligence community. With the U.S. presence so scaled down in Asia, and the Communists needing fewer killers, and more lawyers, they had been sorry but no work. So Xan had begun free-lancing in Japan. In 1974, he obtained Japanese citizenship and a passport and started his new career.

Unlike Tony, Xan did not resent the others he was working with. He simply didn't think about them. He had been hired, willingly, to perform a momentous task, a task for which he would be well paid and that would at last avenge, at least in part, the outraged bodies of his wife and daughters. The others had limited roles to play in support of his operation. Provided they played them with a minimum of foolish error, he would perform his part flawlessly, and within a few days, he would be back in the Orient. Bangkok or Manila, perhaps Singapore. Xan hadn't decided yet. When this one was over, he would need—and would be able to afford—a long rest.

The third man in the room, Ralph Matson, was perhaps the most dangerous of the three. Six feet two, tall and broad, with a big nose and heavy chin, he was the most dangerous because he was highly intelligent. After five years a special agent with the Federal Bureau of Investigation, he found an easy way out after Hoover's death; loyalty to the Chief and all that garbage. By then, he had learned enough to take advantage of everything the Bureau had taught him about criminology. He had started with a little blackmail, men who had not wanted their FBI records made public, but now he had moved on to bigger things. He trusted no man—the Bureau had also taught him that—certainly not the stupid wop, who under pressure might drive backward rather than forward, or the silent slant-eyed yellow hit man. Still nobody spoke.

The door swung open. Three heads turned, three heads that were used to danger and did not care for surprises; they relaxed again immediately when they saw the two men enter.

The younger of the two was smoking. He took the seat at the head of the table as befits a chairman; the other man sat down next to Matson, keeping the Chairman on his right. They nodded acknowledgment, no more. The younger man, Peter Nicholson on his voter-registration card, Pyotr Nicolaivich by birth certificate, looked for all the world like the reputable head of a successful cosmetics

98

ompany. His suit revealed that he went to Chester Barrie. His shoes revealed that he went to Church's of London. His tie revealed that he went to Ted Lapidus. His criminal record revealed nothing. That was why he was at the head of the table. He didn't look upon himself as a criminal; he merely wished to maintain the status quo.

He was one of a small group of Southern millionaires who had made their money in the small-arms trade. Theirs was a giant business: it was the right of every American citizen under Amendment Two of the Constitution to bear arms, and one in every four American males exercised that right. A regular pistol or revolver could be had for as little as $100 but the fancy shotguns and rifles that were a status symbol to many patriots could go up to $10,000. The Chairman and his ilk sold handguns by the millions and shotguns by the tens of thousands. They had persuaded Jimmy Carter to see the arms trade their way, but they knew they were not going to convince Ted Kennedy. The Gun-Control Bill had already squeaked through the House, and unless some drastic action was taken, there was undoubtedly going to be a repeat performance in the Senate. To preserve the status quo, therefore, the Chairman sat at the head of the table.

He opened the meeting formally, as any regular chairman would, by asking for reports from his men in the field. First Matson.

The big nose bobbed, the heavy jaw moved.

"I was tuned into the FBI's Channel One." During his years as an FBI agent, preparing for a career in crime, Matson had stolen one of the Bureau's special portable walkie-talkies. He had signed it out for some routine purpose and then reported that it was lost. He was admonished and had to reimburse the Bureau; it had been a small price to pay for the privilege of listening to FBI communications. "I knew the Greek waiter was hiding somewhere in Washington, and I suspected that because of his leg injury, he would eventually have to go to one of the five hospitals. I guessed he wouldn't end up with a private doctor, too expensive. Then I heard that motherfucker Stames come up on Channel One."

"Cut out the profanity, if you please," said the Chairman.

Stames had given Matson four reprimands during his service with the FBI. Matson did not mourn his death. He started again.

"I heard Stames come up on Channel One, on his way to Woodrow Wilson Medical Center, to ask a Father Gregory to go to the Greek. It was a long shot, of course, but I remembered that Stames was a Greek himself, and it wasn't hard to trace Father Gregory. I just caught him as he was about to leave. I told him the Greek had been discharged from the hospital and that his services wouldn't be needed. And thanked him. With Stames dead, no one is likely to follow that one up and, if they do, they won't be any the wiser. I then went to the nearest Greek Orthodox church and stole the vestments, a hat, a veil, and a cross and I drove to Woodrow Wilson. By the time I arrived, Stames and Colvert had already left. I learned from the receptionist on duty that the two men from the FBI had returned to their office. I didn't ask for too much detail as I didn't want to be remembered. I found out which room Casefikis was in and it was easy to get there unnoticed. I slipped in. He was sound asleep. I cut his throat."

The Senator winced.

"There was a nigger bastard in the bed next to him, we couldn't take the risk. He might have overheard every-

ing, and he might have given a description of me, so I
ut his throat too."

The Senator felt sick. He hadn't wanted these men to
ie. The Chairman showed no emotion, the difference be-
ween a professional and an amateur.

"Then I called Tony in the car. He drove to the Wash-
ngton Field Office and saw Stames and Colvert coming
ut of the building together. I then contacted you, boss,
nd Tony carried out your orders."

The Chairman passed over a packet. It was one hun-
red fifty-dollar bills. All American employees are paid
·y seniority and achievement; it was no different here.

The Chairman nodded and almost said thank you.

"Tony."

"When the two men left the Old Post Office Building,
·e followed them as instructed. They went over Memorial
₃ridge. The German passed them and managed to get
·ell ahead of them. As soon as I realized they were turn-
·g up onto the G.W. Parkway, as we thought they would,
·told Gerbach on the walkie-talkie. He was waiting in a
·lump of trees on the middle strip, with his lights off,
·bout a mile ahead. He turned on his lights and came
·own from the top of the hill on the wrong side of the
·ivided highway. He swung in front of the Feds' car just
·fter it crossed Windy Run Bridge. I accelerated and
·vertook on the left-hand side of the car. I hit them with
·glancing sideways blow at about seventy miles an hour,
·ust as that damn-fool German hit them head-on. You
·now the rest, boss. If he had kept his cool," Tony finished
·ontemptuously, "the German would be here today to
·ake his report in person."

"What did you do with the car?"

"I went to Mario's workshop, changed the engine block

and the license plates, repaired the damage to the fender
sprayed it, and dumped it. The owner probably wouldn'
recognize his own car if he saw it. Then I picked u
another Buick, 1980, good condition."

"Where?"

"New York. The Bronx."

"Good. With a murder there every four hours, the
don't have a lot of time to check on missing cars."

The Chairman flicked a packet over the table. Fiv
thousand dollars in used fifties. "Stay sober, Tony, we'l
be needing you again." He refrained from saying wha
assignment number two would be; he simply said, "Xan.'
He stubbed out his cigarette and lit another one. All eye
turned to the silent Vietnamese. His English was good
though heavily accented. He tended, like so many edu
cated Orientals, to omit the definite article, giving hi
speech a curious staccato effect.

"I was in car with Tony whole evening when we go
your orders to eliminate two men in Ford sedan. We fol
lowed them over bridge and up freeway and when Ge
man swung across path of Ford, I blew their back tire
in under three seconds, just before Tony bounced then
They had no chance of controlling car after that."

"How can you be so sure it was under three seconds?'
queried the Chairman.

"I'd been averaging two-point-eight in practice all day.

Silence. The Chairman passed yet another packet. An
other one hundred fifties, twenty-five hundred dollars fo
each shot.

"Do you have any questions, Senator?"

The Senator did not look up, but shook his hea
slightly.

The Chairman spoke. "From the press reports and fro
our further investigation, it looks as if nobody has co

nected the two incidents, but the FBI just aren't that stupid. We have to hope that we eliminated everybody who heard anything Casefikis might have said, if he had anything to say in the first place. We may just be oversensitive. One thing's for sure, we eliminated everybody connected with that hospital. But we still can't be sure if the Greek knew anything worth repeating."

"May I say something, boss?"

The Chairman looked up. Nobody spoke unless it was relevant, most unusual for an American board meeting. The Chairman let Matson have the floor.

"One thing worries me, boss. Why would Nick Stames be going to Woodrow Wilson?"

They all stared at him, not quite sure what he meant.

"We know from my inquiries and my contacts that Colvert was there, but we don't actually know that Stames was there. All we know is that two agents went and that Stames asked Father Gregory to go. We know Stames was on his way home with Colvert, but my experience tells me that Stames wouldn't go to the hospital himself; he'd send somebody else—"

"Even if he thought it was a serious matter?" interrupted the Chairman.

"He wouldn't know it was a serious matter, boss. He wouldn't have known until the agents had reported back to him."

The Chairman shrugged. "The facts point to Stames going to the hospital with Colvert. He left the Washington Field Office with Colvert driving the same car that left the hospital."

"I know, boss, but I don't like it; I know that we've covered all the angles, but it's possible that three or more men left the Washington Field Office and that there is still

103

at least one agent running around who knows what actually happened."

"It seems unlikely," said the Senator. "As you will see when you hear my report."

The lips compressed in the heavy jaw.

"You're not happy are you, Matson?"

"No, sir."

"Very well, check it out. If you come up with anything report back to me."

The Chairman never left a stone unturned. He looked at the Senator.

The Senator despised these men. They were so small-minded, so greedy. They only understood money, and Kennedy was going to take it away from them. How their violence had frightened and sickened him. He should never have allowed that smooth-talking plausible bastard Nicholson to pump so much into his secret campaign funds, although God knows he would never have been elected without the money. Lots of money, and such a small price to pay at the time: steadfast opposition to any gun-control proposals. Hell, he was genuinely opposed to gun control anyway. But assassinating the President to stop the bill, by God, it was lunacy, but the Chairman had him by the balls. "Cooperate, or be exposed, my friend," he had said silkily. The Senator had spent half a lifetime sweating to reach the Senate and what's more, he did a damned good job there. If they stopped him now he would be finished. A public scandal. Nixon, Agnew, Howe, and himself. He couldn't face it. "Cooperate, my friend, for your own good. All we need is some inside information, and your presence at the Capitol on March 10. Be reasonable, my friend, why ruin your whole life for Kennedy?" The Senator cleared his throat.

"It is highly unlikely that the FBI knows any details

104

about our plans. As Mr. Matson knows, if the Bureau had anything to go on, any reason to think that this supposed threat is any different from a thousand others the President has received, the Secret Service would have been informed immediately. And my secretary has ascertained that the President's schedule for that week remains unchanged. All his appointments will be kept. He will go to the Capitol on the morning of March 10 for a special address to the Senate—"

"But that's exactly the point," Matson interrupted with a contemptuous sneer. "All threats against the President, no matter how far-fetched, are routinely reported to the Secret Service. If they haven't reported anything, it must mean that—"

"It may mean that they don't know a thing, Matson," said the Chairman firmly. "I told you to look into it. Now let the Senator answer a more important question: If the FBI knew the details, would they tell the President?"

The Senator hesitated. "No, I don't think so, or only if they were absolutely certain of danger on a particular day; otherwise they'd go ahead as planned. If every threat or suggestion of a threat was taken seriously, the President would never be able to leave the White House. The Secret Service report to Congress last year showed that there were 1572 threats against the President's life, but thorough investigation revealed that there were no actual known attempts."

The Chairman nodded. "Either they know everything or they know nothing."

Matson persisted. "I am still a member of the Society of Former Special Agents and I attended a meeting yesterday, and no one there knew a damn thing. Someone would have heard something by now. Later, I also had a drink with Grant Nanna, who was my old boss at the Washington

Field Office, and he seemed almost uninterested, which I found strange. I thought Stames was a friend of his, but I obviously couldn't push it too far, since Stames was no friend of mine. I'm still worried. It doesn't make sense that Stames went to the hospital and no one in the Bureau is saying anything about his death."

"Okay, okay," said the Chairman. "If we don't get him on March 10, we may as well quit now. We go ahead as if nothing had happened, unless we hear any rumbles—and that's in your hands, Matson. We'll be there on the day, unless you stop us. Now let's plan ahead. First I'll go over Kennedy's schedule for that day. Kennedy"—no one in that room except for the Senator ever called him the President—"leaves the White House at ten A.M., he passes the FBI Building at three minutes past, he passes the Peace Monument at the northwest corner of the Capitol grounds at five minutes past. He gets out of his car at the east front of the Capitol at six minutes past. Normally, he would go in the private entrance, but the Senator has assured us that he will milk this visit for all it's worth. It takes him forty-five seconds to walk from the car to the top of the Capitol steps. We know that Xan can easily do the job in forty-five seconds. I will be watching at the corner of Pennsylvania Avenue when Kennedy passes the FBI Building. Tony will be there with a car, in case of an emergency, and the Senator will be on the Capitol steps to stall Kennedy, if we need more time. The most important part of the operation is Xan's, which we have worked out to a split second. So listen and listen carefully. I have arranged for Xan to be on the construction crew working on the renovation of the front of the Capitol. And, believe me, with that union it was no mean feat to place an Oriental. Take over, Xan."

Xan looked up. He had said nothing since his last invitation to speak.

"Construction on west front of Capitol has been going on for nearly six months. No one is more enthusiastic about it than Kennedy. He wants it finished in time for his second Inaugural." He grinned. All eyes were upon the little man, intent on every word. "I have been part of work force for just over four weeks. I am in charge of checking all supplies that come onto site, which means I am in site office. From there, it has not been hard to discover movements of everybody connected with construction. The guards are not from FBI, Secret Service, or from CIA, but from Government Building Security Service. They are usually a lot older than normal agents, often retired from one of services. There are sixteen in all, and they work in fours on four shifts. I know where they drink, smoke, play cards, everything; no one is very interested in site because at moment it overlooks nothing and it's on least-used side of Capitol. A little petty theft from site but not much else to excite guards." Xan had total silence. "Right in middle of site is biggest American Hoist Co. crane in world, number eleven-three-ten, specially designed for lifting new parts of Capitol into place. Fully extended, it is three hundred and twenty-two feet, almost double regulation height allowed in Washington buildings. Nobody expect us on west side, and nobody figure we can see that far. On top is small covered platform for general maintenance of pulleys, used only when it is flat and parallel to ground, but platform becomes like a small box in effect. It is four feet long, two feet three inches in width, and one foot five inches in height. I have slept there for last three nights. I see everything, no one can see me, not even White House helicopter."

There was a stunned silence.

"How do you get up there?" asked the Senator.

"Like cat, Senator. I climb. An advantage of being very

small. I go up just after midnight and come down at five. I overlook all Washington and no one can see me."

"Do you have a good view of the Capitol steps from such a small platform?" asked the Chairman.

"Perhaps it will take three seconds," Xan said. "View allows me to see White House as no one has ever seen it. I might have been able to kill Kennedy twice last week. When he is on Capitol steps, it will be easy. I can't miss—"

"What about the other workers on Thursday? They may want to use the crane," the Senator interrupted.

This time the Chairman smiled. "There will be a strike next Thursday, my friend. Something to do with unfair rates for overtime, no work while Kennedy is visiting the Capitol to prove their point. One thing is certain, with no one on the site other than some aging guards, nobody will be eager to climb to the top of a crane that is open to the world except for two feet. From the ground it doesn't look as if a mouse could hide up there. Xan flies to Vienna tomorrow and will report the results of his trip at the final meeting next Wednesday. By the way, Xan, have you got your can of yellow paint?"

"Yes, stole one from site."

The Chairman looked around the table—silence. "Good, we seem to be better organized than last time. Thank you, Xan."

"I don't like it," mumbled Matson. "Something's wrong. It's all too easy, it's all too clever."

"The FBI has taught you to be overly suspicious, Matson. You'll see that we're better prepared than they are, because we know what we're going to do and they don't. Fear not, you'll be able to attend another Kennedy funeral."

Matson's big chin moved up and down. "You're the guy that wants him dead," he said sourly.

"And you're being paid for it," said the Chairman. Right, we meet in five days to go over the final plan. You ill be told where to come on Wednesday morning. Xan ill be back from Austria well before then."

The Chairman smiled and lit another cigarette. The enator slipped out. Five minutes later, Matson left. Five inutes later, Tony left. Five minutes later, Xan left. Five inutes later, the Chairman ordered lunch.

4:00 PM

Marc was too hungry to work efficiently any longer, and he eft the Library in search of some food. When the elevator topped, the opening doors provided a view of the card atalogue: "Harrison–Health" confronted him. Some sub-onscious word association triggered in his mind the wel-ome vision of the beautiful, witty girl he had met the revious day, walking along the corridor in her black skirt nd red shirt, heels tapping on the tiles. A big grin spread cross Marc's face. It was amazing the pleasure it gave im just to know he could call her and see her again, larming to realize just how much he wanted to.

He found the snack bar and munched his way through a amburger, letting his mind play back all the things she ad said, and how she had looked while she was saying hem. Then he called Woodrow Wilson.

"I'm sorry, Dr. Dexter is not on duty today," said a urse. "Can I get Dr. Delgado for you?"

"No," said Marc. "I'm afraid she won't do." He took ut his diary, and dialed Elizabeth Dexter's number. Rather to his surprise, she was there.

"Hello, Elizabeth. It's Marc Andrews. Any hope of buying you dinner tonight?"

"Promises, promises. I continue to live in the hope of the big steak."

"Good. I've had a lousy day, and you may turn out to be the only bright spot in it."

"You sound a bit subdued, Marc. Perhaps you really do have a touch of flu."

"No, I don't think it's flu, but thinking of you makes it hard to breathe. I'd better hang up now, before I turn blue."

It was good to hear her laugh.

"Why don't you come by about eight?"

"Fine. See you this evening, Elizabeth."

"Take care, Marc."

He put the telephone down, suddenly conscious that once again he was smiling from ear to ear. He glanced at his watch: 4:30. Good. Three more hours in the Library, then he could go in pursuit of her. He returned to his reference books and continued to make biographical notes on the sixty-two senators.

His mind drifted for a moment to the President. This wasn't just any President. This was a Kennedy. Could there be a tie-in with John and Robert, the conspiracy theory? Why hadn't Tyson mentioned that? Were there any senators connected with those deaths? Or was this another lunatic working on his own? All the evidence on this inquiry so far pointed to teamwork. Lee Harvey Oswald and Sirhan Sirhan, one dead and one in prison, and still there was no convincing explanation of either assassination. If the third Kennedy was going to be killed, why hadn't Tyson mentioned this possibility?

Some people claimed the CIA was behind JFK's death because he had threatened to hang them out to dry in

)61, after the Bay of Pigs fiasco. Others said Castro had ranged the murder in revenge; it was known that Oswald ad an interview with the Cuban ambassador in Mexico /o weeks before the assassination, and the CIA had own about it all along. Twenty years after the event, and ill no one was certain. And what of the famous Massa- usetts plot against Ted Kennedy? The identity of the en involved had never been disclosed.

A smart guy from L.A., Jay Sandberg, who had roomed ith Marc at law school, had maintained that the con- iracy reached the top, even the top of the FBI: they ew the truth but said nothing.

Maybe Tyson and Rogers were two of those who knew: ey had sent him out on useless errands to keep him oc- upied: he hadn't been allowed to tell anyone the details f yesterday's events, not even Grant Nanna.

If there was a conspiracy, whom could he turn to? Only ne man might listen and that was the President, and there as no way of getting to him. He'd have to call Jay Sand- erg, who had made a study of the Kennedy assassinations. anyone would have a theory, it would be Sandberg. Marc retraced his steps to the pay phone, checked Sand- erg's home number in New York, and dialed the ten igits. A woman's voice answered the telephone.

"Hello," she said coolly. Marc could visualize the cloud f cigarette smoke that went with the voice.

"Hello, I'm trying to reach Jay Sandberg."

"Oh." More cigarette smoke. "He's still at work."

"Can you let me have his number?" asked Marc.

After more smoke, she gave it to him, and the phone icked.

Sheeesh, Marc said to himself, Upper East Side women.

A very different voice, warm Irish-American, answered e phone next.

111

"Sullivan and Cromwell."

Marc recognized the prestigious New York law firm. Other people were getting ahead in the world.

"Can I speak to Jay Sandberg?"

"I'll connect you, sir."

"Sandberg."

"Hi, Jay, it's Marc Andrews. Glad I caught you. I'm calling from Washington."

"Hello, Marc, nice to hear from you. How's life for a G-man? Rat-a-tat-tat and all that."

"It can be," said Marc, "sometimes. Jay, I need some advice on where to find the facts on the Edward Kennedy assassination attempts, particularly the one in Massachusetts in 1979; do you remember it?"

"Sure do. Three people arrested; let me think." Sandberg paused. "All released as harmless. One died in an auto accident in 1980, another was knifed in a brawl in San Francisco, later died in 1981, and the third disappeared mysteriously last year. I tell you it was another conspiracy."

"Who this time?"

"Mafia wanted EMK out of the way in seventy-six so they could avoid an inquiry he was pressing for into the death of those two hoodlums, Sam Giancana and John Rosselli; they don't love him any more now with the way he is running the Gun-Control Bill."

"Mafia? Gun-Control Bill? Where do I find all the facts?" asked Marc.

"I can tell you it's not in the Warren Commission Report or any of the later inquiries. Your best bet is *The Yankee and Cowboy Wars* by Carl Oglesby—you'll find it all there."

Marc made a note.

"Thanks for your help, Jay. I'll get back to you if it doesn't cover everything. How are things in New York?"

"Oh, fine, just fine. I'm one of about a million lawyers cleaning up after the New York bankruptcy. Let's get together soon, Marc."

"Sure, next time I'm in New York."

Marc went back to the Library thoughtfully. It could be CIA, it could be Mafia, it could be a nut, it could be anything. He asked the girl for the Carl Oglesby book. A well-thumbed volume beginning to come apart was supplied. Sheed Andrews & McMeel, Inc., 6700 Squibb Road, Mission, Kansas. It was going to make good reading, but for now back to the senators' life histories, still the immediate task. He spent two more hours trying to eliminate senators or find motives for any of them wanting Kennedy out of the way: he wasn't getting very far.

"You'll have to leave now, sir," said the young librarian, her arms full of books, looking as if she would like to go home. "I'm afraid we lock up at seven-thirty."

"Can you give me two more minutes? I'm very nearly through."

"I guess so," she said, staggering away under a load of Senate Reports, 1971-73, which few but she would ever handle.

Marc glanced over his notes. There were some very prominent names among the sixty-two "suspects," men like Alan Cranston of California, often described as the "liberal whip" of the Senate; Edward W. Brooke of Massachusetts, still the only black senator; Majority Leader Robert C. Byrd of West Virginia, who had ousted Edward Kennedy from the post of Democratic Whip in 1971; Henry Dexter of Connecticut, who had served as a special envoy during Ford's term; Edmund S. Muskie of Maine, the Democratic vice-presidential candidate in 1968; Robert E. Duncan of South Carolina, an urbane, educated man with a reputation for parliamentary skill; Marvin Thornton, who occupied the seat vacated by Kennedy in 1980; Mark O. Hatfield, the liberal and devout Republican from Oregon; Hayden Woodson of Arkansas, one of the new breed of Southern Republicans; William Cain of Nebraska, a staunch conservative who had run as an independent in the 1980 election; and Birch Bayh of Indiana, the man who had pulled Ted Kennedy from a plane wreck in 1967, and probably saved his life. Sixty-two men under suspicion, thought Marc. And six days to go. And the evidence must be iron-clad. There was little more he could do that day.

Every government building was closing. He just hoped the Director had covered as much and could bring the sixty-two names down to a sensible number quickly. Sixty-two names; six days.

He returned to his car in the public parking lot. Four dollars a day for the privilege of being on vacation. He paid the attendant, eased the car out on Pennsylvania Avenue, and headed down 9th Street back toward his apartment on N Street, SW, the worst of the rush hour behind him. Simon was there, and Marc tossed him the car keys. "I'm going out again as soon as I've changed," Marc called over his shoulder as he went up to his eighth-floor apartment.

It wasn't the most luxurious part of town, but the renovated Southwest section of Washington was home for many young, single professionals. It was on the waterfront near the Arena Stage, conveniently located next to a Metro station. Pleasant, lively, not too expensive—the place suited Marc perfectly. He showered and shaved

114

quickly and put on a more casual suit than the one he had worn for the Director. Now for the good part of his life.

When he came back down, the car was turned around so that Marc could, to quote Simon, make a quick get-away. He drove to Georgetown, turned right on 30th, and parked outside Elizabeth Dexter's house. A small red-brick town house, very chic. Either she was doing well for herself or her father had bought it for her. Her father, he couldn't help thinking . . .

She looked as beautiful on the doorstep as she had in his imagination. That was good. She wore a long red dress with a high collar. It set off her dark hair and eyes very well.

"Are you going to come in, or are you just going to stand there like a delivery boy?"

"I'm just going to stand here and admire you," he said. "You know, Doctor, I've always been attracted to beautiful, clever women. Do you think that says something about me?"

She laughed and led him into the pretty house.

"Come and sit down. You look as though you could do with a drink." She poured him the beer he asked for. When she sat down, her eyes were serious.

"I don't suppose you want to talk about the horrible thing that happened to my mailman."

"No," said Marc. "I'd prefer not to, for a number of reasons."

Her face showed understanding.

"I hope you'll catch the bastard who killed him." Again, those dark eyes flashed to meet his. She got up to turn over the record on the stereo. "How do you like this kind of music?" she asked lightly.

"I'm not much on Haydn," he said. "I'm a Mahler freak. And Beethoven, Aznavour. And you?"

She blushed slightly.

"When you didn't turn up last night, I called your office to see if you were there."

Marc was surprised and pleased.

"Finally I got through to a girl in your department. You were out at the time, and besides she said you were very busy, so I didn't leave a message."

"That's Polly," said Marc. "She's very protective."

"And pretty?" She smiled with the confidence of one who knows she is good-looking.

"Good from far but far from good," said Marc. "Let's forget Polly. Come on, you ought to be hungry by now, and I'm not going to give you that steak I keep promising you. I've booked a table for nine o'clock at Tío Pepe. How does that suit you?"

"Lovely," she said. "Since you managed to get your car parked, why don't we walk?"

"Great."

It was a clear, cool evening. Marc needed the fresh air. What he didn't need was the continual urge to look over his shoulder.

"Looking for another woman?" she teased.

"No," said Marc. "Why should I look any further?" He spoke lightly, but he knew he hadn't fooled her. He changed the subject abruptly. "How do you like your work?"

"My work?" Elizabeth seemed surprised, as though she never thought of it in those terms. "My life, you mean? It's just about my entire life. Or has been so far."

She glanced up at Marc with a somber expression on her face. "I hate the hospital. It's a big bureaucracy, old and dirty and a lot of the people there, petty administrative types, don't really care about helping people. To them it's just another way of earning a living. Only yesterday

116

had to threaten to resign in order to convince the
[U]tilization Committee to let an old man stay in the
[h]ospital. He had no home to go back to."

They walked down 30th Street, and Elizabeth con-
[ti]nued to tell him about her work. She spoke with spirit,
[a]nd Marc listened to her with pleasure. She had a pleasant
[s]elf-assurance, yet without a trace of the bitchiness that
[m]ars so many professional women. She was telling him
[a]bout a soulful Yugoslav who would sing incomprehen-
[si]ble Slavic songs of love and of longing as she inspected
[h]is ulcerated armpit and who had finally, in a misplaced
[g]esture of passion, seized her left ear and licked it.

Marc laughed and took her arm as he guided her into
[t]he restaurant. "You ought to demand combat pay," he
[s]aid.

"Oh, I wouldn't have complained, but his singing was
[a]lways out of tune."

The hostess led them upstairs to a table in the center
[o]f the room, near where the floor show would be per-
[fo]rmed. Marc rejected it in favor of a table in the far
[co]rner. He did not ask Elizabeth which seat she would
[p]refer. He sat down with his back to the wall, making a
[la]me excuse about wanting to be away from the noise so
[h]e could talk to her. Marc was sure that this girl would
[n]ot fall too easily for that sort of blarney; she knew
[so]mething was wrong and she sensed his edginess, but she
[di]d not pry.

A young Latino waiter asked them if they would like
[a] cocktail. Elizabeth asked for a Margarita, Marc for a
[s]pritzer.

"What's a spritzer?" asked Elizabeth.

"Not very Spanish, half white wine, half soda, lots of
[ic]e, sort of a poor man's James Bond."

She laughed.

The pleasant atmosphere of the restaurant helped to dispel some of Marc's tension; he relaxed slightly for the first time in twenty-four hours. They chatted about movies, music, and books, and about Yale. Her face, now animated, now quiet, was lovely in the candlelight. Marc was enchanted by her. For all her intelligence and self sufficiency, she had a touching fragility and femininity.

They chose a meal of paella. Marc asked Elizabeth about the way in which her father had become a senator, about his career, and her childhood in Connecticut. The subject seemed to make her uneasy. Her father, he couldn't help remembering, was still on the list. He tried to shift the conversation to her mother. Elizabeth avoided his eyes and even, he thought, turned pale. For the first time, a tiny ripple of suspicion disturbed his affectionate vision of Elizabeth, and made him worry momentarily. She was the first beautiful thing that had happened for quite a while, and he didn't want to distrust her. Was it possible? Could she be involved? No, of course not. He tried to put it out of his mind.

The Spanish floor show came on and was performed with enthusiasm. Marc and Elizabeth listened and watched, unable to speak to each other because of the noise. Marc was happy enough just to sit and be with her; her face was turned away as she looked at the dancers. When the floor show eventually ended, they had both finished the paella and it was 11:15. They ordered dessert and coffee.

"Would you like a cigar?"

Elizabeth smiled. "No, thanks. We've almost beaten you men. We don't have to ape your vile habits as well as your good ones."

"Like that," said Marc. "You're going to be the first woman Surgeon General, I suppose?"

"No, I'm not," she said demurely. "I'll probably be the second or third."

Marc laughed. "I'd better get back to the Bureau, and do great things. Just to keep up with you."

"And it may well be a woman who stops you becoming Director of the FBI," Elizabeth added.

"No, it won't be a woman that stops me becoming Director of the FBI," said Marc, but he didn't explain.

"Your coffee, señorita, señor."

If Marc had ever wanted to sleep with a woman on the first date, this was the occasion, but there was no way that was going to happen, and he wasn't totally sure he would have been happy if it did.

He paid the bill, left a generous tip for the waiter, and congratulated the girl from the floor show, who was sitting in a corner drinking coffee.

The night now had a chill edge. Marc found himself once again looking nervously around him, trying not to make it obvious to Elizabeth. He took her hand as they crossed the street, and didn't let it go when they reached the other side. They walked on, chatting intermittently, both aware of what was happening. He wanted to make love to her very much. Lately, he had been seeing a lot of women, but with none of them had he held their hand either before or afterward. Gradually his mood darkened again. Perhaps fear was making him excessively sentimental.

A car was driving up behind them. Marc stiffened with anticipation. Elizabeth didn't notice. It slowed down. It was going slower as it neared them. It stopped just beside them. Marc undid his middle button and fidgeted,

more worried for Elizabeth than for himself. The doors o
the car opened suddenly and out jumped four teen-agers
two girls, two boys. They darted into a Hamburger Haven
Sweat appeared on Marc's forehead. He shook free o
Elizabeth's touch. She stared at him. "Something's ver
wrong, isn't it?"

"Yes," he said. "Just don't ask me about it."

She sought his hand again, held it firmly, and they
walked on. The oppression of the horrible events of th
previous day bore down on Marc and he did not speal
again. When they arrived at her front door, he was bacl
in the world which was shared only by him and the hulk
ing, shadowy figure of Halt Tyson.

"Well, you have been very charming this evening, when
you've actually been here," she said smilingly.

Marc shook himself. "I'm really sorry."

"Would you like to come in for coffee?"

"Yes and no. Can I take another rain check on that?
don't feel like good company right now."

He still had several things to do before he saw th
Director at 7:00 A.M. and it was already midnight. H
hadn't slept for a day and a half.

"Can I call you tomorrow?"

"I'd like that," she said. "Be sure to keep in touch
whatever happens."

Marc would carry those few words around with hir
like a talisman for the next few days. He could recall he
every word and its accompanying gesture. Were they sai
in fun, were they said seriously, were they said teasingly
Lately, it hadn't been fashionable to fall in love; very fe
people seemed to be getting married and a lot of peopl
who had were getting divorced. Was he really going t
fall madly in love in the middle of all this?

He kissed her on the cheek and turned to leave, his eyes darting up and down the road again. She called after him:

"I hope you find the man who killed my mailman and your Greek."

Your Greek, your Greek, Greek Orthodox priest, Father Gregory. God in heaven, why hadn't he thought of it before. He'd forgotten Elizabeth for a moment as he started to run toward his car. He turned to wave; she was staring at him with a puzzled expression, wondering what she had said. Marc leaped into the car and drove as fast as he could to his apartment. He must find Father Gregory's number. Greek Orthodox priest, what did he look like, the one who came out of the elevator, what did he look like; it was all coming back, there was something wrong with him: what the hell was it? His face was wrong somehow. Of course. Of course. How could he have been so stupid. When he arrived home, he called the Washington Field Office immediately. Polly, on the switchboard, was surprised to hear him.

"Aren't you on leave?"

"Yes, sort of. Do you have Father Gregory's number?"

"Who is Father Gregory?"

"A Greek Orthodox priest whom Mr. Stames used to contact occasionally; I think he was his local priest."

"Yes, you're right. Now I remember."

Marc waited.

She checked Stames's Rolodex and gave him the number. Marc wrote it down, and replaced the phone. Of course, of course, of course. How stupid of him. It was so obvious. Well past midnight, but he had to call. He dialed the number. The telephone rang several times before it was answered.

"Father Gregory?"

"Yes."

"Do all Greek Orthodox priests have beards?"

"Yes, as a rule. Who is this asking such a damn silly question in the middle of the night?"

Marc apologized. "My name is Special Agent Marc Andrews. I worked under Nick Stames."

The man at the other end, who had sounded sleepy, immediately woke up. "I understand, young man. What can I do for you?"

"Father Gregory, last night Mr. Stames's secretary called you and asked you to go to Woodrow Wilson to check a Greek who had a bullet wound in his leg?"

"Yes, that's right—I remember, Mr. Andrews. But somebody else called about thirty minutes later, just as I was leaving, in fact, to tell me I needn't bother because Mr. Casefikis had been discharged from the hospital."

"He'd been what?" Marc's voice rose with each word.

"Discharged from the hospital."

"Did the caller say who he was?"

"No, the man said no more. I assumed he was from your office."

"Father Gregory, can I see you tomorrow morning at eight o'clock?"

"Yes, of course, my son."

"And can you be sure you don't talk to anybody else about this phone call, whoever they say they are?"

"If that is your wish, my son."

"Thank you, Father."

Marc dropped the telephone and tried to concentrate. He was taller than I was, so he was over six feet. He was dark, or was that just his priest's robes? No, he had dark hair, he had a big nose, I remember he had a big nose, eyes, no I can't remember his eyes, he had a big nose, a heavy chin, a heavy chin. Marc wrote everything down he could remember. A big heavy man, taller than me, big nose, heavy chin, big nose, heavy . . . he collapsed. His head fell to the desk and he slept.

5

6:32 AM

Marc had awoken, but he wasn't awake. His head was swimming with incoherent thoughts. The first vision to flash across his mind was Elizabeth; he smiled. The second was Nick Stames; he frowned. The third was the Director. Marc woke with a start and sat up, trying to focus his eyes on his watch. All he could see was the second hand moving: 6:35. Jesus. He shot up from the chair, his stiff neck and back hurting him; he was still dressed. He threw off his clothes and rushed into the bathroom and showered, without taking time to adjust the water temperature. Goddamn freezing. At least it woke him up and made him forget Elizabeth. He jumped out of the shower and grabbed a towel: 6:40. After throwing the lather on his face, he shaved too quickly, mowing down the stubble on his chin. Damn it, three nicks; the aftershave lotion stung viciously: 6:43. He dressed: clean shirt, same cuff links, clean socks, same shoes, clean suit, same tie. A quick look in the mirror: two nicks still bleeding slightly, the hell with it. He bundled the papers on his desk into his briefcase and ran for the elevator. First piece of luck, it was on the top floor. Downstairs: 6:46.

124

"Hi, Simon."

The young black garage attendant didn't move. He was dozing in his little cubbyhole at the garage entrance.

"Morning, Marc. Christ, is it eight o'clock already?"

"No, thirteen minutes to seven."

"What are you up to? Moonlighting?" asked Simon, rubbing his eyes and handing over the car keys. Marc smiled, but didn't have time to answer. Simon dozed off again.

Car starts first time. Reliable Mercedes. Moves onto the road: 6:48. Must stay below speed limit. Never embarrass the Bureau. At 6th Street, held up by lights: 6:50. Cut across G Street, up 7th, more lights. Cross Independence Avenue: 6:53. Corner of 7th and Pennsylvania. Can see FBI Building: 6:55. Down ramp, park, show FBI pass to garage guard, run for elevator: 6:57; elevator to seventh floor: 6:58. Along the corridor, turn right, Room 7074, straight in, past Mrs. McGregor as instructed. She barely glances up; knock on door of Director's office; no reply; go in as instructed. No Director: 6:59; sink into easy chair. Director going to be late; smile of satisfaction. Thirty seconds to seven; glance around room, casually, as if been waiting for hours. Eyes land on grandfather clock. Strikes: one, two, three, four, five, six, seven.

The door opened, and the Director marched in. "Good morning, Andrews." He did not look at Marc, but at the clock on the wall. "It's always a little fast." Silence. The Old Post Office Tower clock struck seven.

The Director settled into his chair, and once again the large hands took possession of the desk.

"We'll start with my news first, Andrews. We have just received some identification on the driver of the

Lincoln that went into the Potomac with Stames and Colvert."

The Director opened a new manila file marked "Eyes only" and glanced at its contents. What was in the file that Marc didn't know about and ought to know about?

"Nothing solid to go on. Hans-Dieter Gerbach, German. Bonn has reported that he was a minor figure in the Munich rackets until five years ago, then they lost track of him. There is some evidence to suggest he was in Rhodesia and hitched up with the CIA for a while. The White-Lightning Brigade. Langley is not helping, I can't see much information coming from them before Thursday. Sometimes I wonder whose side they're on. In 1980, Gerbach turned up in New York, but there's nothing there except rumors and street talk, no record to go on. It would help if he'd lived."

Marc thought of the slit throats in Woodrow Wilson Medical Center and wondered.

"The interesting fact to emerge from the car crash is that both back tires of Stames's and Colvert's car have small holes in them. They could have been the result of the fall down the bank, but our laboratory boys think they are bullet holes. If they are, whoever did the shooting makes Annie Oakley look like a girl scout.

The Director spoke into his intercom. "Have Assistant Director Rogers come in please, Mrs. McGregor."

"Yes, sir."

"His men have found the catering outfit Casefikis was working for, for what that's worth."

The Assistant Director knocked and entered. The Director indicated a chair. Rogers smiled at Marc and sat down.

"Let's have it, Matt."

"Well, sir, the owner of the Golden Duck wasn't exactly

cooperative. Seemed to think I was after him for contravening employers' regulations. I threatened to shut him down if he didn't talk. Finally he admitted to employing a man matching Casefikis's description. February 24, he sent Casefikis to serve at a small luncheon party in one of the rooms at the Georgetown Inn on Wisconsin Avenue. The man who made the arrangement was a Lorenzo Rossi. He insisted on a waiter who couldn't speak English. Paid in cash. We've run Rossi through all the computers—nothing. Obviously a false name. Same story at the Georgetown Inn. The proprietor said the room had been hired for the day of February 24 by a Mr. Rossi, food to be supplied, but no service, cash paid in advance. Rossi was about five feet eight, dark complexion, no distinguishing features, dark hair, sunglasses. The proprietor thought he 'seemed Italian.' No one at the hotel knows or cares who the hell went to lunch in that room that day. I'm afraid it doesn't get us very far."

"I agree. I suppose we could pull every Italian answering that description off the street," said the Director. "If we had five years, not five days. Did you turn up anything new at the hospital, Matt?"

"It's a hell of a mess, sir. The place is full of people coming and going, all day and most of the night. The staff all work shifts. They don't even know their own colleagues, let alone outsiders. You could wander around there all day with an ax over your shoulder and nobody would ask you who you were or what you were doing."

"That figures," said Tyson. "Right, Andrews, what have you been up to for the past twenty-four hours?"

Marc opened his regulation blue-plastic portfolio. He reported that there were sixty-two senators left, the other thirty-eight accounted for, most of them having been out of Washington on February 24. He passed the list of names over to the Director, who glanced through them.

"Some pretty big fish still left in the muddy pond, Andrews. Go on."

Marc proceeded to outline his encounter with the Greek Orthodox priest. He expected a sharp reprimand for failing to remember the matter of the beard immediately. He was not disappointed. Chastened, he continued: "I am seeing Father Gregory at eight o'clock this morning, and I thought I would go on to see Casefikis's widow afterward. I don't think either will have much to offer, but I imagine you want those leads followed up, sir. After that I intended to return to the Library of Congress to try and figure out why any of those sixty-two senators might wish to see an end of President Kennedy."

"Well, to start with, put them in categories," said the Director. "First political party, then committees, then outside interests, then their personal knowledge of the President. Don't forget, Andrews, we do know that our man had lunch in Georgetown on February 24 and that should bring the numbers down."

"But, sir, presumably they all had lunch on February 24."

"Exactly, Andrews, but not all in private. Many of them would have been seen in a public place or lunched officially, with constituents or federal employees or lobbyists. You have to find out who did what, without letting the senator we're after get suspicious."

"How do you suggest I go about doing that, sir?"

"Simple," replied the Director. "You call each of the senators' secretaries and ask if the boss would be free to attend a luncheon on—" he paused "—'The Problems of Urban Environment.' Yes, I like that. Give them a date, say May 5, then ask if they attended either the one given

a," the Director glanced at his calendar, "January 17
· February 24, as some senators who had accepted
dn't attend, and one or two turned up without invita-
ons. Then say a written invitation will follow. All the
cretaries will put it out of their minds unless you write,
d if any of them does remember on May 5, it will be too
te for us to care. One thing is certain: no senator will
· letting his secretary know he is planning to kill the
resident."

The Assistant Director grimaced slightly. "If he gets
ught, sir, all hell will break loose. We'll be back in the
rty-tricks department; he'll be playing the new John
ean and you'll be Haldeman."

"No, Matt, if I tell the President one of his precious
rethren is going to knife him in the back, he won't see
nything particularly dirty in that trick."

"We haven't enough proof, sir."

"You had better get it, Andrews, or we'll all be looking
r a new job, trust my judgment."

Trust my judgment, Marc thought. "May I mention
omething else that bothers me?"

"Of course, Andrews."

"Have you considered the conspiracy theory, sir? This
ssassination may be connected with JFK and even RFK,
d therefore involve the outfits sometimes linked with
e other Kennedy killings, because if the Mafia or—"

"Yes, Andrews, I have considered it many times,
d we still don't know the truth behind the Dallas as-
ssination after almost twenty years and ten million
ollars down the drain on inquiries. If they had given
e that kind of money to buy information, I would have
lved the whole damn mystery within six months. With
n million to play around with, someone would have
ened his mouth. In this case, we have one strong lead:

that a senator may be involved, and we have only fi
days left. If we fail next Thursday, there will be enou
time during the next twenty years to work out any lin
with JFK, and you'll be able to make a fortune writing
book about it."

That may be right, but I'm still going to do a litt
checking myself, whatever you say, Mark thought.

"Andrews, don't get too worried. I have briefed t
head of the Secret Service. I told him no more and no le
than was in your report, as we agreed yesterday, so th
gives us a clear run right through to March 10. I
working on a contingency plan, in case we don't kno
who Cassius is before then; but I won't bore you with
now. I have also talked to the boys from Homicide; the
have come up with very little that can help us. It m
interest you to know that they have seen Casefikis's wi
already. Their brains seem to work a little faster th
yours, Andrews."

"Perhaps they don't have as much on their minds
said the Assistant Director.

"Maybe not. Okay, go see her if you think it mig
help. You may pick up something they missed. Cheer u
you've covered a lot of ground. Perhaps this morning
investigation will give us some new leads to work on.
think that covers everything. Right, Andrews, don't l
me waste any more of your time."

"No, sir."

Marc rose.

"I'm sorry, I forgot to offer you coffee, Andrews."

I didn't manage to drink it the last time, Marc wou
have liked to have said. He left as the Director ordere
coffee for himself and the Assistant Director. He decide
that he too could do with some breakfast and a chance

130

ollect his thoughts. He went in search of the Bureau afeteria.

The Director drank his coffee and asked Mrs. McGregor to send in his personal assistant. The anonymous man appeared almost instantly, a gray folder under his arm. He didn't have to ask the Director what it was that he wanted. He placed the folder on the table in front of him, and left without speaking.

"Thank you," said the Director to the closing door.

He turned back the gray cover and browsed through it for twenty minutes, a chuckle here, and a grunt there, the odd comment to Matthew Rogers. There were facts in it about Marc Andrews of which Marc himself would have been unaware. The Director finished his second cup of coffee, closed the file, and locked it in the personal drawer of the Queen Anne desk. Queen Anne had never held as many secrets as that desk.

Marc finished a much better breakfast than he could have hoped for at the Washington Field Office. There, you had to go across the street to the Lunch Connection, because the snack bar downstairs was so abominable, much in keeping with the rest of the building. Not that he wouldn't have liked to return to it now instead of the underground garage to pick up his car. He didn't notice the man across the street who watched him leave, but he did wonder whether the blue Ford sedan that stayed in his rear-view mirror so long was there by chance. If it wasn't, who was watching who, who was trying to protect who?

He arrived at Father Gregory's church just before 8:00 P.M. and they walked together to the priest's house. Marc said that he had already breakfasted, but it didn't stc the Father from frying two eggs and bacon, plus toas marmalade, and a cup of coffee. Father Gregory cou add very little to what he had told Marc on the telephor the previous night, and he sighed deeply when he wa reminded of the two deaths at the hospital.

"Yes, I read the details in the *Post*." His little hal rim glasses squatted on the end of his stubby nose. H large, red cheeks and even larger basketball belly led tl uncharitable to conclude that Father Gregory had foun much to solace him on earth while he waited for tl eternal kingdom of heaven. When they talked about Nic Stames, a light came into his gray eyes; it was clear th priest and policeman had shared a few secrets, this was n jolly old Jesus freak.

"Is there any connection between Nick's death and tl accident in the hospital?" Father Gregory asked suddenl

The question took Marc by surprise. There was shrewd brain behind the half-rim glasses. Lying to priest, Greek Orthodox or otherwise, seemed someho worse than the usual lies which were intended to prote the Bureau from the general public.

"Absolutely none," said Marc. "Just one of those ho rible auto accidents."

"Just one of those weird coincidences?" said Fath Gregory quizzically, peering at Marc over the top of h glasses. "Is that right?" he sounded almost as unco vinced as Grant Nanna. He continued: "There's one mo thing I would like to mention. Although it's hard to r member exactly what the man said when he called n and told me not to bother to go to the hospital, I'm fair certain he was a well-educated man. I feel sure by tl way he carried it off that he was a professional man, a I am not sure what I mean by that; it's just the stran

eling that he had made that sort of call before; there
us something professional about him."

Father Gregory repeated the phrase to himself—
omething professional about him"—and so did Marc,
hile he was in the car on the way to the house in which
rs. Casefikis was staying. It was the home of a friend,
e friend who had harbored her wounded husband.

Marc drove down Connecticut Avenue, past the Wash-
gton Hilton and the National Zoo, into Maryland.
tches of bright, yellow forsythia had begun to appear
ong the road. Connecticut Avenue turned into Univer-
y Boulevard, and Marc found himself in Wheaton, a
burban satellite of stores, restaurants, gas stations, and
few apartment buildings. Stopped by a red light near
heaton Plaza, Marc checked his notes. 11501 Elkin
reet. He was looking for the Blue Ridge Manor Apart-
ents. Fancy name for a group of squat, three-story
ded-brick buildings lining Blue Ridge and Elkin streets.
s he approached 11501, Marc looked for a parking
ace. No luck. He hovered for a moment, then decided
park in front of a fire hydrant. He draped the radio
icrophone carefully over his rear-view mirror, so that
y observant meter maid or policeman would know that
is was an official car on official business.

Ariana Casefikis burst into tears at the mere sight of
arc's badge. Her English, it turned out, was rather
tter than her husband's. She had already seen two po-
emen. She told them all that she knew nothing. First
e nice man from the Metropolitan Police who had
oken the news to her and been so understanding, then
e Homicide lieutenant who had come a little later and
en much firmer, wanting to know things she hadn't the
intest clue about, and now a visit from the FBI. Her
sband had never been in trouble before and she didn't

know who shot him or why anybody would want to. H
was a gentle, harmless sort of man. Marc believed her.

Mrs. Casefikis looked frail; only twenty-nine, h
clothes unkempt, her hair all over the place, her eyes gr
and still full of tears. The lines on her face showed whe
the tears had been running, running for two days. Sl
and Marc were about the same age. She didn't have
country, and now she didn't have a husband. What w
going to happen to her? If Marc had felt alone, he w
certainly better off than this poor woman. Marc assure
her that she had no immediate cause for worry and th
he would deal personally with the Immigration Office ar
the Welfare people about getting her some income.
seemed to cheer her up and make her a little more respo
sive.

"Now please try to think carefully, Mrs. Casefiki
Have you any idea where your husband was working o
February 23 or 24, the Wednesday and Thursday of la
week, and did he tell you anything about his work?"

She had no idea. Angelo never told her what he was u
to and half the jobs were casual and only for a da
because he couldn't risk staying on without a work permi
being an illegal immigrant. Marc was getting nowher
but it wasn't her fault.

"Will I be able to stay in America?"

"I'll do everything I can to help, Mrs. Casefikis. Th
I promise you. I'll talk to a Greek Orthodox priest I kno
about finding some money to tide you over till I've see
the Welfare people."

Marc opened the door, despondent about the lack c
any hard information either from Father Gregory or fro
Ariana Casefikis.

"The priest already give me money."

134

Marc stopped in his tracks, turned slowly, and faced er. He tried to show no particular interest.

"Which priest was that?" he asked casually.

"He said he help. Man who came to visit me yesterday. ice man, very nice, very kind. He give me twenty dol- rs."

Marc turned cold. The man had been ahead of him gain. Father Gregory was right, there was something pro- essional about him.

"Can you describe him, Mrs. Casefikis?"

"What do you mean?"

"What did he look like?"

"Oh, he was a big man, very dark, I think," she began. Marc tried to remain offhand. It must have been the nan who had passed him in the elevator, the man who ad earlier kept Father Gregory from going to the hospital nd who, if Mrs. Casefikis had known anything at all bout the plot, would no doubt have dispatched her to oin her husband.

"Did he have a beard, Mrs. Casefikis?"

She hesitated. "Most of them do—but I can't remem- er him having one."

Marc asked her to stay in the house, not to leave under ny circumstances. He made an excuse that he was going o check on the Welfare situation and talk to the Immi- ration officials. He was learning how to lie. The clean- haven Greek Orthodox priest was teaching him.

He jumped into the car and drove a few hundred yards o the nearest pay phone on Georgia Avenue. He dialed e Director's private line. The Director picked up the hone.

"Julius."

"What is your number?" asked the Director.

Thirty seconds later the phone rang. Marc went ove
the story carefully.

"I'll send an Identikit man down to you immediately
You go back there and hold her hand. And, Mr. Ar
drews, try to think on your feet. I'd like that twent
dollars. Was it one bill, or several? There may just be
fingerprint on them." The telephone clicked. Ma
frowned. If the phony Greek Orthodox priest wasn't al
ways two steps ahead of him, the Director was.

Marc returned to Mrs. Casefikis and told her that he
case would be dealt with at the highest level; he mus
remember to speak to the Director about it at the ne
meeting, he made a note about it on his pad. Back to th
casual voice again.

"Are you sure it was twenty dollars, Mrs. Casefikis?"

"Oh, yes, I don't see a twenty-dollar bill every da
and I was most thankful at the time."

"Can you remember what you did with it?"

"Yes, I went and bought food from the supermarke
just before they closed."

"Which supermarket, Mrs. Casefikis?"

"Wheaton Supermarket. Up the street."

"When was that?"

"Yesterday evening about six o'clock."

Marc realized that there wasn't a moment to lose. If i
wasn't already too late.

"Mrs. Casefikis, a man will be coming, a colleague o
mine, a friend, from the FBI, to ask you to describe th
kind Father who gave you the money. It will help u
greatly if you can remember as much about him as possi
ble. You have nothing to worry about because we're do
ing everything we can to help you."

Marc hesitated, took out his wallet and gave he
twenty dollars. She smiled for the first time.

136

"Now, Mrs. Casefikis, I want you to do just one last thing for me. If the Greek priest ever comes to visit again, don't tell him about our conversation, just call me at this number."

Marc handed her a card. Ariana Casefikis nodded, but her lackluster gray eyes followed Marc to his car. She didn't understand, or know which man to trust: hadn't they both given her twenty dollars?

Marc pulled into a parking space in front of the Wheaton Supermarket. A huge sign in the window announced that cases of cold beer were sold inside. Above the window was a blue-and-white cardboard representation of the dome of the Capitol. Five days, thought Marc. He went into the store. It was a small family enterprise, privately owned, not part of a chain. Beer lined one wall, wine the other, and in between were four rows of canned and frozen foods. A meat counter stretched the length of the rear wall. The butcher seemed to be minding the store alone. Marc hurried toward him, starting to ask the question before he reached the counter.

"Could I please see the manager?"

The butcher eyed him suspiciously. "What for?"

Marc showed his credentials.

The butcher shrugged and yelled over his shoulder, "Hey, Flavio. FBI. Wants to see you."

Several seconds later, the manager, a large red-faced Italian, appeared in the doorway to the left of the meat counter. "Yeah? What can I do for you, Mr. uh . . ."

"Andrews, FBI." Marc showed his credentials once again.

"Yeah, okay. What do you want, Mr. Andrews? I'm Flavio Guida. This is my place. I run a good, honest place."

"Yes, of course, Mr. Guida. I'm simply hoping you can

help me. I'm investigating a case of stolen money, and we have reason to believe that a stolen twenty-dollar bill was spent in this supermarket yesterday and we wonder now if there is any way of tracing it."

"Well, my money is collected every night," said the manager. "It's put into the safe and deposited in the bank first thing in the morning. It would have gone to the bank about an hour ago, and I think——"

"But it's Saturday," Marc said.

"No problem. My bank is open till noon on Saturday. It's just a few doors down."

Marc thought on his feet.

"Would you please accompany me to the bank immediately, Mr. Guida?"

Guida looked at his watch and then at Marc Andrews.

"Okay. Give me just half a minute."

He shouted to an invisible woman in the back of the store to keep an eye on the cash register. Together he and Marc walked to the corner of Georgia and Hickers. Guida was obviously quite excited by the whole episode.

At the bank Marc went immediately to the chief cashier. The money had been handed over thirty minutes before to one of his tellers, a Mrs. Townsend. She still had it in piles ready for sorting. It was next on her list. She hadn't had time to do so yet, she said rather apologetically. No need to feel sorry, thought Marc. The supermarket's take for the day had been just over five thousand dollars. There were twenty-eight twenty-dollar bills. Christ Almighty, the Director was going to tear him apart, or to be more exact, the fingerprint experts were. Marc counted the twenty-dollar notes using gloves supplied by Mrs. Townsend and put them on one side—he agreed there were twenty-eight. He signed for them, gave the receipt to the chief cashier, and assured him they would be returned in the very near future. The bank manager came over and took charge of the receipt and the situation.

"Don't FBI men usually work in pairs?"

Marc blushed. "Yes, sir, but this is a special assignment."

"I would like to check," said the manager. "You are asking me to release five hundred and sixty dollars on your word."

"Of course, sir, please do check."

Marc had to think quickly. He couldn't ask the manager of a local bank to ring the Director of the FBI. It would be like charging your gasoline to the account of Henry Ford.

"Why don't you ring the FBI's Washington Field Office, sir, ask for the head of the Criminal Section. Mr. Grant Nanna."

"I'll do just that."

Marc gave him the number, but he ignored it and looked it up for himself in the Washington directory. He got right through to Nanna. Thank God he was there.

"I have a young man from your Field Office with me. His name is Marc Andrews. He says he has the authority to take away twenty-eight twenty-dollar bills. Something to do with stolen money."

Nanna also had to think quickly. Deny the allegation, defy the alligator—Nick Stames's old motto.

Marc, meanwhile, offered up a little prayer.

"That's correct, sir," said Nanna. "He has been instructed by me to pick up those notes. I hope you will release them. We will return them as soon as possible."

"Thank you, Mr. Nanna. I'm sorry to have bothered you. I did feel I ought just to check; you never can be sure nowadays."

"Not at all, a wise precaution, sir. We wish everybody

139

would take it." The first truth he'd uttered, thought Grant Nanna.

The bank manager replaced the receiver, put the pile of twenty-dollar bills in a brown envelope, accepted the receipt, and shook hands with Marc apologetically.

"You understand I had to check?"

"Of course," said Marc. "I would have done the same thing."

He thanked Mr. Guida and the manager and asked them both not to mention the matter to anybody. They nodded with the air of those who know their duty.

Marc returned to the FBI Building immediately. He went to the Director's office. Mrs. McGregor nodded at him. A quiet knock on the door, and he went in.

"Sorry to interrupt you, sir."

"Not at all, Andrews. Have a seat. We were just finishing."

Matthew Rogers rose and looked carefully at Andrews and smiled.

"I'll try and have the answers for you by lunch, Director," he said, and left.

"Well, young man, do you have our Senator in the car downstairs?"

"No, sir, but I have these."

Marc opened the brown envelope and put twenty-eight twenty-dollar bills on the table.

"Been robbing a bank, have you? A federal charge, Andrews."

"Almost, sir. One of these notes, as you know, was given to Mrs. Casefikis by the man posing as the Greek Orthodox priest."

"Well, that will be a nice little conundrum for our fingerprint boys; fifty-six sides with hundreds, perhaps thousands of prints on them. It's a long shot and it will take considerable time, but it's worth a try." He was careful not to touch the notes. "I'll have Sommerton deal with it immediately. We'll also need Mrs. Casefikis's prints. I think I'd better put an agent on her house in case our big man returns." The Director was writing and talking at the same time. "It's just like the old days when I ran a field office. I do believe I'd enjoy it if it wasn't so serious."

"Can I mention just one other thing while I'm here, sir?"

"Yes, go ahead, Andrews." Tyson didn't look up, just continued writing.

"Mrs. Casefikis is worried about her status in this country. She has no money, no job, and now no husband. She may well have given us a vital lead and she has certainly been as cooperative as possible. I think we should help."

The Director pressed a button.

"Send Elliott in, and ask Mr. Sommerton from Fingerprints to come up."

Ah, thought Marc, the anonymous man has a name.

"We'll do what we can. I'll see you Monday at seven, Andrews. I'll be home all weekend if you need me. Don't stop working."

"Yes, sir."

Marc left. He stopped at the Riggs Bank and changed fifteen dollars into dimes. The teller looked at him curiously.

"Have your own pinball machine?"

Marc smiled.

He spent the rest of the morning and most of the afternoon with a diminishing pile of dimes, calling the weekend-duty secretaries of the sixty-two senators who

141

had been in Washington on February 24. All of them were most gratified that their senator should be invited to an Environmental Conference; the Director was no fool. At the end of sixty-two phone calls, his ears were numb. Marc studied the results . . . thirty senators had eaten in the office or with constituents, fifteen had not told their secretaries where they were having lunch or had mentioned some vague "appointment," and seventeen had attended luncheons hosted by groups as varied as the National Press Club, Common Cause, and the NAACP. One secretary even thought her boss had been at that particular Environmental Luncheon on February 24. Marc certainly had no reply to that.

With the Director's help he was down to fifteen senators.

He returned to the Library of Congress, and once again made for the quiet reference room. The librarian did not seem the least bit suspicious of all the questions about particular senators and committees and procedure in the Senate; she was used to graduate students who were just as demanding and far less courteous.

Marc went back to the shelf that held the *Congressional Record*. It was easy to find February 24: it was the only thumbed number in the pile of unbound latest issues. He checked through the fifteen remaining names. On that day, there had been one committee in session, the Foreign Relations Committee: three senators on his list of fifteen were members of that committee, and all three had spoken in committee that morning, according to the *Record*. The Senate itself had debated two issues that day: the allocation of funds in the Energy Department for solar-energy research, and the Gun-Control Bill. Some of the remaining twelve had spoken on one or both issues on the floor of the Senate: there was no way of eliminating any of the fifteen, damn it. He listed the fifteen names on fifteen sheets of paper, and read through the *Congressional Record* for every day from February 24 to March 3. By each name he noted the senator's presence or absence from the Senate on each working day. Painstakingly, he built up each senator's schedule; there were many gaps. It was evident that senators do not spend all their time in the Senate.

The young librarian was at his elbow. Marc glanced at the clock: 7:30. Throwing-out time. Time to forget the senators and to see Elizabeth. He called her at home.

"Hello, lovely lady. I think it's time to eat again. I haven't had anything since breakfast. Will you take pity on my debilitated state, Doctor, and eat with me?"

"And do what with you, Marc? I've just washed my hair. I think I must have soap in my ears."

"Eat with me, I said. That will do for the moment. I just might think of something else later."

"I just might say no later," she said sweetly. "How's the breathing?"

"Coming on nicely, thank you, but if I go on thinking what I am thinking right now, I may break out in pimples."

"What do you want me to do, pour cold water in the phone?"

"No, just eat with me. I'll pick you up in half an hour, hair wet or dry."

They found a small restaurant called Mr. Smith's in Georgetown. Marc was more familiar with it in the summer, when one could sit at a table in the garden at the back. It was crowded with people in their twenties. The perfect place to sit for hours and talk.

"God," said Elizabeth. "This is just like college; I thought we had grown out of that."

"I'm glad you appreciate it." Marc smiled.

143

"It's all so predictable. Folksy wooden floors, butcher-block tables, plants, Bach flute sonatas. Next time we'll try McDonald's."

Marc couldn't think of a reply, and was saved only by the appearance of a menu.

"Can you imagine, four years at Yale, and I still don't know what *ratatouille* is," said Elizabeth.

"I know what it is, but I wasn't sure how to pronounce it."

They both ordered chicken, baked potato, and salad.

"Look, Marc, there, that ghastly Senator Thornton with a girl young enough to be his daughter."

"Perhaps she is his daughter."

"No civilized man would bring his daughter here." She smiled at him.

"He's a friend of your father's, isn't he?"

"Yes, how do you know that?" asked Elizabeth.

"Common knowledge." Marc regretted his question.

"Well, I'd describe him as more of a business associate. He made his money manufacturing guns. Not the most attractive kind of man."

"But your father owns part of a gun company."

"Daddy? Yes, I don't approve of that either, but he blames it on my grandfather who founded the firm. I used to argue with him about it when I was at school. Told him to sell his stock and invest it in something socially useful, saw myself as a sort of Major Barbara."

"How is your dinner?" a hovering waiter asked.

"Um, just great, thanks," said Elizabeth looking up. "You know, Marc, I once called my father a war criminal."

"He was against the war, I thought."

"You seem to know an awful lot about my father," said Elizabeth looking at him suspiciously.

Not enough, thought Marc, and how much could you

really tell me? If Elizabeth picked up any sign of his anxiety, she didn't register it but simply continued.

"He voted to approve the Defense Budget in seventy-nine, and I didn't sit at the same table with him for almost a month. I don't think he even noticed."

"How about your mother?" asked Marc.

"She died when I was fourteen, which may be why I'm so close to my father," Elizabeth said. She looked down at her hands in her lap, evidently wanting to drop the subject. Her dark hair shone as it fell across her forehead.

"You have very beautiful hair," Marc said softly. "I wanted to touch it when I first saw you. I still do."

She smiled. "I like curly hair better." She leaned her chin on her cupped hands and looked at him mischievously. "You'll look fantastic when you're forty and fashionably gray at the temples. Provided you don't lose it all first, of course. Did you know that men who lose their hair at the crown are sexy, those who lose it at the temples, think, and those who lose it all over, think they are sexy?"

"If I go bald at the crown, will you accept that as a declaration of intent?"

"It might be a long wait."

On the way back to her house he stopped, put his arm round her and kissed her, hesitantly at first, unsure of how she would respond.

"You know, I think I am half in love with you already, Elizabeth," he murmured into her soft, warm hair. "What are you going to do with your latest victim?"

She walked on without speaking for a little way.

"Maybe I am half in love with you, too," she said, so quietly that he could barely catch the words. "More than half in love. And that isn't a word I use a lot."

They walked on hand in hand, silently, happily, slowly. Three not very romantic men were following them.

In the pretty living room, on the cream-colored sofa, he kissed her again.

The three unromantic men waited in the shadows outside.

6

9:00 AM

Marc spent Sunday morning putting the finishing touches to his report for the Director. He began by tidying his desk; he could never think clearly unless everything was in place. He gathered all his notes together and put them in a logical sequence. He completed the task by two o'clock, without noticing that he had missed lunch. Slowly he wrote down the names of the fifteen senators who were left, six under the heading Foreign Relations Committee, nine under Gun-Control Bill—Judiciary Committee. He stared at the lists, hoping for inspiration but none came. One of these men was a killer and there were only four days left to find out which one. He put the papers into his brief-case, which he locked in his desk.

He went into the kitchen and made himself a sandwich. He looked at his watch. What could he do that would be useful for the rest of the day? Elizabeth was on duty at the hospital. He picked up the phone and dialed the number. She could only spare a minute, due in the operating theater at three o'clock.

"Okay, Doctor, this won't take long and it shouldn't hurt. I can't call you every day just to tell you that you are

147

lovely and intelligent and that you drive me crazy, so listen carefully."

"I'm listening, Marc."

"Okay. You are beautiful and bright and I'm crazy about you . . . What, no reply?"

"Oh, I thought there might be more. I'll say something nice in return when I'm three inches away from you, not three miles."

"Better make it soon, or I am going to crack up. Off you go, and cut out someone else's heart."

She laughed. "It's an ingrown toenail, not very romantic."

She hung up. Marc roamed about the room, his mind jumping from fifteen senators, to Elizabeth, back to one Senator. Wasn't it going just a little too well with Elizabeth? Was one Senator looking for him, rather than the other way around? He cursed and poured himself Michelob. His mind switched to Barry Colvert; on Sunday afternoons they usually played squash. Then to Nick Stames, Stames who had unknowingly taken his place. If Stames were alive now, what would he do? . . . A remark that Stames had made at the office party last Christmas came flashing across Marc's mind: "If I'm not available, the second best crime man in this goddamn country is George Stampouzis of *The New York Times*"—another Greek, naturally. "He must know more about the Mafia and the CIA than almost anyone on either side of the law."

Marc dialed Information in New York, and asked for the number, not quite sure where it was leading him. The operator gave it to him.

"Thank you."

"You're very welcome."

He dialed it.

"Crime desk, George Stampouzis, please." They put him through.

"Stampouzis," said a voice. They don't waste words on *The New York Times*.

"Good afternoon. My name is Marc Andrews. I'm calling from Washington. I was a friend of Nick Stames; in fact, he was my boss."

The voice changed. "Yes, I heard about the terrible accident, if it was an accident. What can I do for you?"

"I need some inside information. Can I come and see you immediately?"

"Does it concern Nick?"

"Yes."

"Sure, can you meet me at eight o'clock, northeast corner of Twenty-first and Park Avenue South?"

"Easy," said Marc looking at his watch.

"I'll be waiting for you."

The Eastern Airlines shuttle flight arrived a few minutes after seven. Marc made his way through the crowd milling around the baggage pickup and headed for the taxi stand. A potbellied, middle-aged, unshaven New Yorker with an unlit cigar stub bobbing up and down in his mouth drove him into Manhattan. He never stopped talking the whole way, a monologue that required few replies. Marc could have used the time to compose his thoughts.

"This country's full of shit," said the bobbing cigar.

"Yes," said Marc.

"And this city is nothing more than a bankrupt garbage hole."

"Yes," said Marc.

"And that son of a bitch Kennedy's to blame. They ought to string him up."

Marc froze. It was probably said a thousand times a day; someone in Washington was saying it and meaning it.

The cab pulled up to the curb.

"Thirteen dollars even," said the bobbing cigar.

Marc put a ten and a five into the little plastic drawer in the protective screen that divided driver from passenger, and climbed out. A heavy-set man in his mid-fifties and wearing a tweed overcoat, headed toward him. Marc shivered. He had forgotten how cold New York could be in March.

"Marc Andrews?"

"Yes. Good guess."

"When you spend your life studying criminals, you begin to think like them." He was taking in Marc's suit. "G-men are certainly dressing better than they did in my day."

Marc looked embarrassed. Stampouzis must know that an FBI agent was paid almost double the salary of a New York cop.

"You like Italian food?" He didn't wait for Marc's reply. "I'll take you to one of Nick's old favorites." He was already on the move. They walked the long block in silence, Marc's step hesitating as he passed each restaurant entrance. Suddenly, Stampouzis disappeared into a doorway. Marc followed him through a run-down bar full of men who were leaning on the counter and drinking heavily. Men who had no wives to go home to, or if they did, didn't want to.

Once through the bar, they entered a pleasant, brick walled dining area. A tall, thin Italian guided them to corner table: obviously Stampouzis was a favored customer. Stampouzis didn't bother with the menu.

"I recommend the shrimp marinara. After that, you're on your own."

Marc took his advice and added a *piccata al limone* and half a carafe of Chianti. Stampouzis drank Colt 45. They talked of trivia while they ate. Marc knew the residual Mediterranean creed after two years with Nick Stames—never let business interfere with the enjoyment of good food. In any case, Stampouzis was still sizing him up, and Marc needed his confidence. When Stampouzis had finished an enormous portion of zabaglione and settled down to a double espresso with Sambuca on the side, he looked up at Marc and spoke in a different tone.

"You worked for a great man, a rare lawman. If one-tenth of the FBI were as conscientious and intelligent as Nick Stames, you would have something to be pleased about in that brick coliseum of yours."

Marc looked at him, about to speak.

"No, don't add anything about Nick; that's why you're here, and don't ask me to change my opinion of the Bureau. I've been a crime reporter for over thirty years and the only change I've seen in the FBI and the Mafia is that they are both bigger and stronger." He poured the Sambuca into his coffee, and took a noisy gulp. "Okay. How can I help?"

"Everything off the record," said Marc.

"Agreed," said Stampouzis. "For both our sakes."

"I need two pieces of information. First, are there any senators with close connections in organized crime and second, what is the attitude of the mob to the Gun-Control Bill?"

"Jesus, you only want the earth. Where shall I begin? The first is easier to answer directly, because the truth is that half the senators have loose connections with organized crime, which I call the Mafia, however out-of-date that is. Some don't even realize it but if you include accepting campaign contributions from businessmen and large corporations directly or indirectly associated with crime, then every President is a criminal. But when the Mafia needs a senator they do it through a third party, and even that's rare."

"Why?" queried Marc.

"The Mafia needs clout at the state level, in courts, with deals, local by-laws, all that. They're just not interested in foreign treaties and the approval of Supreme Court justices. In a more general way, there are some senators who owe their success to links with the Mafia, the ones who have started as civil-court judges or state assemblymen and received direct financial backing from the Mafia. It's possible they didn't even realize it; some people don't check too carefully when they are trying to get elected. Added to this are cases like Arizona and Nevada, where the Mafia runs a legit business, but God help any outsiders who try to join in. Finally, in the case of the Democratic party, there's organized labor, especially the Teamsters Union. There you are, Marc, thirty years' experience in ten minutes."

"Great background. Now can I ask you some specifics If I name fifteen senators, will you indicate if they could fall into any of the categories you have mentioned?' Marc asked.

"Maybe. Try me. I'll go as far as I feel I can. Jus don't push me."

"Percy."

"Never," said Stampouzis.

"Thornton."

He didn't move a muscle.

"Bayh."

"Not that I have ever heard."

"Duncan."

"No idea. I don't know much about South Carolina politics."

"Church."

"Frank Sunday-School? Scout's Honor Church? You've got to be kidding."

"Glenn."

"Nope. Only loses his balance in the bathtub, far as I can tell."

Marc went down the list. Stevenson, Biden, Moynihan, Woodson, Clark, Mathias. Stampouzis shook his head silently.

"Dexter."

He hesitated. Marc tried not to tense.

"Trouble, yes," Stampouzis began. "But Mafia, no."

He must have heard Marc sigh. Marc was anxious to know what the trouble was; he waited but Stampouzis didn't add anything.

"Byrd."

"Not his style."

"Pearson."

"You're joking."

"Thank you," said Marc. He paused. "Now to the Mafia's attitude toward the Gun-Control Bill."

"I'm not certain at the moment," began Stampouzis. "The Mafia is no longer monolithic. It's too big for that and there has been a lot of internal disagreement lately. The old-timers are dead set against it because of the obvious difficulty of getting guns legally in the future, but they are more frightened by the riders to the bill, like mandatory sentences for carrying an unregistered gun. The Feds will love that; for them it's the best thing since tax evasion. They will be able to stop any known criminal, search him, and if he is carrying an unregistered gun,

153

which he is almost certain to be, wham, he's in the court-house. On the other hand, some of the young Turks are looking forward to it, a modern-day Prohibition for them. They will supply unregistered guns to unorganized hood-lums and any mad radical who wants one, another source of income for the mob. They also believe the police won't be able to enforce the law and the cleaning-up period will take a decade. Does that get near to answering the question?"

"Yes, very near," said Marc.

"Now, my turn to ask you a question, Marc."

"Same rules?"

"Same rules. Are these questions directly connected with Nick's death?"

"Yes," said Marc.

"I won't ask any more then, because I know what to ask and you're going to have to lie. Let's just make a deal. If this breaks into something big, you'll see I get an exclusive over those bastards from the *Post*."

"Agreed," said Marc.

Stampouzis smiled and signed the check; the last comment had made Marc Andrews a legitimate expense.

Marc looked at his watch; with luck he would make the last shuttle from La Guardia. Stampouzis rose and walked to the door; the bar was still full of men drinking heavily, the same men with the same wives. Once on the street, Marc hailed a cab. This time, a young black pulled up beside him.

"I'm halfway there," said Stampouzis, puzzling Marc. "If I pick up anything that I think might help, I'll call you."

Marc thanked him and climbed into the cab.

"La Guardia, please."

Marc rolled down the window, Stampouzis stared in briefly.

"It's not for you, it's for Nick." He was gone.

The journey back to the airport was silent.

When Marc eventually reached his own apartment, he tried to put the pieces together in his mind ready for the Director tomorrow. He glanced at his watch. Christ, it was already tomorrow.

7

7:00 AM

The Director listened to all of Marc's research in attentive silence and then added his own startling piece of information.

"Andrews, we may be able to narrow your list of fifteen even further. Last Thursday morning a couple of agents picked up an unauthorized transmission on one of our KGB channels. Either temporary interference from some commercial station caused us to tune in a different frequency momentarily or else some guy has an illegal transmitter for our frequency. The only thing our boys heard was: 'Come in, Tony. I just dropped the Senator off for his committee meeting and I'm . . .' The voice stopped transmitting abruptly and we couldn't find it again. Perhaps the conspirators have been listening in on our conversations, and this time one of them without thinking started to transmit on our frequency as well; it's easy enough to do. The agents who heard it filed a report concerning the illegal use of our frequency, nothing else."

Marc was leaning forward in his chair.

"Yes, Andrews," said the Director. "I know what's

156

going through your mind. Ten-thirty A.M. The message was sent at ten-thirty A.M."

"Ten-thirty A.M., March 3," said Marc urgently. "Let me just check . . . which committees would have been meeting . . ." He opened his file. "Dirksen Building . . . that hour . . . I have what we need here somewhere, I know . . . three possibilities, sir. The Foreign Relations and Government Operations committees were in session that morning. On the floor of the Senate they were debating the Gun-Control Bill: that's taking up a lot of their time right now."

"Now we may be getting somewhere," said the Director. "Can you tell from your records how many of your fifteen were there on March 3 and what they were doing?"

Marc leafed through the fifteen sheets of paper and slowly divided them into two piles. "Well, it isn't conclusive, sir, but I have no record of these eight"—he placed his hand on one of the piles—"being in the Senate that morning. The remaining seven were there. None on the Government Operations Committee. Two on Foreign Relations—Pearson and Percy, sir. The other five are Bayh, Byrd, Dexter, Duncan, and Thornton. They were all on the floor. And they were all on the Judiciary Committee, Gun-Control Bill, as well."

The Director grimaced. "Well, as you say, Andrews, it's hardly conclusive. But it's all we have, so you concentrate on those seven. With only four days, it's a chance we will have to take. Don't get too excited just because we had one lucky break, and double-check that those eight were not in Dirksen that morning. Now, I am not going to risk putting seven senators under surveillance. Those folks on the Hill are suspicious enough of the FBI as it is. We'll have to use different tactics. Politically, we can't take a chance on a full-scale investigation. I'm afraid we'll have to find our man by using the only clues we're certain of—where he was on February 24 at lunchtime, and this ten-thirty Judiciary Committee meeting last week. So don't bother with the motive—we can't second-guess that, Andrews. We don't have time. Just keep looking for ways of narrowing the list, and spend the rest of the day at the Foreign Relations Committee and the floor of the Senate. Talk to the staff directors. There is nothing they don't know—public or private—about the senators.

"Yes, sir."

"And one more thing which may interest you: I'm having dinner with the President tonight. Perhaps I'll glean some information from him which might help us reduce the number of suspects."

"Will you tell the President, sir?"

"No, I don't think so. I still believe we have the matter under control. I see no reason for worrying him at this stage, certainly not until I think we're likely to fail."

Finally the Director passed over an Identikit picture of the Greek priest. "Mrs. Casefikis's version," he said. "What do you think of it?"

"It's not a bad likeness at all," said Marc. "Maybe a little uglier than that. Those men really know their job."

"What worries me," said the Director, "is I've seen that damn face before. So many criminals have come across my path that to remember one of them is impossible. Maybe it will come to me, maybe it will come to me."

"I know," said Marc, "and I was only twenty-four hours behind him. It hurts."

"Think yourself lucky, young man. If you had been ahead of him, I think Ariana Casefikis would now be dead and so might you. That would have hurt a whole lot more. I've still got a man on Mrs. Casefikis's home just in case he returns, but I think he is far too professional a bastard to risk that."

Marc agreed. Professional bastard, professional bastard.

The red light on the internal telephone winked.

"Yes, Mrs. McGregor?"

"You'll be late for your appointment with Senator Inouye."

"Thank you, Mrs. McGregor." He put the phone down. "I'll see you at the same time tomorrow, Marc." It was the first time he had called him Marc. "Leave no stone unturned; only four days left."

Marc took the elevator down and left the building by his usual route. He didn't notice he was being followed from the other side of the street. He went to the Senate Office Building and made appointments to see the staff directors of the Foreign Relations and Judiciary committees. The earliest either could manage was the following morning. Marc returned to the Library of Congress to research more thoroughly the personal histories of the seven senators left on his list. They were a rather varied bunch, from all over the country, with little in common; one of them had nothing in common with the other six, but which one? Percy—it didn't add up. Thornton— Stampouzis obviously didn't care for him but what did that prove. Bayh—a close friend of Kennedy's. Duncan— Stampouzis said he was against the Gun-Control Bill, but so was almost half the Senate. Dexter—what was the trouble Stampouzis wouldn't tell him about? Perhaps Elizabeth would enlighten him tonight. Byrd—a strangely intense, driven man who had gradually disavowed his conservative past. The quintessential party man, and apparently clean, though he had no affection for Kennedy, that was for sure. Pearson—if he turned out to be the villain, no one would believe it: thirty-three years in the Senate, and always playing honest Casca in public and private.

Marc sighed—the long weary sigh of a man who has come to an impasse. He glaced at his watch: 10:45; he must leave immediately if he was to be on time. He returned the various periodicals, *Congressional Records,* and Ralph Nader reports to the librarian, and hurried across the street to the parking lot to pick up his car. He drove quickly down Constitution Avenue and over Memorial Bridge—how many times had he done that this week? Marc glanced in his rear-view mirror and thought he recognized the car behind him, or was it just the memory of last Thursday?

Marc parked his car at the side of the road. Two Secret Service men stopped him. He produced his credentials and walked slowly down the path just in time to join a hundred and fifty other mourners standing around two graves, freshly dug to receive two men who a week ago were more alive than most of the people attending their burial. The Vice President, former Senator Dale Bumpers, was representing the President. He stood next to Norma Stames, a frail figure in black, being supported by her two sons. Bill, the eldest, stood next to a giant of a man, who must have been Barry Colvert's father. Next was the Director, who glanced around and saw Marc, but didn't acknowledge him. The game was being played out even at the graveside.

Father Gregory's vestments fluttered slightly in the cold breeze. The hem was muddy, for it had rained all night. A young chaplain in white surplice and black cassock stood silently at his side.

"I am the image of Thine inexpressible glory, even though I bear the wounds of sin," Father Gregory intoned.

His weeping wife bent forward and kissed Nick Stames's pale cheek and the coffin was closed. As Father Gregory prayed, Stames's and Colvert's coffins were lowered slowly, slowly into their graves. Marc watched sadly: it might have been him going down, down; it should have been him.

"With the saints give rest, O Christ, to the souls of Thy servants, where there is neither sickness nor sorrow, nor sighing, but Life everlasting."

The final blessing was given, the Orthodox made the sign of the cross and the mourners began to disperse.

After the service Father Gregory was speaking warmly of his friend Nick Stames and expressed the hope that he and his colleague Barry Colvert had not died without purpose; he seemed to be looking at Marc as he said it.

Marc saw Nanna, Aspirin, Julie, and the anonymous man, but he had no desire to speak to them. He slipped quietly away. Let the others mourn the dead; his job was to find their living murderers.

Marc drove back to the Senate, more determined than ever to find out which senator should have been present at that poignant double funeral. Had he stayed, he would have seen Matson talking casually to Grant Nanna, saying what a good man Stames was and what a loss he would be to law enforcement.

Marc spent the afternoon at the Foreign Relations Committee listening to Pearson and Percy. If it were either of them, they were cool customers, going about their job without any outward signs of anxiety. Marc wanted to cross their names off the list but he needed one

161

more fact confirmed before he could. When Pearson finally sat down, Marc felt limp. He needed to relax tonight if he was going to survive the next three days. He left the committee room and called Elizabeth to confirm their dinner date. He then called the Director's office and gave Mrs. McGregor the telephone numbers at which he could be reached: the restaurant, his home, Elizabeth's home. Mrs. McGregor took the numbers down without comment.

Two cars tailed him on his way back: a blue Ford sedan and a black Buick. When he arrived home, he tossed the car keys to Simon, dismissed the oppressive but familiar sensation of being continually watched, and started thinking of more pleasant things, an evening with Elizabeth.

The Director was checking his dinner jacket, ready for dinner with the President of the United States.

6:30 PM

Marc walked down the street thinking about the evening ahead of him. Jesus, I adore that girl. That's the one thing I am certain of at the moment. If only I could get rid of the nagging doubt about her father—even about her.

He went into Blackistone's and ordered a dozen roses, eleven red, one white. The girl handed him a card and an envelope. Quickly, he wrote Elizabeth's name and address on the envelope, and he pondered the blank card fragments of sentences and poems flashing through his mind. Finally, he smiled. He wrote, carefully:

> Haply I think on thee, and then my state,
> Like to the lark at break of day arising
> From sullen earth, sings hymns at heaven's gate.
>   P.S. Modern version. Is it at long last love?

"Have them sent at once, please."

"Yes, sir."

Good. Back home. What to wear? A dark suit? Too formal. The light-blue suit? Too much like a fag, should never have bought it in the first place. The denim suit—latest thing. Shirt. White, casual, no tie. Blue, formal, tie. White wins. Too virginal? Blue wins. Shoes: black slip-on or laces? Slip-on wins. Socks: simple choice, dark blue. Summing up: denim suit, blue shirt, dark-blue tie, dark-blue socks, black slip-on shoes. Leave clothes neatly on bed. Shower and wash hair—I like curly hair better. Damn, soap in eyes. Grope for towel, soap out, drop towel, out of shower. Towel around waist. Shave; twice in one day. Shave very carefully. No blood. Aftershave. Dry hair madly with towel. Curls all over the place. Back to bedroom. Dress carefully. Get tie exactly—that won't do, tie again. Better, this time. Pull up zipper—could stand to lose inch around waist. Check in mirror. Seen worse. To hell with modesty, have seen a whole lot worse. Check money, credit cards. No gun. All set. Bolt door. Press button for elevator.

"Can I have my keys, please, Simon?"

"Well, goddamn." Simon's eyes opened very wide. "Found yourself a new fox!"

"You better not wait up, because if I fail, Simon, I'm going to attack you."

"Thanks for the warning, Marc. Tough it out, man."

Beautiful evening, climb into car, check watch: 7:34.

The Director checked his dinner jacket again.

I miss Ruth. Housekeeper does a great job, but not the same thing at all. Pour a scotch, check clothes. Tuxedo just pressed—a little out of fashion. Dress shirt back from the cleaners. Black tie to be tied. Black shoes, black socks, white handkerchief—all in order. Turn on shower. Ah, how to get something useful out of the President? Damn, where's the soap. Have to get out of shower and soak bathmat and towel. Only one towel. Grab soap, revolting smell. Nowadays, they only make it for queers. Wish I could still get army surplus. Out of the shower. Overweight; I need to lose about fifteen pounds. Body too white. Hide it quickly and forget. Shave. Good old trusty cutthroat. Resolve never to shave twice a day except when dining with the President. Good. No damage. Get dressed. Fly buttons; hate zippers. Now to tie black tie. Try to forget that Ruth could always do it the first time, perfectly. Damn it, try again. Success at last. Check wallet. Don't really need money, credit cards, or anything else. Unless the President's going through hard times. Tell housekeeper I'll be back about eleven. Put on overcoat. Special agent there with car, as always.

"Good evening, Sam, beautiful evening."

The only chauffeur in the employ of the FBI opened the back door of the Ford sedan.

Climb into car, check watch: 7:45.

Drive slowly—lots of time—don't want to be there early—never seems to be any traffic when you have all the time in the world—hope roses have arrived—take longer route to Georgetown, past Lincoln Memorial and up Rock Creek and Potomac Parkway—it's prettier—at least con yourself that's why you're doing it. Don't run yellow lights, even though man behind you is obviously late and gesticulating. Obey the law—con yourself again—you'd shoot through the lights if you were running late for her. Never embarrass the Bureau. Careful of trolley lines in Georgetown, so easy to skid on them. Turn right at end of street and find parking space. Circle slowly looking for perfect spot—no such thing. Double-park and hope no traffic cop's around. Stroll nonchalantly toward house—bet she's still in the tub. Check watch: 8:04. Perfect. Ring doorbell.

"We're running a bit late, Sam." Perhaps unwise to say that because he'll break the speed limit and might embarrass the Bureau. Why is there so much traffic when you're in a hurry? Damn Mercedes in front of us at the circle, stopping even before the lights have turned red. Why have a car that can do a hundred and twenty miles per hour if you don't even want to do thirty? Good, the Mercedes has turned off toward Georgetown. Probably one of the beautiful people. Down Pennsylvania Avenue. At last the White House in sight. Turn onto West Executive Avenue. Waved on by guard at gate. Pull up to West Portico. Met by Secret Service man in dinner jacket. His tie looks better than mine. I'll bet it's a clip-on. No, come to think of it, it's regulation to have to tie them in the White House. Damn it, the man must be married. Didn't do it himself. Follow him through foyer to West Wing Reception Room past Remington sculpture. Met by another Secret Service man also in dinner jacket. Also better tie. I give up. Escorted to elevator. Check watch: 8:06. Not bad. Enter West Sitting Hall.

"Good evening, Mr. President."

165

"Hello, lovely lady."

She looks beautiful in that blue dress. Fantastic creature. How could I have any suspicions about her?

"Hello, Marc."

"That's a terrific dress you're wearing."

"Thank you. Would you like to come in for a minute?"

"No, I think we'd better go, I'm double-parked."

"Fine, I'll just grab my coat."

Open car door for her. Why didn't I just take her by the hand into the bedroom and make mad passionate love to her. I would have happily settled for a sandwich. That way we could do what we both want to do and save time and trouble.

"Did you have a good day?"

"Very busy. How about you, Marc?"

Oh, managed to think about you for a few hours while I got some work done, but it wasn't easy.

"Busy as all hell. I wasn't sure I was going to be able to make it."

Start car, right on M Street to Wisconsin. No parking spaces. Past Roy Rogers' Family Restaurant. Let's just get some chicken and go home.

"Aah, success."

Hell, where did that Volkswagen come from?

"What rotten luck. You'll find another one."

"Yes, but four hundred yards away from the restaurant."

"The walk will do us good."

Did the roses come? I'll put that florist's girl in jail in the morning if she didn't send them.

"Oh, Marc, how rude of me not to mention it before, thank you for those glorious roses. Are you the white one? And the Shakespeare?"

"Think nothing of it, lovely lady."

Liar. So you liked the Shakespeare, but what was your answer to the Cole Porter? Enter supersmooth French restaurant. Rive Gauche. Gauche is right. A Fed in a place like this? Bet it'll cost an arm and a leg. Full of snotty waiters with their hands out. What the hell, it's only money.

"Did you know that this place is responsible for making Washington the French-restaurant capital of America?"

Trying to impress her with a little inside dope.

"No, why?"

"Well, the owner keeps bringing his chefs over from France. One by one they quit and go off to start their own restaurants."

"You G-men really do carry around a store of useless information."

Look for the maître d'.

"Table in the name of Andrews."

"Good evening, Mr. Andrews. How nice to see you."

Damn man's never seen me before and probably will never see me again. Which table is he going to give me? Not too bad. She might even believe I've been here before. Slip him a five-dollar bill.

"Thank you, sir. Enjoy your dinner."

They settled back in the deep-red leather chairs. The restaurant was crowded.

"Good evening. Would you care for an apéritif, sir?"

"What will you have, Elizabeth?"

"Scotch on the rocks, please."

"One scotch on the rocks and I'll have a spritzer."

Glance at menu. Chef Michel Laudier. The restaurant motto: *Fluctuat nec mergitur*. Oh, I'll *mergitur,* all right, over charges, service charges. Ouch. And she has no way of knowing. This is one of those sexy places where the man is given a menu with the prices.

167

"I'll have a first course, but only if you'll join me."

"Of course, I'm going to have one, lovely lady."

"Good, I'll have the avocado . . ."

Without prawns?

". . . with prawns, and then . . ."

. . . Caesar salad?

". . . the filet mignon Henri IV—rare please."

$17.50. To hell with it, she's worth every penny. I think I'll have the same.

"Have you decided, sir?"

"Yes, we'll both have the avocado with prawns and the filet mignon Henri IV, rare."

"Would you care to look at the wine list?"

No, thank you, I'll have a beer.

"Would you like some wine, Elizabeth?"

"That would be lovely, Marc."

"A bottle of Hospice de Beaune, *soixante-neuf*, please."

I bet he can tell the only damn French I learned at school was the numbers.

"Very good, sir."

The first course arrived and so did the sommelier with the wine.

If you think you're going to sell us two bottles, you damn frog, think again.

"Shall I serve the wine, sir?"

"Not yet, thank you. Open it and then serve it with the main course."

"Certainly, sir."

"Your avocado, Mademoiselle."

Prawns go before the fall.

"Good evening, Halt. How's life at the Bureau?"

"We're surviving, sir."

What banal remarks the mighty make to each other.

The Director glanced around the pleasant blue-and-gold room. H. Stuart Knight, the head of the Secret Service, stood alone at the far end. On the sofa, by the window overlooking the West Wing and the Executive Office Building, sat the Attorney General, Marian Edelman, talking to Senator Birch Bayh, the man who had succeeded Ted Kennedy as chairman of the Judiciary Committee. The hackneyed phrase "boyish good looks," which had been applied to Bayh constantly during his campaigning in the 1976 Democratic presidential primaries, was still an accurate description. The thin, gaunt senator from Massachusetts, Marvin Thornton hovered over his colleague and Marian Edelman.

My God, Let me have men about me that are fat. . . .

"You see I've invited Thornton."

"Yes, sir."

"We must talk him around on the Gun-Control Bill."

The West Sitting Hall was a comfortable room on the family floor of the White House, adjacent to the First Lady's bedroom. It was an honor to be entertained in this part of the White House. And to eat in the family dining room, rather than the President's dining room downstairs, was a special compliment, since the former was usually reserved for strictly family dining.

"What will you drink, Halt?"

"Scotch on the rocks."

"Scotch on the rocks for the Director and an orange juice for me. I'm watching my weight."

Doesn't he know orange juice is the last thing to drink you're dieting.

"What's the latest voting position, Mr. President?"

"Well, the numbers are forty-eight for and forty-seven against at the moment, but it's got to go through on the nth or I'll have to forget it until the next session. That's my biggest worry at the moment, what with my European tour and the New Hampshire primary less than a year off. I would have to drop it until I was re-elected. I can't afford it to be the main election issue in eighty-four. I want it out of the way and seen to be working by then."

"Let's hope it passes on the tenth. It would certainly make my job easier, Mr. President."

"Marian's too."

"Another drink, Halt?"

"No, thank you, sir."

"Shall we go in to dinner?"

The President led his five guests into the dining room. The wallpaper in the room depicted scenes from the American Revolution. It was furnished in the Federal style of the early nineteenth century.

I am never bored with the beauty of the White House.

The Director gazed at the plaster-composition mantel designed by Robert Welford of Philadelphia in 1815. It bore the famous report of Commodore Oliver Hazard Perry after the Battle of Lake Erie during the War of 1812: "We have met the enemy, and they are ours."

"Five thousand people went through this building today," H. Stuart Knight was saying. "Nobody really grasps the security problems. This building may be the home of the President, but it still belongs to the people and that makes for a peck of difficulties."

If he knew everything . . .

The President sat at the head of the table, the Attorney General at the other end, Bayh and Thornton on one side, the Director and Knight on the other. The first course was avocado with prawns.

I always get sick when I eat prawns.

"It's good to see my law officers together," said the President. "I want to take this opportunity to discuss the

170

Gun-Control Bill, which I am determined will pass on March 10. That's why I invited Birch and Marvin here tonight, because their support will influence the fate of this bill."

March 10 again. Perhaps Cassius has to keep to a deadline. Seem to remember Thornton being firmly against this bill, and he's on Andrews' list of seven.

"The rural states are going to be a problem, Mr. President," Marian Edelman was saying. "They're not going to hand over their guns all that readily."

"A long amnesty period, say about six months, might be the answer," the Director offered. "So the law remains unaffected for a statutory period. It's what always happens after a war. And the public-relations boys can keep announcing that hundreds of weapons have been handed in to local police stations."

"I agree," said the President.

"It's going to be a hell of an operation," said the Attorney General, "with seven million members of the National Rifle Association and probably fifty million firearms in America."

They all nodded.

The second course arrived.

Dover sole. Obviously the President is serious about his diet.

"Coffee or brandy, sir?"

"Don't let's bother," said Elizabeth, touching Marc's hand gently. "Let's have it at home."

"Nice idea."

He smiled into her eyes and tried to guess what was going on in her mind. . . .

"No, thank you. Just the check."

The waiter scurried away obediently.

They always scurry away obediently when you ask for the check. She hasn't let go of my hand.

"A delicious meal, Marc. Thank you very much."

"Yes, we must come here again sometime."

The check arrived. Marc glanced at it in rueful bemusement.

$67.20, plus tax. If you can understand how a restaurant gets to its final figure you deserve to be Secretary of the Treasury. Hand over the American Express Card. The little piece of blue paper comes back to sign. Make it up to $80.00 and forget it until the envelope marked American Express arrives in the mail.

"Good night, Mr. Andrews." Much bowing and scraping. "I hope we will see you and Mademoiselle again soon."

"Yes, indeed."

You'll need a very good memory to recognize me next time. Open car door for Elizabeth. Will I do this when we're married? Christ, I'm thinking about marriage.

"I think I must have eaten too much. I'm rather sleepy."

Now what does that mean? You could take that about twenty different ways.

"Oh really, I feel ready for anything."

A bit clumsy, maybe. Look for parking space again. Good. There's one right in front of the house and n Volkswagen to stop me grabbing it. Open car door fo Elizabeth. She fumbles with front-door keys. Into kitcher Kettle on.

"What a nice kitchen."

Silly remark.

"I'm glad you like it."

Equally silly.

Into living room.

Good, there are the roses.

172

"Hello, Samantha. Come and say hello to Marc."

Christ Almighty, she has a roommate after all this. Disaster.

Samantha rubbed up against Marc's leg and purred.

Relief. Samantha is Siamese, not American.

"Where shall I sit?"

"Anywhere."

She's no help at all.

"Black or with cream, darling?"

"Darling." The odds must be better than 50–50.

"Black, please, with one sugar."

"Amuse yourself till the water boils. I'll only be a few minutes."

"More coffee, Halt?"

"No thank you, sir, I have to be getting home, if you'll excuse me."

"I'll walk you to your car. There are one or two things I'd like to discuss with you."

"Yes, of course, Mr. President."

The Marines at the West Entrance came to attention. A man in a dinner jacket hovered in the shadows behind the pillars.

"I'll need your backing a hundred per cent for this Gun-Control Bill, Halt. The committee is bound to be pushing for your views. And although the numbers are still with us on the floor of the House, I don't want any last-minute hiccups; I'm running out of time."

"I'll be with you, sir. I've wanted it since the death of your brother." It was the first time that evening anyone had mentioned JFK.

"Have you any particular worries about it, Halt?"

"No, sir. You deal with the politics and sign the bill, and I'll carry it out."

"Any advice, perhaps? . . ."

"No, I don't think so."

Beware the ides of March.

". . . although it's always puzzled me, Mr. President, why you left the bill this late, if something goes wrong on March 10 and if you were to lose next year's election, we would all be back at square one."

"I know, Halt, but I had to decide between my Medicare Bill, which was a controversial enough way to start an administration, and pushing a Gun-Control Bill through at the same time; I might have ended up losing both. To tell you the truth, it had been my intention to start the bill in committee a year earlier, but no one could have anticipated Nigeria attacking South Africa without warning, and America finally having to decide where she stood in Africa."

"You sure stuck your neck out on that one, Mr. President, and I confess at the time I thought you were wrong."

"I know, Halt. I had a few sleepless nights myself. But, getting back to the Gun-Control Bill: don't ever forget that Dexter and Thornton have run the most successful two-man filibuster in the history of the Senate. By March 10, this damn bill will have been going the rounds for nearly two years despite the tacit support of Senator Byrd as Majority Leader. But I'm not too worried. I think we'll pull it off on March 10. I can't foresee anything that can stop it, can you, Halt?"

The Director hesitated. "No, sir."

The first lie I have ever told the Chief. Would an investigating commission believe my reasons if the President is dead in three days' time?

"Good night, Halt, and thank you."

"Good night, Mr. President, and thank you for an excellent dinner."

The Director stepped into his car. The special agent in the driver's seat looked around at him.

"An important message has just come in for you, sir. Could you return to the Bureau immediately?"

Not again.

"All right, but it might be simpler to keep a bed in the place, except someone would accuse me of trying to live rent-free on taxpayers' money."

The driver laughed; the Director had obviously had a good dinner, which was more than he had had.

Elizabeth brought the coffee in and sat down by him.

Only the brave deserve the fair. Lift arm casually, place at the back of the couch, touch her hair lightly.

Elizabeth rose. "Oh, I nearly forgot. Would you like a brandy?"

No, I don't want a brandy. I want you to come back.

"No, thank you."

She settled back into Marc's shoulder.

Can't kiss her while she's got the coffee cup in her hand. Ah, she's put the cup down. Hell, she's up again.

"Let's have some music."

Christ Almighty, what next!

"Great idea."

"How about 'In Memory of Sinatra'?"

"Great."

. . . "This time we almost made the pieces fit . . . didn't we . . . gal?"

It's got to be absolutely the wrong song. Ahh, she's back. Try the kiss again. Damn, still more coffee. The cup's down at last. Gentle. Yes, very nice. Christ, she's beautiful. Long kiss—are her eyes open?—no, closed. She's enjoying it—good—longer and even better.

"Would you like some more coffee, Marc?"

175

No no no no no no no.

"No, thank you."

Another long kiss. Start moving hand across back—I've been this far before with her—can't possibly be any objection—move hand to leg—pause—what fabulous legs and she's got two of them. Take hand off leg and concentrate on kissing.

"Marc, there's something I have to tell you."

Oh, Christ! It's the wrong time of the month. That's all I need now.

"Uh-mh?"

"I adore you."

"I adore you too, darling."

He unzipped her skirt, and caressed her gently.

She began to move her hand up his leg.

Heaven is about to happen.

Ring, ring, ring, ring.

Jee-sus!

"It's for you, Marc."

"Andrews?"

"Sir."

"Julius."

Shit.

"I'm coming."

8

1:00 AM

The man standing in a corner of the churchyard was trying to keep warm in the cold of the early March morning by slapping himself on the back. He had seen Gene Hackman do it in a movie and it had worked. It wasn't working. Perhaps he needed the big Warner Brothers arc light Mr. Hackman had had to help him. He considered the matter, but continued slapping.

There were actually two men on surveillance, Special Agent Kevin O'Malley and Assistant Field Supervisor Pierce Thompson, both selected by Tyson for their ability and discretion. Neither had shown any sign of surprise when the Director had instructed them to tail a fellow FBI man and report back to Elliott. It had been a long wait for Marc to emerge from Elizabeth's house, and O'Malley didn't blame him. Pierce left the churchyard and joined his colleague.

"Hey, Kevin, have you noticed someone else tailing Andrews?"

"Yeah. Matson. Why?"

"I thought he was retired."

"He is. I just assumed old Halt was making sure."

177

"I guess you're right. I wonder why Tyson didn't tell us."

"Well, the whole operation's pretty irregular. No one seems to be telling anyone anything. You could ask Elliott."

" 'You could ask Elliott.' You might as well ask the Lincoln Memorial."

"Or you could ask the Director."

"No, thank you."

A few minutes passed by.

"Think we should talk to Matson?"

"You remember the special orders. No contact with anyone. He probably has the same orders, and he would report us without thinking about it. He's a bastard, you know."

O'Malley was the first to see Marc leaving the house and could have sworn he was carrying one shoe. He was right and Marc was running, so he began to follow him. Must avoid getting burned, thought O'Malley. Marc would have known, had he seen him, that he was FBI. Marc stopped at the pay phone; his pursuer disappeared into some new shadows, to continue his vain attempts to keep warm. He was thankful for the brisk walk, which had helped a little.

Marc had only two dimes; the others were all lying uselessly on the floor by the side of Elizabeth's couch. Where had the Director phoned from? Could it have been the Bureau? That didn't make sense, what would he be doing there at this time of night? Wasn't he supposed to be with the President? Marc looked at his watch. He one-fifteen. He must be at home; if he isn't I'll be out of dimes. Marc put on his other shoe. Easy slip-on. He cursed, and tossed one of the dimes; President Roosevelt I call the Bureau. *E pluribus unum,* then I call him

178

home. The coin landed—President Roosevelt. Marc dialed the Director's private number at the Bureau.

"Yes."

God bless President Roosevelt.

"Julius?"

"Come in immediately."

That didn't sound very friendly. Perhaps he had just returned from the President with some important new information, or maybe something at the dinner had given him indigestion.

Marc walked quickly to his car, checking his shirt buttons and tie as he went. His socks felt uncomfortable, as if one of the heels was in the arch of his foot. He passed the man in the shadows, who watched as Marc returned to his car and hesitated. Should he return to Elizabeth and say, say what? He looked up at the light in the window, took a deep breath, cursed again, and fell into the bucket seat of the Mercedes. There hadn't even been time for a cold shower.

It took only a few minutes to reach the Bureau. There was very little traffic, and with the streets so quiet, the new computerized lights meant no stopping.

Marc parked the car in the basement garage of the FBI and immediately there was the anonymous man, the anonymous man who obviously was waiting for him. Didn't he ever go to bed? A harbinger of bad tidings, probably, but he didn't let him know, because as usual he didn't speak. Perhaps he's a eunuch, Marc thought. Lucky man. They shared the elevator to the seventh floor. The anonymous man led him noiselessly to the Director's office; wonder what he does for a hobby, thought Marc. Probably a prompter at the National Theater for the Deaf.

"Mr. Andrews, sir."

The Director offered no greeting. He was still in evening clothes and looked as black as thunder.

"Sit down, Andrews."

Back to Andrews, thought Marc.

"If I could take you out into the parking lot, stick you up against the wall, and shoot you, I would."

Marc tried to look innocent; it had usually worked with Nick Stames. It didn't seem to cut any ice with the Director.

"You stupid, unthinking, irresponsible, reckless idiot."

Marc decided he was more frightened of the Director than he was of those who might be trying to kill him.

"You've compromised me, the Bureau, and the President," continued the Director. Marc could hear his heart pounding. If he could have counted it, it would have been a hundred and twenty. Tyson was still in full cry. "If I could suspend you or just dismiss you, if only I could do something as simple as that. How many senators are there left, Andrews?"

"Seven, sir."

"Name them."

"Duncan, Bayh, Thornton, Byrd, Percy, Dex . . . Dexter, and . . ." Marc went white.

"Summa cum laude at Yale, and you have the naïveté of a boy scout. When we first saw you with Dr. Elizabeth Dexter, we, in our stupidity, knowing she was the doctor on duty on the evening of March third at Woodrow Wilson, assumed in our stupidity"—he repeated it even more pointedly—"that you were onto a lead, but now we discover that she not only is the daughter of one of the seven senators whom we suspect of wanting to murder the President but, as if that's not enough, we find out you're having an affair with her."

180

Marc wanted to protest but couldn't get his lips to move.

"Can you deny you've slept with her, Andrews?"

"Yes, sir," Marc said very quietly.

The Director was momentarily dumbfounded. "Young man, we wired the place; we know exactly what went on."

Marc leaped out of his chair, stunned dismay yielding to fierce anger. "I couldn't have denied it," he cried, "if you hadn't interrupted me, you bastard. Have you forgotten what it feels like to love someone, if you ever knew? Fuck your Bureau, and I don't use that word very often, and fuck you. I've been working sixteen hours a day and I'm not getting any sleep at night. Someone may be trying to murder me and I find that you, the only man I trusted, have ordered your anonymous pimps to play Peeping Tom at my expense. I hope you all roast in hell. I'd rather take on the whole Mafia."

Marc was angrier than he had ever been in his life. He collapsed back into the chair, and waited for the consequences. His only strength was that he no longer cared. The Director was equally silent. He walked to the window and stared out. Then he turned slowly; the heavy shoulders, the large head were turning toward him. This is it, thought Marc.

The Director stopped about a yard away from him, looking him square in the eyes, the way he had done from the first moment they had met.

"Forgive me," said the Director. "I'm becoming paranoid about the whole problem. I've just left the President, healthy, fit, full of plans for the future of this country, only to be told that his one hope of carrying out those dreams is sleeping with the daughter of one of the seven men who might at this very moment be planning to assassinate him. I didn't think much further than that."

A big man, thought Marc.

The Director's eyes hadn't left him.

"Let's pray it's not Dexter. Because if it is, Marc, you may well be in the same danger." He paused again. "By the way, those anonymous pimps have been guarding you day and night, also on a sixteen-hour day, without a break. Some of them even have wives and children. Now we both know the truth. Let's get back to work, Marc, and let's try and stay sane for three more days. Just remember to tell me everything."

Marc had won. No, Marc had lost.

"There are seven senators left." The words were slow and tired, the man was still on edge. Marc had never seen him like this and doubted that many members of the Bureau had.

"My discussions with the President have strengthened my suspicion that the link between March tenth and the Senator is the Gun-Control Bill. The chairman of the Judiciary Committee, who handled the planning stages of the bill, was there—Senator Bayh. He's still on the list. You had better see what he and our other suspects on that committee had to say about the bill—but keep your eye on Pearson and Percy at Foreign Relations as well." He paused. "Only three days to go. I intend to stick to my original plan and let things run just as they are for the moment. I'm still in a position to cancel the President's schedule for the tenth at the very last minute. Do you wish to add anything, Marc?"

"No, sir."

"What are your plans?"

"I should be seeing the staff directors of both the Foreign Relations and Judiciary committees tomorrow, since I may have a clearer idea then on how to approach the problem and what to be looking for."

"Good. Follow them both up meticulously, just in case I've missed something."

"Yes, sir."

"We've had our fingerprint men working overtime on those twenty-eight bills; at the moment, they are only looking for the prints of Mrs. Casefikis. That way at least we will know which one might have our man's on it. They have found over a thousand prints, so far, but none fit Mrs. Casefikis's. I'll brief you the moment I hear anything. Now let's call it a day, we're both bushed. Don't bother to come in at seven tomorrow"—the Director looked at his watch—"I mean today. Make it seven A.M. on Wednesday and make it on time because then we'll have only one full day left."

Marc knew he was being invited to leave but there was something he wanted to say. The Director looked up and sensed it immediately.

"Save it, Marc. Go home and get some rest. I'm a tired old man, but I would like those bastards, each and every one of them, behind bars on Thursday night. For your sake, I hope to God Dexter is not involved. But don't close your eyes to anything, Marc. Love may be blind, but let's hope it's not deaf and dumb."

A very big man, thought Marc.

"Thank you, sir. I'll see you on Wednesday morning."

Marc drove his car quietly out of the FBI's garage. He was drained. There was no sign of the anonymous man. He stared in the rear-view mirror. A blue Ford sedan was following him, and this time it seemed obvious. How could he ever be sure whose side they were on. In three more days, he might know. This time next week he'd know everything or nothing. Would the President be alive or dead?

Simon, still on duty at the entrance to the apartment house, gave Marc a cheerful grin. "Make it, man?"

"Not exactly," he replied.

"I could always call up my sister, if you're desperate." Marc tried to laugh.

"A generous offer, but not tonight, Simon." He tossed the car keys over and headed for the elevator. Once locked and bolted into his apartment, he strode into his bedroom, pulled off his shirt and tie, picked up the phone and dialed seven digits slowly. A gentle voice answered.

"You still awake?"

"Very much so."

"I love you." He put the phone down and slept.

8:04 AM

The phone was ringing, but Marc was still in a deep sleep. It continued to ring. Eventually he awoke, focused on his watch: 8:05. Damn, probably the Director asking where the hell he was; no, he hadn't wanted to see him this morning, isn't that what they agreed? He grabbed the phone.

"You're awake?"

"Yes."

"I love you, too."

He heard the phone click. A good way to start the day, though if she knew he was going to spend it investigating her father . . . And almost certainly the Director was investigating her.

Marc let the cold shower run on and on until he was fully awake. Whenever he was awakened suddenly, h always wanted to go back to sleep. Next week, he promised himself. There were one hell of a lot of things he was going to do next week. He glanced at his watch: 8:25. No Wheaties this morning. He flicked on the television to see if he had missed anything going on in the rest of the world; he was sitting on a news story that would make Walter Cronkite fall off his CBS chair. What was the man saying?

". . . and now one of the greatest achievements of mankind, the first pictures ever taken from the planet Jupiter by an American spacecraft. History in the making, but first, this message from Jell-O, the special food for special children."

Marc turned it off, laughing. Jupiter, along with Jell-O, would have to wait until next week.

Because he was running late, he decided to take the Metro from the Waterfront Station next to his apartment. It was different when he had been going in early and had the roads to himself, but at 8:30, the cars would be bumper to bumper the whole way. Washington's subway system had begun operation in the downtown area in 1976. By 1980, many of the outlying stations had been completed.

The entrance was marked with a bronze pylon sporting an illuminated M. Marc stepped onto the escalator, which took him from street level down to the Metro station. The tunnellike station reminded him of a Roman bath, gray and dark with a honeycombed, curved ceiling. Sixty cents. Rush-hour fare. And he needed a transfer. Seventy-five cents. Marc fumbled in his pockets for the exact fare. No bus or subway in Washington provides change, because drivers or attendants who carry coins and bills are easy prey for robbers. Must remember to stock up on dimes when I get to the Bureau, he thought, as he stepped onto another escalator and was deposited at track level. During rush hour, 6:30–9:00 A.M., the trains arrived every five minutes. Round lights on the side of the platform began to flash to indicate the train was approaching. The doors opened automatically. Marc joined the crowd in a colorful, brightly lit car, and five minutes later heard his destination announced on the public-address system: Gallery Place. He stepped out onto the platform and waited for a red line train. The green line worked perfectly on mornings when he was going to the Washington Field Office, but to get to Capitol Hill, he had to switch. Four minutes later, he emerged into the sunshine at Union Station Visitors' Center, the bustling command post for bus, train, and subway travel in and out of Washington; it was functioning far better than its critics had predicted in 1977. The Dirksen Senate Office Building was three blocks away, down First Street, at the corner of Constitution. That was quick and painless, thought Marc, as he went in the Constitution Avenue entrance. Why do ever bother with a car at all?

He walked past two members of the Capitol police who were inspecting briefcases and packages at the door, and pressed the Up-button at the public elevator.

"Four, please," he said to the elevator operator.

The Foreign Relations Committee hearing was scheduled to begin shortly. Marc pulled the list of "Today Activities in the House and Senate," which he had torn out of *The Washington Post,* from his coat pocket. "Foreign Relations: 9:30 A.M. Open. Hearing on U.S. policy toward the Common Market; administration representatives. 4229 DOB." As Marc walked down the hall Senator Frank Church of Idaho stepped into Suite 4229 and Marc followed him into the hearing room.

Church, who had established a national reputation for

himself in 1975 as chairman of the Senate Select Committee to Study Government Operations with Respect to Intelligence Activities, had tried unsuccessfully to wrest the Democratic nomination away from Jimmy Carter in 1976. The retirements of Mike Mansfield in 1976 and John Sparkman in 1978 had elevated Church to the chairmanship of the powerful Foreign Relations Committee. The trim six-foot senator was considered an intelligent and thoughtful man, whose exuberant rhetorical excesses masked a shrewd mind.

The hearing room had light-colored wood paneling, accented by green marble on the lower part of the wall and around the door. At the end of the chamber, there was a semicircular desk of the same light wood, which was raised one step above the rest of the room. Fifteen burnt-orange chairs. Only about ten of them were occupied. Senator Church took his seat, but the assorted staff members, aides, newsmen, and administrative officials continued to mill around. On the wall behind the senators hung two large maps, one of the world, the other of Europe. At a desk immediately in front of and below the senators' sat a stenotypist, poised to record the proceedings verbatim. In front, there were desks for witnesses.

More than half the room was given over to chairs for the general public, and these were nearly all full. An oil painting of George Washington dominated the scene. That man must have spent the last ten years of his life posing for portraits, thought Marc.

Senator Church whispered something to an aide and rapped his gavel for silence. "Before we begin," he said, "I'd like to notify Senate staff members and the press of a change in schedule. Today and tomorrow, we will hear testimony from the State Department concerning the

European Common Market. We will then postpone the continuation of these hearings until next week, so the committee may devote its attention to the pressing and controversial issue of arms sales to Africa."

By this time, almost everyone in the room had found a seat, and the government witnesses were glancing through their notes. Marc had worked on Capitol Hill one summer during college, but even now he could not help feeling annoyed at the small number of senators who showed up at these hearings. Because each senator served on three or more committees and innumerable sub- and special committees, they were forced to specialize and to trust the expertise of fellow senators and staff members in areas outside their own specialty. So it was not at all unusual for committee hearings to be attended by three or two or sometimes even only one senator.

The subject under debate was a bill to dismantle the North Atlantic Treaty Organization. Portugal and Spain had gone Communist, like two well-behaved dominoes at the turn of the decade. The Spanish bases went soon after; King Juan Carlos was living in exile in England. NATO had been prepared for the Communist takeover in Portugal, but when Italy finally installed a Fronte Popolare government in the Quirinal, things began to fall apart. The Papacy, trusting to tried-and-proven methods, locked itself behind its gates, and American Catholic opinion forced the United States to cut off financial aid to the new Italian government. The Italians retaliated by closing her NATO bases.

The economic ripples of the Italian collapse were thought to have influenced the French elections of 1981 which had led to a victory for Mitterand and the Socialists supported by the Communists. The more extreme form of socialism had recently been repudiated in Holland and some Scandinavian countries. The Germans were happy with their social democracy. But in 1982, Senator Pearson was declaring that America's only real ally in NATO was Britain, where a Tory government had won an upset victory in the February 1982 general election.

The British Foreign Secretary, Edward Heath, had argued forcefully against the formal breakup of NATO. Such a move would sever Great Britain from her alliance with the United States, and commit her solely to the EEC, seven of whose fifteen members were now Communist or close to it. Senator Pearson thumped the table. "We should take the British view seriously in our considerations and not be interested only in immediate strategic gains."

After an hour of listening to Church and Pearson questioning State Department witnesses about the political situation in Spain, Marc slipped out the door and went into the Foreign Relations Committee suite down the hall. The secretary informed him that Lester Kenneck, the committee staff director, was out of the office. Marc had telephoned him the day before, leaving the impression that he was a student doing research for his dissertation.

"Is there someone else who could give me some information about the committee?"

"I'll see if Michael Bradley, one of our staff members, might be able to help you." She picked up the telephone and, several moments later, a thin bespectacled man emerged from one of the back rooms.

"What can I do for you?"

Marc explained that he would like to see other members of the committee in action, particularly Percy. Bradley smiled patiently. "No problem," he said. "Come back tomorrow afternoon or Thursday for the discussion about arms sales to Africa. Senator Percy will be here, I guarantee. And you'll find it much more interesting than the Common Market stuff. In fact, the meeting may be closed to the public. But I'm sure if you come by here and talk to Mr. Kenneck, he'll arrange for you to sit in."

"Thank you very much. Would you by any chance happen to know if Percy and Pearson were present at the hearing on February 24, or last Thursday?"

Bradley raised his eyebrows. "I have no idea. Kenneck might know."

Marc thanked him. "Oh, one more thing. Could you give me a pass for the Senate gallery?" The secretary stamped a card and wrote in his name. Marc headed for the elevator. Arms sales. Africa, he thought. Thursday's too late. Damn. How the hell am I supposed to know why one of these guys would want to kill Kennedy? Could be some crazy military thing, or a severe case of racism. It doesn't make any sense. Not why, but who, he reminded himself. As he walked, Marc almost knocked over one of the Senate pages, who was running down the corridor clutching a package. The Congress operates a page school for boys and girls from across the nation who attend classes and work as "gophers" in the Capitol. They all wear dark-blue-and-white and always give the impression of being in a hurry. Marc stopped just in time and the boy scooted around him without even breaking stride.

Marc took the elevator to the ground floor and walked out of the Dirksen Building onto Constitution Avenue. He made his way across the Capitol grounds, entered the Capitol on the Senate side, underneath the long marble expanse of steps, and waited for the public elevator.

"Busy day," said the guard. "Lots of tourists here to watch the gun-control debate."

Marc nodded. "Is there a long wait upstairs?"

"Yes, sir, I think so."

The elevator arrived, and on the gallery level a guard ushered Marc into line with a horde of gaping visitors. Marc was impatient. He beckoned to one of the guards.

"Listen, officer," he said, "I have a regular public pass for the gallery, but I'm a student from Yale doing research. Think there is any way you could get me in?"

The guard nodded sympathetically.

A few minutes later, Marc was seated in the chamber. He could see only part of the floor. The senators were seated at desks in semicircular rows facing the Chair. Even while someone was speaking, staff members and senators wandered around, giving the impression that the really significant maneuvering took place in hushed tones, not in dramatic debate.

The Judiciary Committee had reported out the bill two weeks before, after prolonged hearings and discussion. The House had already passed similar legislation, which would have to be reconciled with the stricter Senate version if it was to be approved.

Senator Dexter was speaking. My future father-in-law? Marc wondered. He certainly didn't look like a killer, but then which senator did? He had given his daughter her glorious dark hair, although there was a little white at his temples. Not as much as there ought to be, thought Marc—a politician's vanity. And he had also given her his dark eyes. He seemed fairly contemptuous of most of the people around him, tapping the desk with his long fingers to emphasize a point.

"In our discussion about this bill, we have side-stepped a critical, perhaps the most crucial, consideration. And that is the principle of Federalism. For the past fifty years, the federal government has usurped many of the powers once wielded by the states. We look to the President, the Congress, for answers to all our problems. The

Founding Fathers never intended the central government to have so much power, and a country as wide and diverse as ours cannot be governed democratically or effectively on that basis. Yes, we all want to reduce crime. But crime differs from place to place. Our constitutional system wisely left the business of crime control to state and local jurisdiction, except for those federal criminal laws which deal with truly national matters. But crimes committed with guns are of a local nature. They ought to be legislated against and enforced at the local level. Only at the state and local levels can the attitude of the people and the specific characteristics of the crime problem be understood and dealt with by public officials.

"I know that some of my colleagues will argue that since we require registration of cars and drivers, we ought also to register guns. But, gentlemen, we have no national car- or driver-registration law. These matters are left to the states to determine. Each state should be allowed to decide for itself, taking into account the interests of its people, what is reasonable and necessary."

Senator Dexter monopolized the floor for twenty minutes before yielding to the Chair, occupied today by Senator Hayakawa, who recognized Senator Bayh. Next to Bayh sat a tall blue-eyed man. Not a staff member, thought Marc. Former California Senator John Tunney. What the hell is he doing here? Tunney and Edward Kennedy had been roommates at the University of Virginia Law School. Tunney's son was named after his godfather, Edward Kennedy. Tunney had been an articulate advocate of gun-control measures before he lost to the Republican Hayakawa in a close race in 1976. had served on the Judiciary Committee. Glad he's not on the list. What's Tunney doing here? Marc wondered. Just helping Bayh? Two friends of Kennedy. Bayh pulled

192

Kennedy out of a plane wreck, saving his life, how could he possibly be involved in a plot to—Bayh had finished his preliminary remarks, and launched into a prepared speech.

". . . have consistently decried the killing in the Middle East, in Africa, in Northern Ireland, in Chile. We ended the bloodshed in Vietnam. But when are we going to confront the killing that takes place in our own communities, our own streets, our own homes, every day of every year?" Bayh paused and looked at Senator Duncan from South Carolina, one of the leading opponents of the bill. "Are we waiting for another national tragedy to compel us to take action? Only after the assassination of John Kennedy was Senator Thomas Dodd's Handgun-Control Bill taken seriously by a Senate committee. No legislation was passed. After the Watts riots of August 1965, in which purchased, not looted guns were used, the Senate held hearings about control of handguns. No action was taken. It took the slaying of Martin Luther King, Jr., before the Judiciary Committee passed legislation, controlling interstate sale of handguns as a rider to the omnibus Crime-Control Bill. The Senate approved the bill. The House concurred after RFK was murdered. In response to the violence of 1968, we enacted the Handgun-Control Act. But the act, gentlemen, contained a huge loophole—it did not regulate domestic production of these weapons, because at that time eighty per cent of available handguns were manufactured overseas. In 1972, after George Wallace was shot with a Saturday-night Special, the Senate finally acted to close the loophole. But the bill died in a House committee.

"Now, ten years later, having disregarded the fact that the late Senator Stennis was seriously wounded in 1973 by a man wielding a handgun, and that the Ambassador from Zimbabwe was shot on the streets of Washington only ten months ago, disregarding the fact that someone in America is killed or injured by gunfire every two minutes, we are still without an effective gun-control law. What are we waiting for? Someone to assassinate the President?" He paused for effect. "The American people favor gun-control legislation. Every poll indicates that this is the case, and it has been true for a decade. Why do we allow the National Rifle Association to manipulate us, to persuade us that they and their views are compelling when in fact they are hollow? What has happened to our capacity for the clear weighing of alternatives, and for outrage at the violence in our society?"

Marc, along with many other observers, was astonished by the impassioned outburst. His impression from the newspapers was that Bayh was something of a light-weight, even though he had been a key figure on a number of constitutional issues and in the fight against two of Nixon's Supreme Court appointees, Haynsworth and Carswell. Tunney was smiling.

Senator Duncan of South Carolina, an urbane, quietly distinguished man, asked to be recognized. "Will the distinguished Senator from Indiana yield?"

Bayh nodded to the Chair.

Duncan addressed his colleagues in a soft, firm voice.

"This bill completely negates the concept of self-defense. It asserts that the only legitimate reason for owning a handgun, a shotgun, or a rifle is for sporting purposes. But I would like to ask my distinguished colleagues from the urban states to consider for a moment—just a moment—the plight of a family on a farm in Iowa or on a homestead in Alaska which needs a gun in the house to protect itself. Not for sport, but for self-defense. In my estimation, they have a right to take that ste

194

For what we face in this country, in urban as well as rural areas, is increasing lawlessness. That is the root problem—lawlessness—not the number of guns in circulation. Increased lawlessness means more crimes involving guns, to be sure. But guns do not cause crimes, people cause crimes. If we want to fight crime, we should investigate its root causes instead of trying to take guns away from people who would use them legally. As many a bumper sticker in this great land proclaims, 'If guns are outlawed, only outlaws will have guns.' "

Senator Thornton of Massachusetts, thin and gaunt, with greasy black hair, whom Marc remembered from Mr. Smith's Restaurant, had only just begun to express his agreement with the views of Senator Dexter and Senator Duncan when six lights around the numbers on the clock at Marc's end of the chamber came alive. A buzzer sounded six times to signal that morning business had concluded. The "morning hour" on the floor of the Senate, from midday until no later than 2:00 P.M., was set aside for the presentation of petitions and memorials, reports of standing and select committees, and introduction of bills and resolutions. Up until 1964, committees were not allowed to meet during morning hour.

Senator Hayakawa looked at his watch. "Excuse me, Senator Thornton, but it is noon and now that morning business is over, a number of us are expected to appear in committee to debate the Clean Air Bill which is on the Calendar for this afternoon. Why don't we reconvene at two-thirty? As many of us who can get away from the committee at that time can meet back here to discuss this bill. It's important that we move as quickly as possible on this legislation, as we are still hoping to vote on it this session."

The Senate floor was cleared in a minute. The actors had

said their lines and only those who had to get the Theater ready for the afternoon performance remained. Marc asked the guard which was Henry Lykham, the other staff director he had to see. The doorman in the official blue uniform of the Senate Security Staff pointed to a short fat man with a thin mustache and a jolly open face sitting firmly in a large seat at the far side of the gallery making notes and checking papers. Marc strolled over to him, unaware that a pair of eyes behind dark glasses followed his every movement.

"My name is Marc Andrews, sir."

"Ah, yes, the graduate student. I'll be free in a moment, Mr. Andrews."

Marc sat down and waited. The man in dark glasses left the chamber by the side door.

"All right, Mr. Andrews, how about some lunch?"

"Great," replied Marc. He was taken to the ground floor, to G-211, the Senators' Dining Room. They found a table at the side of the room. Marc chatted convincingly about the hard work a committee staff director must have to do, while others get the praise and publicity. Henry Lykham readily agreed. They both chose their meal from the fixed menu; so did the man three tables away, who was watching them both carefully. Marc told the committee staff director that he intended to write his thesis on the Gun-Control Bill if it became law, and that he wanted some interesting inside information that the general public wouldn't get from the newspapers. "Therefore, Mr. Lykham," he concluded, "I have been advised to speak to you."

The fat man beamed; he was duly flattered, as Marc had hoped, and he began.

"There is nothing I can't tell you about this bill or the bunch of politicians involved in it."

Marc smiled, recalling the testimony given by Anthony Ulasewicz, a retired NYPD detective, at the Watergate Hearings. He had studied the hearings in an elective seminar at Yale. A particular remark came to mind. Ulasewicz had said something to the effect: Why bother to bug the place? Politicians and officials will tell you anything you want to know, over the phone, they'll even want to send it to you in the mail, whoever you are.

Senator Sam Irvin of North Carolina, the committee chairman, had reprimanded him for treating the committee lightly and turning the matter into a joke. It's no joke—it's the truth, was Ulasewicz's reply.

Marc asked which of the eleven senators on the committee were for the bill. Only four of them had been present at the morning discussion. From his research, Marc was fairly certain about the opinions of most of them but he wanted his assessments confirmed.

"Among the Democrats, Bayh, Burdick, Stevenson, and Glenn will vote for the measure. Abourezk, Byrd, and Moynihan are keeping their own counsel, but will probably come through in support of the administration position. They voted for the bill in committee. Thornton is the only Democrat who may vote against it. You heard him start to speak in favor of Dexter's states' rights position. Well, for Thornton, young man, it's not a matter of principle. He wants it both ways. Massachusetts has a strong state gun-control measure, so he can claim that his stance means that states can take whatever action they deem necessary to protect their citizens. But Massachusetts also has a number of firearms companies—Smith and Wesson, GKN Powdermet, Harrington and Richardson—which would be seriously affected by a federal gun-control act. The specter of unemployment, you know. As long as those companies can sell their wares outside Massachusetts,

197

they're okay. So Thornton fools his constituents into thinking they can control guns and manufacture them at the same time. Strange games being played by the man who took the President's Senate seat. You'll remember he won that special election in 1980. He's just not Kennedy caliber." Lykham chuckled. "Pun intended. As for the Republicans, Mathias of Maryland will vote for the bill. He's a very liberal guy—I'll never understand why he stays in the GOP. McCollister of Nebraska is against, along with Woodson of Arkansas. Duncan and Dexter you heard. No question where they stand. Duncan knows damn well that his constituents wouldn't tolerate gun control and will vote him out if he goes with it. Hard to tell if he's been brainwashed by the NRA, because he seems to be sincere when he talks about the idea of self-defense. He's a strange guy. Everyone in this place regards him as a dyed-in-the-wool conservative, but no one really knows him. He hasn't been here all that long. He succeeded Sparkman, who retired in 1978—bit of an unknown quantity."

Marc let him talk on. Lykham was enjoying the role of the expert, the man who knew everything. Normally, he sat for hours in the Hearing Room, unable to say a word, listening and making notes and occasionally whispering a suggestion in the ear of the chairman. Only his wife listened to his opinions and she never understood their significance. Lykham was delighted to have found an academic who had come to him for the facts.

"Dexter talks a good game—smooth character, that one. He beat the guy who was appointed to fill Ribicoff's term when Abe was picked by the President for a roving ambassadorship. Surprise winner. Wouldn't have thought that Connecticut would be represented by two Republicans. Guess all those rich New Yorkers moving to Stamford are making a difference. Anyway, just between the two of us, Andrews, I have my suspicions about the purity of his principles. Do you know how many gun companies there are in Connecticut? Remington, Colt, Olin, Winchester, Marlin, Sturm-Ruger. Now, that never stopped Senator Ribicoff from voting for gun control, but Dexter . . . well, he owns a big slice of a gun company, that's no secret. Something's biting him at the moment, he's as grouchy as hell. Maybe it's something to do with this bill, because he hasn't missed a session yet."

Marc sensed a sick feeling in his stomach. My God, Elizabeth's father? He just didn't want to believe it.

"So you think the bill will be passed?" said Marc in a conversational tone.

"No question, while the Democrats are in control. The minority report was vicious, but it'll get a majority on the tenth. There wasn't much doubt about that after the House put it through. By Thursday, nothing can stop it. The Majority Leader is only too aware of the importance the President attaches to this bill."

Byrd, thought Marc. He's on the list. "Could you tell me a little about the Majority Leader? He was on the Judiciary Committee, right? Where does he stand?"

"That's an interesting question, Andrews. Senator Byrd is a humorless, driven, ambitious individual. He has ulcers. He was born in poverty, always makes a point of emphasizing his origins, so much so that some of his colleagues call him Uriah Heep. In the 1940s, when he was only nineteen, he belonged to the Ku Klux Klan; yet he managed to overcome that handicap and rise to the most powerful post in the Senate in a party dominated by liberals. He got where he is because he's a team player. He does favors for other senators, and always has. He's diligent, conscientious about meeting their needs. His attention to detail has paid off in spades. He has always supported the Democratic—

with a capital D—position. And he's a very effective Majority Leader.

"Now, the strange thing about the current situation is that he's managing the program of a man he detests. He's always disliked the Kennedys, though he tries to play it down. In 1967, he had a bitter exchange with RFK on the Senate floor, and in 1971 he ousted EMK from his post as Majority Whip. No love lost in that relationship, but now that they have to work together, Byrd has fallen into line. With his background, it's unlikely that he's genuinely in favor of gun control, but he hasn't spoken out against the bill, naturally, because he has been shepherding it through the Senate for the President. He's done it very efficiently. He's scheduled it early, avoided recesses—"

"Sorry to intrrupt you, Mr. Lykham, but what do you mean he's avoided recesses? The committee didn't sit round the clock, surely?"

"No, young man, I was referring to a technical, procedural distinction between adjournment and recess. You see, the Senate usually recesses from one day to the next. The day after a recess, the unfinished business of the previous day is in order; the morning business can be dispensed with. Whenever the Majority Leader opts for recess rather than adjournment, he thereby lengthens the 'legislative day.' And since bills reported from committee must lay over one legislative day before a motion to consider is in order, the recess can be used to delay action on a particular measure. The so-called legislative day can extend for days, weeks, conceivably even months. This bill has been put through in the minimum possible time. If the President doesn't get support on the tenth, he will not have time to put it up again before he goes for re-election. will be a victory for those against the bill. And he may not be re-elected if the polls are to be believed. Americans g

200

sick of their presidents very quickly nowadays. So it's the tenth or forget it."

"What could stop it on the tenth?"

"Nothing I can think of offhand, except the death of the President, which could recess the Senate for seven days. Still the President looks pretty fit to me, perhaps a little overweight, not that I'm one to comment."

Marc was about to question Lykham about Bayh, when the staff director glanced at his watch.

"Look at the time," Lykham expostulated, "I must get back. I have to be the first, you know, get everything in order, so those senators think that we haven't been away at all."

Marc thanked him. Lykham picked up the check and signed it.

"Anytime you want more help or information, don't hesitate to get in touch."

"I certainly will," said Marc.

The fat staff director waddled away at what for him was full speed. Marc pondered over his coffee. The man three tables away had finished his and was waiting for Marc's next move. Those damn bells were ringing again. Only one this time, indicating that the yeas and nays were being tallied on the Senate floor. As soon as the vote was over, the senators would be flocking back to committee meetings. The bell brought Marc sharply out of his thoughts.

Once again he returned to the Dirksen Building and the Foreign Relations Committee Suite, where he asked if he could see Mr. Kenneck.

"Who shall I say is asking for him?" the receptionist inquired.

"Andrews, I'm a Yale student."

She picked a phone up and pressed two digits, informed the listener what Marc had told her.

201

"He's in Room 4491."

Marc thanked her and left for Room 4491, which was only a few doors down the corridor.

"Well, Andrews, what can I do for you?"

Marc was taken aback by the suddenness of his question; he recovered.

"I'm doing some research for a thesis, Mr. Kenneck, on the work of senators, and Mr. Lykham said you were the man to speak to. I wondered if Senators Percy and Pearson were in the Senate on Thursday, March 3, at ten-thirty, for the Foreign Relations Committee?"

Kenneck bent over a red leather-bound book. "Percy— no," he paused. "Pearson—no. Anything else, Mr. Andrews?" He obviously hadn't any time to waste.

"No, thank you."

Marc headed for the Library. That was sudden; now he was down to five senators, if the Bureau was right about what they had overheard on the illegal radio transmission when their man must have been in the Senate on the morning of March 3. He checked his notes: each one of the remaining suspects—Bayh, Byrd, Dexter, Duncan, and Thornton—had sat on the Judiciary Committee on the Gun-Control Bill and was in the Senate for the debate. Five men and a motive?

He was followed out of the room and into the elevator that took him to the ground floor. He used the pay phone across the hall from the elevator, near the Constitution Avenue entrance, to call the Director.

He dialed the Director's private number.

"Julius."

"What's your number?"

Marc gave it. A few seconds later the Director called him back.

"Percy and Pearson are off. I'm down to five and th

one thing they have in common is that all of them were on the committee of the Gun-Control Bill."

"Good," said the Director. "Much as I had expected. Getting better, Marc, but your time is running out, only about forty-eight hours left."

"Yes, sir."

The phone clicked.

He waited for a moment and then dialed Woodrow Wilson. There was the usual interminable wait while they found Elizabeth. What could he say about last night? What if the Director were right and her father—

"Dr. Dexter."

"When do you finish work tonight, Liz?"

"Five o'clock, lover," she said mockingly.

"May I pick you up?"

"If you like, now that I know your intentions are pure and honorable."

"Listen, we have to get something straight about that. I've told you how I feel; it was true yesterday and it's true now."

"See you at five, Marc."

"See you at five, Liz."

Marc put Elizabeth out of his mind by a conscious effort of will, and walked across the street to the Capitol grounds. He sat down under a tree on the grassy area between the Supreme Court and the Capitol. Protected, he thought, by law and legislature, bounded by Constitution and Independence. Who would dare to take him on here in front of the Capitol, the favored haunt of Senate staff, law clerks, and the Capitol police? A blue-and-white sightseeing tourmobile passed by on First Street, blocking his view of the fountains in front of the Supreme Court. Tourists gaped at Washington's white-marbled splendor. "And on your right, ladies and gentlemen, the United States Capitol. The cornerstone of the original building was laid in 1793. The British burned the Capitol building on August 24, 1814. . . ."

And some crazy senator defiled it on March 10, 1983, added Marc silently as the tourmobile moved on. Foreboding oppressed him: it really is going to happen, we can't stop it. Comes Caesar to the Capitol . . . Blood on the steps.

He forced himself to look at his notes. Bayh, Byrd, Dexter, Duncan, Thornton. He had two days to transform five into one. The conspirator he sought was Cassius, not Brutus. Bayh, Byrd, Dexter, Duncan, and Thornton. Where were they at lunchtime on February 24? If he knew the answer, he would know which four men were innocent and which man was so desperate that he would plot to assassinate the President. Even if we find out which man is behind this, he thought, as he stood up and brushed the grass from his pants, how do we stop the murder? Obviously, the Senator isn't going to do the killing himself. We must keep the President away from the Capitol. The Director must have a plan, he surely wouldn't let it go that far. Marc closed his file and walked to the Metro.

Once home, he picked up his car and drove slowly to Woodrow Wilson. He looked in the rear-view mirror. A different car was following him today, a black Buick. Someone looking after me again, he thought. He arrived at the hospital at 4:45 but Elizabeth wasn't free yet, so he went back to his car and turned on the evening news. An earthquake in the Philippines that had killed one hundred and twelve people was the lead story. President Kennedy was confident of support for the Gun-Control Bill. The Dow-Jones Index had moved up three points to 1211. The

Yankees beat the Dodgers in a spring training game, what's new?

Elizabeth came out of the hospital looking depressed and jumped in beside him.

"What can I say about last night?" Marc asked.

"Nothing," said Elizabeth. "It was like reading a book with the last chapter torn out. Who tore it out, Marc?"

"Perhaps I've brought the last chapter with me," said Marc, avoiding the question.

"Thanks, but I don't think I'll be in the mood for another bedtime story for a while," she replied. "The last one gave me a bad dream."

Elizabeth was very quiet and Marc could get little response from her. He turned right off Independence and stopped the car on one of the side streets on the Mall, facing the Jefferson Memorial and the sunset.

"Is it last night?" asked Marc.

"Partly," she said. "You made me feel pretty silly walking off like that. I don't suppose you're going to tell me what it was all about?"

"I can't do that," said Marc uneasily. "But believe me, had nothing to do with you. At least that's almost—" He stopped abruptly.

Never embarrass the Bureau.

" 'At least that's almost' what? Almost true? Why was at call so important?"

"Let's stop this and go eat."

Elizabeth didn't reply.

He started the car again. Two cars pulled out at the me time as he did. A blue Ford sedan and a black Buick. They're certainly making sure today, he thought. Perhaps e of them is just looking for a parking space. He anced at Elizabeth to see if she'd noticed them too; no,

205

why should she, only he could see in the rear-view mirror. He drove to a small, warm Japanese restaurant on Wisconsin Avenue. He couldn't take her home while the damned Bureau had the place bugged. Deftly, the Oriental waiter sliced the fat shrimps, cooked them on the metal slab in the center of their table. He flicked each shrimp as he finished it onto their plates, giving them small, delicious bowls of sauces in which to dip the pieces. Elizabeth brightened under the influence of the hot sake.

"I'm sorry to react so strongly. I have a lot on my mind at the moment."

"Like to tell me about it?"

"I can't, I'm afraid. It's personal and my father has asked me not to discuss it with anyone yet."

Marc froze. "Can't you tell me?"

"No. I guess we'll both have to be patient."

They went to a drive-in movie and sat in the comfortable semidarkness, arms companionably intertwined. Marc sensed she didn't wish to be touched, and indeed he was in no mood to do so. They were both concerned about the same man, but for different reasons—or was it the same reason? And how would she react if she discovered that he had been investigating her father since the day after they met. Maybe she knew. Damn it, why couldn't he simply believe in her? Surely, she wasn't setting him up. He could remember very little about the film, and when it ended he took her home and left immediately. Two cars were still following him.

"Hi, stud!" A figure jumped out of the shadows. Marc swung around and checked his holster nervously.

"Oh, hi, Simon."

"Listen, man, I can show you some dirty postcards if you're still desperate, 'cause it seems that you're just not

206

good enough, man. I had a black one last night, I'm having a white one tonight."

"How can you be so sure?" said Marc.

"I check in advance, man, I ain't got time to waste with my pretty body." Simon burst out laughing. "Think about me when you go to bed tonight, all alone, Marc, 'cause I sure will have forgotten you. Cool your jets, man."

Marc threw him the keys and watched him as he walked toward the Mercedes swinging his hips, dancing and laughing.

"You ain't got it, baby, whatever it is."

"Bullshit! You're a jive-ass bastard," Marc said, and laughed.

"Now, you're just jealous, man, or prejudiced," said Simon, as he revved up the car and moved to a parking space. As he passed Marc, he shouted, "Either way, I'm the winner."

Marc wondered if he ought to apply for a job as a garage attendant at the apartment building. It seemed to have its compensations. He looked around; something moved; no, it was just his nerves or his imagination. Once in his room, he wrote his report for the morning session with the Director and fell into bed.

Two days to go.

9

1:00 AM

The phone rang. Marc was just falling asleep, still in tha
world between sleeping and waking. The phone insisted
Try to answer it, it could be Julius.

"Hello," he said, yawning.

"Marc Andrews?"

"Yes," he said wearily, shifting himself to a more com
fortable position in the bed, fearing if he woke up fully h
would never get back to sleep.

"It's George Stampouzis. Sorry to wake you, but I'v
come up with something I thought you would want
know immediately."

Stampouzis's statement was like cold water. Marc w:
wide awake instantly.

"Right, don't say anything else, I'll call you from a p:
phone. What's your number?" Marc wrote it down on t
back of a Kleenex box, the only thing he could reac
He threw on a bathrobe, forced his feet into a pair
tennis shoes, and started for the door. He opened the do
looked both ways. Christ, he was getting paranoid. The
was no sound in the hall; there wouldn't be if someo
was waiting for him. He took the elevator down to
garage level, where there was a pay phone. Simon v

asleep on the chair—how did he manage it? Marc had found it hard enough to sleep in bed.

He dialed the 212 area code.

"Hello, Stampouzis. Andrews."

"You G-men always play games at one in the morning? I would have thought you'd figured out a better system by now."

Marc laughed; the sound echoed in the garage; Simon twitched.

"What can I do for you?"

"I traded some information today, now you owe me two stories." Stampouzis paused. "The Mafia had nothing to do with Stames's death, and they are not going overboard for the Gun-Control Bill, although they basically oppose it. So now you know everything. I wouldn't have gone this far for anyone but Nick, so make sure you handle it right."

"I'm doing my best," Marc replied. "Thanks for the help."

He put the phone on the hook and walked back to the elevator, thinking about the tousled bed which he hoped was still warm. Simon was still asleep.

5:50 AM

"It's for you, sir."

"What?" mumbled the Director, still half-asleep.

"The phone, sir, it's for you." His housekeeper was standing at the doorway in her bathrobe.

"Ugh. What time is it?"

"Ten to six, sir."

"Who is it?"

"Mr. Elliott, sir."

"Right, switch it through."

"Yes, sir."

Elliott had woken him up. A decision he would never have taken unless it was necessary.

"Good morning, Elliott, right, what is it?" He paused. "Can you be sure? That changes the whole situation. What time is he due in? Seven, of course. I'll see you at six-thirty."

The Director put the phone down, and sat on the edge of the bed, and said very loudly: "Damn," which by the Director's standards was extreme. His big feet placed firmly on the floor, his large hands splayed on his equally large thighs, he was deep in thought. Eventually he arose put on a robe, and disappeared into the bathroom, repeating the expletive several times.

Marc also had a phone call, not from the anonymous man, but from Elizabeth. She wanted to see him urgently They agreed to meet at eight o'clock in the lobby of the Mayflower. It was certain no one would recognize him there, but he wondered why Elizabeth had chosen that particular meeting place.

Marc took off his robe and returned to the bathroom.

The Senator took an early-morning phone call as well not from the anonymous man or from Elizabeth, but from the Chairman, who was arranging their midday meeting for the final briefing at the Sheraton Hotel Silver Spring. The Senator agreed, replaced the phone and roamed around the room in his robe thinking.

"Coffee for three, Mrs. McGregor. Are they both here?" the Director asked as he passed her.

"Yes, sir."

Mrs. McGregor looked very chic in a new turquoise, two-piece suit, but the Director hadn't noticed. He went into his office.

"Good morning, Matt. Good morning, Marc." When should he drop the bomb? He decided to let Andrews speak first. "Right, let's hear what you've found out."

"I think we've cut our list down to five senators, sir— Bayh of Indiana, Byrd of West Virginia, Dexter of Connecticut, Duncan of South Carolina, and Thornton of Massachusetts. The common feature here is opposition to the Gun-Control Bill, which as we know, sir, is likely to become law on March 10. Assassination of the President would be about the only way of holding that up."

"I would have thought that would be the one act that would make certain the bill went through," said Matthew Rogers.

"You tell that to two Kennedys, Martin Luther King, and George Wallace and see what they say," responded the Director. "Continue, Marc."

Marc summarized what Lykham and Stampouzis had told him about each man, and explained his elimination of the two other men on the list of seven—Pearson and Percy. "That's it, sir, unless, of course, we are approaching this thing in the wrong way and heading down a blind alley. And as far as I'm concerned that is entirely possible. I'm boxing with shadows."

The Director nodded and waited.

Marc continued: "I was going to spend today trying to hear them in action in the Senate. I wish I could think of a good way of finding out where they were at lunchtime on February 24, short of asking them outright, that is."

"Don't go anywhere near any of them. That would be a sure way to shut down the whole plot. Now, Marc, I must warn you my news is not good, so settle back and prepare for the worst. We are beginning to think our man is Dexter," said the Director.

Marc went cold. "Why, sir?" he managed to get out.

The Assistant Director leaned forward to speak. "I have had some men checking out the Georgetown Inn, very unobtrusively. We didn't expect to turn anything up. We questioned all the day staff and they couldn't help. Early this morning, just to be thorough, we interviewed the night staff. Turned out that one of the night porters, who was off duty during the day, of course, is pretty sure he saw Senator Dexter hurrying along a street away from the hotel some time like two-thirty in the afternoon on February 24."

Marc was stunned. "How did he know it was Senator Dexter?"

"The man was born and raised in Wilton, Connecticut, knows his face well. I'm afraid there's something else, too; there was a young woman with him whose rough description tallies with his daughter."

"That's not proof," said Marc. "It's all circumstantial."

"Maybe," said the Director, "but it's an unfortunate coincidence for Senator Dexter. Remember his involvement in the arms business; it won't do his finances much good if the Gun-Control Bill goes through; in fact our inquiries show he stands to lose a fortune, so we have motive as well."

"But, sir," Marc argued, carried away by the need to believe in Elizabeth, "do you really think that a senator would plot to kill the President just to keep one of his companies afloat? There are so many less drastic ways stall the bill. He could try to tie it up in committee. Or organize a filibuster—"

"He already has tried—and failed, Marc," Matthew Rogers interrupted.

"The other four senators may have more powerful motives we don't happen to know about. It doesn't have to be Dexter," continued Marc, sounding unconvinced.

"Marc, I understand what you're saying. You do have a point. Under ordinary circumstances I'd agree that it seems unlikely, but we have to go on the evidence we have, even if it's slim and no more than circumstantial. And there's something else. On the night of March third, when Casefikis and the postman were killed, Dr. Dexter's name was not marked on the duty register. She should have finished work at five o'clock, but for some unfathomable reason she stayed an extra two hours, treated the Greek—who was not her patient—and then went home. Now it's possible that she was just conscientious and working overtime, or that she was filling in for someone else temporarily, but there are a hell of a lot of coincidences here, Marc. I'm bound to say if one is dispassionate about it, the odds are stacked heavily against Senator Dexter—and his daughter."

Marc did not reply.

"Now listen and listen carefully," the Director went on. "I know you want to believe that all this is coincidence and that it's one of the other four—but I only have twenty-six hours left before the President leaves the White House, and I have to face the facts as they present themselves. I want to catch the man involved, whoever he is, and I'm not willing to risk the life of the President to do it. When are you seeing the girl next?"

Marc looked up. "Eight o'clock at the Mayflower."

"Why? Why the Mayflower?"

"I don't know, sir. She just said that it was important."

"Um, well I think you ought to go and then report bac[k] to me immediately."

"Yes, sir."

"I don't understand why it's the Mayflower, Andrew[s]. Be careful."

"Yes, sir."

"It's ten to eight, you'd better be on your way. I[n]cidentally, we're still having no luck with the twent[y] dollar bills. We're down to the last eight, but no prin[t] from Mrs. Casefikis. Better news on the German, Gerbac[h]. We've established beyond a doubt that he had no conne[c]tion with the CIA during his stay in Rhodesia or at t[he] time of his death, so that's one more problem out of t[he] way."

Marc didn't give a damn about the twenty-dollar bil[l,] the German driver, the Mafia, or the CIA. All his ha[rd] work was leading them straight to Dexter. He left t[he] office more despondent than he had been when he ca[me] in.

Once back on the street, he decided to walk to [the] Mayflower in the hope of clearing his head. He di[d] notice that two men were following him down Penns[yl]vania Avenue, past the White House, on to the hotel.

At the press of a button, Elliott entered the Direct[or'] office.

"Elliott, you were right about the Mayflower. Wh[at's] been done about it?"

"There are two men already there, sir, and one foll[ow]ing Andrews."

"It's the first time in thirty-six years that I've hated [my] job," said the Director. "You've done very well, Elli[ott]

and soon I'll be able to tell you what this whole damn thing is about."

"Yes, sir."

"Follow up these five names. Leave no stone unturned."

"Yes, sir."

"Thank you."

Elliot slid out of the room.

Damn man has no heart. Can't have a right-hand man without a heart. Makes him damn useful in this strange situation, though. When this thing's all over, I'll transfer him back to Ohio and—

"You said something, sir?"

"No, Mrs. McGregor, I'm just going quietly mad. Don't worry about me. When the men in the white coats come to take me away, just sign the forms in triplicate and look relieved."

Mrs. McGregor smiled.

"I like your new suit," the Director said.

She blushed. "Thank you, sir."

Marc pushed through the revolving doors of the Mayflower Hotel, his eyes searching the lobby for Elizabeth. How he wanted to see her and how he wanted to stop being devious and clear things up. It's all circumstantial, he insisted to himself. He couldn't spot her and chose a comfortable seat outside the bar, which was all packed up.

On the far side, a man was buying *The Washington Post* from the newspaper stand. Marc didn't notice that he wasn't reading it. Elizabeth was heading toward him with Senator Dexter by her side. Hell, that was all he needed.

"Hello, Marc." She kissed him gently on the cheek.

Judas showing the Pharisees which one was to be killed? The unkindest cut of all.

"Marc, I'd like you to meet my father."

"Good morning, sir."

"Good morning, Marc, it's good to meet you. Elizabeth has told me quite a bit about you."

And what would you be able to tell me, thought Marc. Where were you on February 24? Where will you be tomorrow?

"Marc, are you all right?" Elizabeth inquired.

"Yes, fine. I'm so sorry, Senator, it's good to meet you."

The Senator was looking at him strangely.

"Well, I must get going, dear—I have a busy schedule. I look forward to our usual lunch tomorrow."

"See you then, Father. Thanks for the breakfast and the chat."

"Good-by, Marc. See you again soon, I hope." Senator Dexter looked at him expressionlessly.

"Maybe," replied Marc quietly

They watched him leave. So did three other people. One of them left to make a phone call.

"Marc, what's the matter with you? Why were you so brusque with my father? I especially wanted you to meet him."

"I'm sorry, I'm just tired."

"Or is there something you're not telling me?" said Elizabeth.

"I could ask you the same question."

"What are you talking about?"

"Oh, I don't know, let's forget it," said Marc. "Why did you want to see me so urgently?"

"Simply because I wanted you to meet my father. What's so strange about that? Why the hell did I bother?

She got up and ran down the corridor, pushing her

through the revolving door at the end. Three men saw her leave. One followed her, two stuck with Marc. He walked slowly toward the doors. The doorman saluted him punctiliously.

"Cab, sir?"

"No, thanks, I'll walk."

The Director was on the phone and waved Marc to the large leather chair. He sank down in it, his mind fuzzy. The Director put the phone down and looked at him.

"So now you've met Senator Dexter, and I must tell you that either Dr. Dexter knows nothing or she's the greatest actress alive."

"You saw everything," said Marc.

"Of course, and more. She was just in an automobile accident, two minutes ago. That phone call was the details."

Marc jumped out of his seat.

"She's all right. A couple of hundred dollars' worth of damage to the front of her Fiat and not a mark on the bus she hit. Sensible girl. Wears a seat belt. She's on her way to work now in a cab, or rather, she thinks it's a cab."

Marc sighed, resigned to whatever would happen next. "Where is Senator Dexter?" he asked.

"He's gone to the Senate. Made one phone call when he got there, but it wasn't of any significance."

Marc was beginning to feel like a puppet. "What do you want me to do now?"

There was a knock on the door and the anonymous man appeared. He handed a note to the Director, who read it quickly.

"Thank you."

The anonymous man left. Marc feared the worst. The Director placed the note on the desk and looked up.

"Senator Thorton has called a press conference at ten-thirty in Senate Committee Room 2228. Better get down there immediately. Phone me as soon as he has said his piece. The questions from the press afterward will be irrelevant; they always are."

Marc walked to the Senate, once again hoping it would clear his head. He wanted to ring Elizabeth and ask if she was all right after the accident; he wanted to ask her a hundred questions, but he only wanted one answer. Three men also walked to the Senate, two of them taking half of the route each, and the third walking the whole way. All three of them arrived eventually in Room 2228 none of them was there to hear Senator Thornton's statement.

The room was already well lit by Idreg lights for the television cameras, and the members of the press were chatting among themselves. It was a packed house, even though Senator Thornton had not yet arrived. Marc wondered what he had to say, whether it would throw any light on his own problems. Point the guilty finger at Thornton perhaps, give a motive he could go back to the Director with. He thought, as he looked at the senior reporters, that they might have a shrewd idea or even a tip from one of Thornton's staff as to the contents his statement. But he didn't want to ask them any questions for fear of being remembered. With an entrance that would have pleased Caesar himself, Senator Thornton came in, all smiles, behind three aides and a private secretary. He certainly was making the most of it. His dark hair was covered with grease, and he had put what he obviously imagined to be his best suit, green w a blue pin-stripe. No one had briefed him on what to wear when facing color television—only dark clothes, as plain as possible—or if he had been briefed, he hadn't listened.

He sat in a large throne of a chair at the far end of the room, his feet only just touching the ground. He was surrounded by arc lights and the TV acoustics men put microphones around him and in front of him. Suddenly, three more vast Idreg lights were thrown on. Thornton was sweating already, but still smiling. The three television networks agreed that they were ready for the Senator. Thornton cleared his throat.

"Ladies and gentlemen of the press . . ."

"That's a pompous remark to start with," said a correspondent in front of Marc, writing every word down in shorthand. Marc looked more closely, he thought he recognized the face. It was Sinclair of *The Washington Post*. Senator Thornton now had complete silence from the room.

"I have just left a long discussion with the President of the United States and because of that meeting, I wish to make a statement to the press and television." He paused. "My criticisms of the Gun-Control Bill and my vote against it in committee were motivated by a desire to represent my constituents and their genuine fear of unemployment . . ."

". . . and your own genuine fear of unemployment," remarked Sinclair, *sotto voce*. "What bribe did the President offer you at dinner on Monday?"

The Senator cleared his throat again. "The President has promised that after this legislation is passed, and domestic production of guns is prohibited, he will sponsor legislation to give financial assistance to gun manufacturers and their employees, in the hope that the facilities of the gun industry can be turned to other, less dangerous uses than the production of weapons of destruction. The President's concern has made it possible for me not to vote against this piece of legislation. I have for some considerable time been of two minds . . ."

"True enough," said Sinclair.

". . . about this bill, because of my genuine fear of the freedom and ease with which criminals can obtain firearms."

"It didn't worry you yesterday. Just what contracts did the President promise," murmured the correspondent, "or did he say he would help you win re-election to his old seat this year?"

"And the problem for me has always been in the balance . . ."

". . . a little bribe tipped the balance."

Sinclair now had his own audience, which was enjoying his offerings far more than those of the Senator from Massachusetts.

"Now that the President has shown such understanding I feel able to announce with a clear conscience . . ."

". . . so clear we can see right through it," more Sinclair.

". . . that I can support my party's position. I will not be opposing the President on the floor of the Senate tomorrow."

Wild applause from scattered parts of the room sounding—and looking—suspiciously like aides in strategic spots.

"I shall, ladies and gentlemen," Senator Thornton continued, "rest an easier man tonight. . . ."

"And a richer one," added Sinclair.

"I should like to end by thanking the members of press for attending. . . ."

"We had to; it was the only show in town."

Laughter broke out around the *Post* correspondent, but it didn't reach Thorton.

"And I would like to say that I will be delighted to answer any questions. Thank you."

"Bet you don't answer any of mine."

Most of the other reporters left the room immediately, in order to catch the early editions of the afternoon papers, already going to press around the country. Marc joined them but glanced over the famous journalist's shoulder. He had been scribbling in longhand.

"Friends, Romans, country bumpkins, lend me your ears; I come to bury Kennedy, not to praise him." Not exactly front-page material.

Three other men who had been at the press conference followed Marc out of the room. He ran to the nearest pay telephones, halfway down the hall; they were all being used by newspapermen anxious to get their copy out, and there was a long line behind them. Another line had formed by the two phones at the end of the hall. Marc took the elevator to the ground floor; same problem; his only chance would be the pay phone in the Russell Building across the street. He ran all the way; so did three other men. When he got there, a middle-aged woman stepped into the booth a pace ahead of him, and put her two dimes in.

"Hello . . . it's me. I got the job. . . .Yeah, pretty good. . . . Mornings only. . . . Start tomorrow. . . . but I can't complain, money's not bad."

Marc paced up and down while the three men caught their breath. At last, the woman finished talking and, with a big smile all over her face, she walked away, oblivious to Marc or his problems. At least someone is confident about tomorrow, Marc thought. He glanced around to be sure that there was no one near him, though he thought he recognized a man standing by the Medicare poster; perhaps it was one of his colleagues from the FBI. He had seen that face behind the dark glasses somewhere. He was getting better protection than the President. He dialed the Director's private line and gave him his pay-phone number. The phone rang almost immediately.

"Thornton's off the list, sir, because he has—"

"I know, I know," said the Director. "I've just been on the phone and been briefed on what Thornton said. It's exactly what I would have expected him to say if he's involved. It certainly does not get him off my list; if anything, I'm a little more suspicious. Keep working on all five this afternoon and contact me the moment you come up with anything; don't bother to come in."

The phone clicked. Marc felt despondent. He depressed the cradle and waited for the dial tone, put two more dimes in, and dialed Woodrow Wilson. The nurse on duty went on a search for Elizabeth, but returned and said that no one had seen her all day. Marc hung up, forgetting to say thank you or good-by. He took the elevator down to the basement cafeteria to have lunch. His decision gained the restaurant two more customers; the third man already had a lunch date, for which he was running late.

1:00 PM

Only Tony and Xan were on time at the Sheraton Hotel Silver Spring. They had spent many hours together, seldom spoke; Tony wondered what the Nip thought about all the time. Tony had had a busy schedule checking

outes for the final day, getting the Buick perfectly
uned—and chauffeuring the Chairman and Matson; they
ll treated him like a damn cab driver. His skill was equal
o theirs anytime, and where the hell would they be with-
ut him? Those fucking FBI men would still be around
eir necks, if it wasn't for him. Still, the whole damn
ing would be over by tomorrow night and he could get
way and spend some of his hard-earned money. He
ouldn't make up his mind whether it would be Miami or
as Vegas. Tony always spent his money before he got it.
he Chairman came in, a cigarette hanging from his
outh as always, looked at them, and asked brusquely
here Matson was. Both shook their heads. Matson always
orked alone. He trusted no one. The Chairman was angry
d made no attempt to hide it. The Senator followed, just
few moments later, looking equally annoyed, but he
dn't even notice that Matson wasn't there.

"Why don't we start?" demanded the Senator. "I find
is meeting inconvenient as it is, since it's the final day
debate on the bill."

The Chairman looked at him with contempt. "We're
ssing Matson and his report is vital."

"How long will you wait?"

"Two minutes."

They waited in silence. They had nothing to say to each
er; each man knew why he was there. Exactly two
nutes later, the Chairman lit another cigarette and asked
ny for his report.

'I've checked the routes, boss, and it takes a car going
twenty-two miles per hour three minutes to get from
south exit of the White House onto E Street and down
nsylvania Avenue to the FBI Building and another
e minutes to reach the Capitol. It takes forty-five
onds to climb the steps and be out of range. On average

six minutes forty-five seconds in all. Never under five minutes thirty seconds, never over seven minutes. That's trying it at midnight, one o'clock, and two o'clock in the morning, remembering the routes are going to be even clearer for Kennedy."

"What about after the operation?" asked the Chairman.

"It's possible to get from the crane through basement passageways to the Rayburn Building and from there to the Capitol South Metro Station in two minutes at best and three minutes fifteen seconds at worst—depends on elevators and congestion. Once the VC—" He stopped himself. "Once Xan is in the Metro, they'll never find him; in a few minutes, he can be on the other side of Washington."

"Are you sure they won't catch him in three minutes fifteen seconds?" asked the Senator, whose personal interest in Xan was nonexistent, but he didn't trust the little man not to sing if he was caught.

"Assuming they know nothing, they won't know which way to turn for the first five minutes," answered the Chairman.

Tony continued: "If it goes as planned, you won't even need the car and I'll dump it and disappear."

"Agreed," said the Chairman. "But I trust the car is in perfect condition?"

"Sure is, ready for Daytona."

The Senator mopped his brow, which was surprising since it was a cold March day.

"Xan, your report," said the Chairman.

Xan went over his plan in detail; he had rehearsed for the last two days. He had slept in the head of the crane both nights and the gun was already in place. The men were going on a twenty-four-hour strike starting six that evening. "By six tomorrow, I will be on other side of America and Kennedy will be dead."

"Good," said the Chairman, stubbing out his cigarette and lighting another one. "I will be on the corner of Ninth and Pennsylvania and I will contact you on my watchband-radio when I arrive at nine-thirty and again when Kennedy's car passes me. When your watch starts vibrating, he will be three minutes away, giving you three minutes and forty-five seconds in all. How much warning do you need?"

"Two minutes and thirty seconds will be enough," said Xan.

"That's cutting it a bit close, isn't it?" inquired the Senator, still sweating.

"It may be, in which case you'll have to delay him on the steps because we don't want to expose Xan more than necessary," said the Chairman. "The longer he is in view, the greater the chance the Secret Service helicopters will have of spotting him."

The Senator turned his head toward Xan. "You say you've been rehearsing every day?"

"Yes," replied Xan. He still saw no reason to use more words than necessary, even when addressing a United States Senator.

"Then why don't people notice you carrying a rifle or at least a gun box?"

"Because gun has been taped to platform on top of crane three hundred and twenty feet out of harm's way since I got back from Vienna."

"What happens if the crane comes down? They'll see it right away."

"No, I in yellow overalls and rifle is in eight parts and has been painted yellow and is taped to underpart of platform. Even with strong field glasses, it looks like part of crane. When I picked up latest sniper rifle from Dr. Schmidt of Helmut, Helmut, and Schmidt, even he was surprised by can of yellow paint."

They all laughed except the Senator.

"How long does it take you to assemble it?" continued the Senator, probing for a flaw, something he always did when questioning so-called experts in Senate committees.

"Two minutes to put rifle together and thirty seconds to get into perfect firing position; two more minutes to dismantle gun and retape it. It's a five point six by sixty-one millimeter Vomhofe Super Express rifle, and I'm using a seventy-seven-grain bullet with a muzzle speed of three thousand four hundred and eighty feet per second, which is two thousand foot-pounds of muzzle energy which, in layman's language, Senator, means if there is no wind, will aim one and one half inches above Kennedy's forehead at two hundred yards."

"Are you satisfied?" the Chairman asked the Senator.

"Yes, I suppose so," he said, and sank into a brooding silence, still wiping his brow. Then he thought of something else and was about to start his questioning again when the door flew open and Matson rushed in.

"Sorry, boss. I've been following something up."

"It better be good," snapped the Chairman.

"It could be bad, boss, very bad," said Matson between breaths.

They all looked anxiously at him.

"Okay, let's have it."

"His name is Marc Andrews," said Matson.

"And who is he?" asked the Chairman.

"The FBI man who went to the hospital with Colver."

"Could we start at the beginning?" the Chairman asked.

Matson took a deep breath. "You know I've alwa

226

been bothered about Stames going to the hospital with Colvert—it didn't make sense, a man of his seniority.

"Yes, yes," said the Chairman impatiently.

"Well, Stames didn't go. His wife told me. I went by to say how sorry I was, and she told me everything Stames had done that evening, right down to eating some moussaka. The FBI told her not to say anything to anyone but she thinks that I'm still with the Bureau, and she doesn't remember, or maybe she never knew, that Stames and I were not exactly friends. I've checked on Andrews and I've been following him for the last forty-eight hours. He's listed in the Washington Field Office as on leave for two weeks, but he's been spending his leave in a very strange way. I've seen him at FBI Headquarters, he's going around with a female doctor from Woodrow Wilson, and he's been nosing around at the Senate."

The Senator flinched.

"The good doctor was on duty the night that I got rid of the Greek and the black bastard."

"So they know everything," said the Chairman quickly. "Why are we still here?"

"Well, that's the strange part. I arranged to have a drink with an old buddy from the Secret Service; he's on duty tomorrow with Kennedy and nothing has changed. It is painfully obvious that the Secret Service have no idea about tomorrow, so either the FBI know one hell of a lot or nothing, but if they do know everything, they're not letting the Secret Service in on it."

"What did you learn from your contacts in the FBI?" asked the Chairman.

"Nothing. Nobody knows anything, even when they're kind drunk."

"How much do you think Andrews knows?" continued the Chairman.

"I think he's fallen for our friend the doctor and knows very little. He's running around in the dark," Matson replied. "It's possible he's picked up something from the Greek waiter. If so, he's working on his own, and that's not FBI policy."

"I don't follow," said the Chairman.

"Bureau policy is to work in pairs or threes, so why aren't there dozens of men on it? Even if there were only six or seven, I would have heard about it and so would at least one of my contacts in the FBI," said Matson. "I think they may know about some attempt on the President, but I don't think they have a clue when—or where."

"Did anyone mention the date in front of the Greek?" asked the Senator nervously.

"I can't remember, but there's only one way to be sure that they know absolutely nothing," said the Chairman.

"What's that, boss?" asked Matson.

The Chairman paused, lit another cigarette, and said "Kill Andrews."

There was silence for a few moments. Matson was the first to recover.

"Why, boss?"

"Simple logic. If he is connected with an FBI investiga tion, then they will change tomorrow's schedule. The would never risk letting Kennedy ride in a car one inc outside the White House gates. Just think of the conse quences involved; if they know of an assassination a tempt on the President and they haven't made an arre to date and they haven't informed the Secret Service . .

"That's right," said Matson. "They would find som excuse and cancel at the last minute."

"Exactly, so if Kennedy comes out of the gates, we w kill him because they know nothing. If he doesn't, we' going to be a long way away for a long time, because they know far too much for our health."

The Chairman turned to the Senator, who was now sweating profusely.

"Now, you just make sure that you're on the steps of the Capitol to stall him if necessary and we'll take care of the rest," he said harshly. "If we don't get him tomorrow, we have wasted one hell of a lot of time and money, and we sure are not going to get another chance like this."

The Senator groaned. "I think you're insane, but I won't waste time arguing. I have to get back to the Senate before somebody notices that I'm missing."

"Settle down, Senator. We have it all under control; we can't lose either way."

"Maybe you can't, but at the end of the day I might be the fall guy."

The Senator left without another word. The Chairman waited in silence for the door to close.

"Now we've got that punk out of the way, let's get down to business. Let's hear all about Marc Andrews and what he's been up to."

Matson gave a detailed description of Marc's movements during the past forty-eight hours. The Chairman took in every detail.

"Right, it's good-by, Mr. Andrews, and then we'll monitor the FBI's reaction. Now listen carefully, Matson. This is the way we'll do it: you will return to the Senate right now and . . ."

Matson listened intently, taking notes and nodding from time to time.

"Any questions?"

"No, boss."

"If they let the President out of the White House after

that, they know nothing. One more thing before we finish. If anything does go wrong tomorrow, we'll all take care of ourselves. Understood? No one ever talks; compensation will be made at a later date, in the usual way."

They all nodded.

"And one final point: if there is a foul-up, there's one man who certainly won't take care of us, so we'll have to be prepared to take care of him. I propose we do it in the following way. Xan, if Kennedy . . ."

They all listened in silence; no one disagreed.

"Now I think it's time for lunch. No need to let that son of a bitch spoil our eating habits. Sorry you're missing it, Matson; just make sure it's Andrews' last lunch."

Matson smiled. "It will give me a good appetite," he said, and left.

The Chairman picked up the phone. "We're ready for lunch now, thank you." He lit another cigarette.

2:15 PM

Marc finished his lunch. Two other men finished their sandwiches and rose to leave. Marc returned to the Senate. He wanted to catch Henry Lykham before the floor debate started. He hoped that Lykham would have something else to reveal after having had a night to sleep on it. He also needed copies of the Judiciary Committee Gun-Control Hearings so that he could study the questions asked by Bayh, Byrd, Dexter, Duncan, and Thornton. Perhaps they would reveal another missing piece of the jigsaw. Marc somehow doubted it. He was becoming convinced that politicians rarely revealed anything. Marc a rived only a few minutes before the session was scheduled to begin. He asked a page to find Lykham in the antechamber.

Lykham bustled out a few moments later. It was obvious he didn't need any interruptions ten minutes before the session. So they had no chance for a chat even if he had thought of anything. But Marc did manage to find out where to obtain transcripts of the committee hearings and discussions.

"You get them from the committee office down the hall."

Marc thanked him and walked upstairs to the gallery, where his new friend, the guard, had saved him a seat. The place was packed. Senators were entering the chamber and taking their places, so he decided to pick up the transcripts later.

The Vice President called for order and Senator Dexter looked around the room slowly and dramatically, sweeping the chamber with his eyes to be assured of everyone's attention. When his eyes alighted on Marc he looked a little surprised, but he soon recovered to begin his final arguments against the bill.

Marc was embarrassed and wished he had taken a seat in the back, beyond the range of Dexter's piercing glance. The debate dragged on. Bayh, Byrd, Dexter, Duncan, Thornton. They all wanted a final word before tomorrow's vote.

Marc listened to them all but learned nothing new. He seemed to be at a dead end. All that was left to do that day was to go and pick up transcripts of the hearings. He would have to read them through the night and he doubted, having listened to the five speak twice already, that they'd tell him anything. But what other lead did he have? Everything else was being covered by the Director.

He walked down the hall to the elevator, left the Capitol by the ground-floor exit, and made his way across the Capital grounds to the Dirksen Building.

"I would like transcripts of the Gun-Control Hearings, please."

"All of them?" asked the disbelieving secretary.

"Yes," replied Marc.

"There were six all-day sessions."

Christ, he thought, it will be worse than all night; still, it would be only the questions and statements of Bayh, Byrd, Dexter, Duncan, and Thornton.

"Sign or pay?"

"I wish I could sign," he said jokingly.

"Well, are you an official of any kind?"

Yes, thought Marc. But I can't admit it.

"No," said Marc, and took out his wallet.

"If you asked for these through one of the senator from your state, you could probably get them for nothing Otherwise that'll be ten dollars, sir."

"I'm in a hurry," said Marc. "Guess I'll have to pay."

He handed over the money. Senator Stevenson appeared in the doorway connecting the hearing room the committee office.

"Good afternoon, Senator," said the secretary, turnin away from Marc.

"Hi, Debbie. Would you happen to have a copy of th Clean Air Bill as it was reported out of the subcommitte before the committee markup?"

"Certainly, Senator, just a moment." She disappear into a back room. "It's the only copy we have at moment. Can I trust you with it, Senator?" She laughe "Or should I make you sign for it?"

Even senators sign, thought Marc. Senators sign everything. Henry Lykham signs for everything, no wo

ler my taxes are so high. But I imagine they have to pay
or the food later. The food. My God, why didn't I think
of it before. Marc started running.

"Sir, sir, you've left your hearings." But it was too late.

"Some kind of nut," said the secretary to Senator
tevenson.

"Anyone who wants to read all those hearings must
e crazy to begin with," said Senator Stevenson, staring
t the pile of paper Marc had left behind him.

Marc went straight to Room G-211, where he had
nched with Lykham the previous day. The door was
arked "Officials' Dining Room." There were only two
three attendants in evidence.

"Excuse me, I wonder if you could tell me, is this
here the senators eat?"

"I'm sorry, I don't know. You'd have to talk to the
stess. We're just cleaning up."

"Where might I find the hostess?"

"She's not here. Gone for the day. If you come back
norrow, maybe she can help you."

"Okay." Marc sighed. "Thanks. But one more thing—is
re another Senate dining room?"

"Yeah, the big one in the Capitol. S-109, but you won't
able to get in."

Marc ran back to the elevator and waited impatiently.
en he reached the basement level, he jumped out and
ked past the entrance to the labyrinthine tunnels which
nect all the office buildings on Capitol Hill. Past the
r marked "Tobacco Shop," he raced toward the large
—"Subway Cars to Capitol." The subway car, actually
an open train with compartments, was about to leave.
c stepped into the last compartment and sat down

opposite a couple of Senate staffers who were jabbering away about some bill or other, with an air of "we belong." A few moments later, a bell signaled their arrival and the train came to a stop at the Senate side of the Capitol. Easy life, thought Marc. These guys never even have to wander out into the cold, cruel world. They just shuttle back and forth between votes and hearings. The basement on this side looked just like the basement on the other side, dull yellow, with exposed plumbing. And a Pepsi machine, it must have made Coca-Cola mad that Pepsi had the concession for the Senate. Marc bounded up the small escalator and waited for the public elevator, while a couple of men with a certain air of importance were ushered into the elevator marked "Senators Only."

Marc got off on the ground floor, and looked around perplexed. Nothing but marble arches and corridors. Where was the Senate Dining Room? He asked one of the Capitol policemen.

"Just walk straight ahead, take the first corridor on the left. It's narrow, the first one you get to." He pointed.

Marc tossed a thank-you over his shoulder and found the narrow corridor. He passed the kitchens and a sign which announced "Private—Press Only." Straight ahead, in large letters on a wooden sign, he saw another "Senators Only." An open door on the right led into the anteroom, decorated with a chandelier, a rose-colored, patterned carpet, and green leather furniture, all dominated by the colorful, crowded painting on the ceiling. Through another door, Marc could see white tablecloths, flowers, the world of gracious dining. A matronly woman appeared in the doorway.

"What can I do for you?" she asked, raising her brows inquisitively.

"I'm doing a thesis on the working life of a senator,"

ny Ph.D." Marc took out his wallet and showed his
Yale I.D. Card, covering the expiration date with his
thumb.

The lady was not visibly impressed.

"I really only want to look at the room. Just to get the
feel of the place."

"Well, there are no senators in here at the moment, sir.
There almost never are this late on a Wednesday. They go
back to their home states on Thursdays for a long weekend. The only thing that is keeping any of them here is
that Gun-Control Bill."

Marc had managed to edge himself into the center of
the room. A waitress was clearing a table. She smiled at
him.

"Do senators sign for their meals? Or do they pay cash?"

"Almost all of them sign, and they pay at the end of the
month."

"How do you keep track?"

"No problem. We keep a daily record." She pointed to a
large book marked *Accounts*. Marc knew that twenty-three
senators had lunched that day because their secretaries
had told him so. Had any other senator done so without
bothering to inform his secretary? He was a yard away
from finding out.

"Could I just see a typical day? Just out of interest," he
asked with an innocent smile.

"I'm not sure I'm allowed to let you look."

"Only a glance. When I write my thesis, I want people
to think that I really know what I'm talking about, that
I've seen for myself."

He looked at the woman pleadingly.

"Okay," she said grudgingly, "but please be quick."

"Oh, pick any old day, let's say February 24."

She opened the book and thumbed through to February

235

24. "A Thursday," she said. Stevenson, Muskie, Moyni-han, Heinz, names rang one after the other. Dole, Hat-field, Byrd. So Byrd lunched at the Senate that day. H read on. Thornton, Bayh—Bayh as well. More name: Church, Reynolds, McGovern. So his statement this morn-ing was for real. The hostess closed the book. No Dunca: no Dexter.

"Nothing very special, is it?" she said.

"No," said Marc. He thanked the woman and le quickly.

In the street he hailed a taxi. So did one of the thre men following him; the other two went off to get their car

Marc arrived at the Bureau a few moments later, pa the driver, showed his credentials at the entrance, a: took the elevator to the seventh floor. Mrs. McGreg smiled. The Director must be alone, thought Marc. I knocked and went in.

"Well, Marc?"

"Bayh, Byrd, and Thornton are not involved, sir."

"The first two don't surprise me," said the Direct "It never made any sense that they were, but I'd have a side bet on Thornton. Anyway, how did you dispose all three?"

Marc described his brainstorm about the Senate Din Room, and wondered what else he had overlooked.

"You should have worked all of that out three days shouldn't you, Marc?"

"Yes, sir."

"So should I," said the Director. "So we're dow Dexter and Duncan. It will interest you to know that men, along with most of the senators, intend to b Washington tomorrow and both are attending the c mony at the Capitol.

"Amazing," he mused, "even at that level, men lil

watch their crimes enacted. Let's go over it once again, Andrews. The President leaves the south entrance at ten A.M. unless I stop him, so we have seventeen hours left and one last hope. The boys in Fingerprints have found the bill with Mrs. Casefikis's prints on it. The twenty-second, we may be lucky—with still another half dozen to go we wouldn't have had a hope before ten o'clock tomorrow. There are several other prints on the bill, and they will be working on it all through the night. I expect to be at home by midnight. If you come up with anything, call me. I want you here at eight-fifteen tomorrow. There's very little you can do now. But don't worry too much; I have twenty agents working on it, though none of them knows all the details. And I'll only let the President near the danger zone if we have a fix on these villains."

"I'll report at eight-fifteen then, sir," said Marc.

"And, Marc, I strongly advise you not to see Dr. Dexter. I don't want to blow this whole operation at the last moment, because of your love life. No offense intended."

"No, sir."

Marc left, feeling slightly superfluous. Twenty agents now assigned to the case. How long had the Director had them working without telling him? Twenty men trying to find out whether it was Dexter or Duncan, without knowing why. Still, only he and the Director knew the whole story, and he feared the Director knew more than he did. Perhaps it would be wiser to avoid Elizabeth until the following evening, but he knew he couldn't do it. He considered the implications of calling her. He picked up his car, and drove back to the Dirksen Building and then remembered he had to pick up the hearings' transcripts he had left at the Committee Office. When he got there he found himself drawn toward the telephone booths. He had to call her, he had to find out how she was after her accident. He dialed Woodrow Wilson.

"Oh, she went home—some time ago."

"Thank you," Marc said. He could feel his heart beat as he dialed her Georgetown number.

"Elizabeth?"

"Yes, Marc." She sounded—cold? frightened? tired? A hundred questions were racing through his mind.

"Can I come and see you right now?"

"Yes." The telephone clicked.

Marc left the booth, conscious of the sweat on the palms of his hands. One more job to do before he could see Elizabeth, pick up those damned papers from the Senate Gun-Control Hearings, must tie up all the loose ends.

He walked toward the elevator and thought he could hear footsteps behind him. Of course, he could hear footsteps behind him: there were people behind him. When he reached the elevator, he pressed the Up-button and glanced around at the footsteps. Among the crowd of Senate staffers, congressmen, and sightseers, two men were watching him—or were they protecting him? There was a third man in dark glasses staring at a Medicare poster, even more obviously an agent, to Marc's quick eyes, than the other two.

The Director had said that he had put twenty agents on the case, and three of them appeared to be watching Marc. Hell. Soon they would be following him back to Elizabeth and Marc did not doubt that the Director would hear about it immediately. Marc resolved that no one was going to follow him back to Elizabeth's. It was none of their damned business. He'd shake the three of them off. He needed to see her in peace, without prying eyes and malicious tongues. He thought quickly as he waited

238

see which of the two elevators would arrive first. Two of the agents were now walking toward him, but the one by the Medicare poster remained motionless. Perhaps he wasn't an operative after all, but there certainly was something familiar about him. He had the aura of an agent; other agents can sense it with their eyes shut.

Marc concentrated on the elevator. The arrow on his right lit up and the doors opened slowly. Marc shot in and stood facing the buttons and stared out at the corridor. The two operatives followed him into the elevator, and stood behind him. The man by the Medicare poster started walking toward the elevator. The doors were beginning to close. Marc pressed the Open-button, and the doors parted again. Must give him a chance to get in, and have all three of them together, Marc thought, but the third man did not respond. He just stood, staring, as if waiting for the next elevator. Perhaps he wanted to go down and wasn't an agent at all. Marc could have sworn . . . The doors began to close and at what Marc thought was the optimum point, he jumped back out. Wrong. O'Malley managed to squeeze himself out as well, while his partner was left to travel slowly but inevitably up to the eighth floor. Now Marc was down to two tails. The other elevator arrived. The third agent stepped into it immediately. Very clever or innocent, Marc thought, and waited outside. O'Malley was at his shoulder—which one next?

Marc strolled into the elevator and pressed the Down-button, but O'Malley was able to get in easily. Marc pressed the Open-button and sauntered back out. O'Malley followed him, face impassive. The third man remained motionless in the elevator. They must be working together. Marc jumped back in and jabbed the Close-button hard. The doors closed horribly slowly, but O'Malley had walked two paces away and was not going to make it. As the doors slammed together, Marc smiled. Two gone, one standing on the ground floor helpless, the other heading for the roof, while he was descending to the basement alone with the third.

O'Malley caught up with Pierce Thompson on the fifth floor. Both were out of breath.

"Where is he?" cried O'Malley.

"What do you mean, where is he? I thought he was with you."

"No, I lost him on the first floor."

"Shit, he could be anywhere," said Thompson. "Whose side does the smart-ass think we are on? Which one of us is going to tell the Director?"

"Not me," O'Malley said. "You're the senior officer you tell him."

"No way I'm telling him," Thompson said. "And let that bastard Matson take all the credit—you can be sure he's still with him. No, we're going to find him. You take the first four floors and I'll take the top four. Bleep immediately when you spot him."

When Marc reached the basement, he stayed in the elevator. The third man walked out and seemed to hesitate. Marc's thumb was jammed on the Close-button again. The door responded. He was on his own. He tried to make the elevator bypass the ground floor but he couldn't someone else wanted to get in. He prayed it was not one of the three men. He had to risk it. The doors opened and he walked out immediately. No agents in sight, no one studying the Medicare poster. He ran toward the revolving doors at the end of the corridor. The guard on duty looked at him suspiciously and fingered the holster of his gun. Through the revolving doors and out into the open

240

unning hard. He glanced around. Everyone was walking, no one was running. He'd made it.

Pennsylvania Avenue—he dodged in and out of the raffic amid screeching tires and angry expletives. He eached the parking lot and jumped into his car, fumbling or some change. Why did they make pants that you ouldn't get your hands into when you sat down? He uickly paid for his ticket and drove toward Georgetown —and Elizabeth. He glanced in the rear-view mirror. No ord sedan in sight. He'd done it. He was on his own. He niled. For once he had beaten the Director. He drove ast the lights at the corner of Pennsylvania and 14th just they were changing. He began to relax.

A black Buick ran the lights. Lucky there were no affic cops around.

When Marc arrived in Georgetown, his nervousness re-rned, a new nervousness associated with Elizabeth and r world, not with the Director and his world. When he essed the bell on her front door, he could still hear his art beating.

Elizabeth appeared. She looked drawn and tired and ln't speak. He followed her into the living room.

"Have you recovered from your accident?"

"Yes, thank you. How did you know I'd had an ac-ent?" she asked.

Marc thought quickly. "Called the hospital. They told there."

"You're lying, Marc. I didn't tell them at the hospital, I left early after a phone call from my father."

Marc couldn't look her in the eyes. He sat down and ed at the rug. "I . . . I don't want to lie to you, abeth. Please don't."

"Why are you following my father?" she demanded.

"He thought you looked familiar when he met you at th Mayflower. You've been haunting his committee meeting and you've been watching the debates in the Senate."

Marc didn't answer.

"Okay, don't explain. I'm not completely blind. I draw my own conclusions. I'm part of an FBI assignmer My, you've been working late hours, haven't you, Age Andrews? For a man singled out to work a senato daughters' beat, you're pretty goddamn inept. Just h many daughters have you seduced this week? Did you g any good dirt? Why don't you try the wives next? Yo boyish charm might be more effective on them. Althou I must confess, you had me fooled, you lying bastard."

Despite a considerable effort to maintain the icy cont with which she had launched her attack, Elizabeth bit lip. Her voice caught. Marc still couldn't look at her. heard the anger and the tears in her voice. In a mome the chilling frost had covered her emotion again.

"Please get out, Marc. Now. I hope I never lay eyes you again. Perhaps then I can recover some of my s respect. Just go; crawl back into the slime."

"It's just not true, Elizabeth."

"I know, you poor maligned agent, you love me myself. There's no other girl in your life," she said bitte "At least not until you're transferred to a new case. W this case is finished. Go find somebody else's daughte seduce with your lies about love."

He couldn't blame her for her reaction. But he wa so desperately to make her understand. How coul expect her to trust him when he too had been torr suspicion, wondering about her, wondering if he c believe . . .

"Elizabeth, that's just not true." He was going to her.

"Oh, that's very persuasive, Mr. Andrews. It's just not true that you've been investigating my father. It's just not true that you've been seeing me during the same period. It's just not true that—"

"It's just not true. I love you," said Marc, "but I can't prove it."

"You've lied to me all along. You're going to harm my father and you expect me to believe you love me? Go find someone else." She collapsed into the chair. "Go, go for God's sake, go."

Marc wanted to touch her, to hold her and explain everything, but he knew he couldn't say anything. In twenty-four hours, he could tell her—tell her what?—would she even want to listen? He went to the door and left quietly. He was glad she couldn't see his face. He'd lost her.

He drove home in a daze. The occupants of the car following him were fully alert. When he arrived, Marc left the car keys with Simon and took the elevator to his apartment.

The black Buick was parked a hundred yards from the building. The two men could see the light in Marc's apartment. He dialed six of the seven digits of her number, but then he put the phone back on the hook and turned off the light. One of the men in the Buick lit another cigarette, inhaled, and checked his watch.

10

5:00 AM

The Director woke suddenly. He lay there, frustrate
there was nothing he could do at this hour except look
the ceiling and think, and that didn't help much. He we
over again and again in his mind the events of the p:
seven days, always leaving until last the thought of canc
ing the whole operation, which would probably mean ev
now that the Senator and his cohorts would get av
scot-free. Perhaps they already knew and had disappea
to lick their wounds and prepare for another day. Eit!
way it remained his problem.

The Senator woke at 5:35 in a cold sweat—not that
had really slept for more than a few minutes at any
time. It had been an evil night, thunder and lightn
and sirens. It was the sirens that had made him sweat.
was even more nervous than he had expected to be
fact at 3:00 A.M. he had nearly dialed the Chairma:
say that he couldn't go through with it, despite the (
sequences that the Chairman had so delicately, bu
frequently, adumbrated. But the vision of the Presi
dead beside him reminded the Senator that everyl
could remember exactly where he was when JFK

244

assassinated, and he himself was never going to be able to forget where he was when EMK died. Even that seemed less appalling than the thought of his own name in the headlines, his public image irreparably damaged, and his career ruined. Even so, he nearly called the Chairman, as much for reassurance as anything, despite their agreement that they had contacted each other for the last time until the following morning, when the Chairman would be in Miami.

Five men had already died but that had caused only a ripple: Kennedy's death would reverberate around the world. How many people remembered the two nameless men who were killed by the train carrying Robert Kennedy's body to Washington? Nobody; but everyone remembered Robert's death.

The Senator stared out of the window for some time, focusing on nothing, then turned away. He kept looking at his watch, wishing he could stop time. The second hand moved relentlessly—relentlessly toward 10:06. He busied himself with breakfast and the morning paper. The *Post* informed him that many buildings had caught fire during the night in one of the worst storms in Washington's history, and the Lubber Run in Virginia had overflowed its banks, causing heavy property damage. There was little mention of Kennedy. He wished he could read tomorrow's papers today.

The first call the Director received was from Elliott, who informed him that the recent activities of Senators Dexter and Duncan revealed nothing new about the situation—not that the anonymous man knew exactly what the situation was. The Director grumbled to himself, finished his egg—sunny-side up—and read the *Post*'s description of the demonic weather that had assailed

Washington during the night. He glanced out of the window at the day, now clear and dry. A perfect day for an assassination, he thought. The bright day that brings forth the adder. How late could it be left before letting everyone know everything? The President was to leave the White House at ten o'clock. The Director would have to brief the head of the Secret Service, H. Stuart Knight, and, if necessary, the President at least two hours before that. To hell with it, he would leave it to the last minute and make a full explanation afterward. He was willing to risk his career to catch this pernicious Senator red-handed. But risking the President's life . . .

He drove to the Bureau soon after 6:00. He wanted to be there a full two hours before Andrews to study all the reports he had ordered the evening before. Not many of his senior aides would have had much sleep last night though they were probably still wondering why. They would know soon enough. His deputy Associate Director for Investigation, his Assistant Director for Planning and Evaluation, and the head of the Criminal Section of that division would help him decide if he should go ahead or cancel. His Ford sedan slid down the ramp to the underground parking lot and his special parking place.

Elliott was there to meet him at the elevator—he was always there, never late. He's not human, he'll have to go, thought the Director, if I don't have to go first. He suddenly realized that he could be handing his resignation in to the President that night. Which President? He put out of his mind—that would take care of itself in its own time, he must take care of the next five hours.

Elliott had nothing useful to say. Dexter and Duncan had both received and made phone calls during the night and early morning, but nothing incriminating had been

246

picked up. No other information was forthcoming. The Director asked where the senators were at that moment.

"Both eating breakfast at their homes. Dexter in Kensington, Duncan in Alexandria. Six agents have been watching them since five o'clock this morning and have been detailed to them all day."

"Good. Report back to me immediately if anything happens."

"Of course, sir."

The fingerprint man was next. When he arrived, the Director first apologized for keeping him up all night, though the man's face and eyes looked more alight and alive than his own had been in the shaving mirror that morning.

Five feet four inches tall, slight and rather pale, Daniel Sommerton began his report. He was like a child with a toy. For him, working with prints had always been a passion as well as a job. The Director remained seated while Sommerton stood. If the Director had stood, he would not have been head and shoulders above him, but head, shoulders, and chest above him.

"We have found seventeen different fingers and three different thumbs, Director," he said gleefully. "We're putting them through the Ninhydrin rather than the iodine-fume process, since we were unable to do them one at a time for technical reasons that I won't bother you with."

He waved his arm to imply that he would not waste a scientific explanation on the Director, who would have been the first to acknowledge that it would have been one wasted.

"We think there are two more prints we might identify," Sommerton continued, "and we will have a read-out for you on all of them within two, at most three hours."

The Director glanced at his watch—already 6:45.

"Well done. That won't be a minute too soon. Get me the results—even if they are negative—as quickly as possible, and please thank all of your staff for working through the night."

The fingerprint expert left the Director, anxious to return to his seventeen fingers and three thumbs. The Director pressed a button and asked Mrs. McGregor to send in the Assistant Director for Planning and Evaluation.

Two minutes later, Walter Williams was standing in front of him.

Five feet eleven, fair with a thin pallid face, dominated by a magnificent high-domed forehead, lined with amusement not grief, Williams was known in the Bureau either as the Brain or W.W. His primary responsibility was to head the Bureau's think tank of six lesser but still impressive brains. The Director often confronted him with hypothetical questions to which he would later provide an answer that usually proved, in retrospect, to be the right one. The Director placed great faith in his judgment, but he could not take any risks today. W.W. had better come up with a convincing answer to his hypothetical question of last night or his next call would be to the President.

"Good morning, Director."

"Good morning, W.W. What is your decision concerning my little problem?"

"Most interesting, Director . . . I feel, to be fair, the answer is simple, even when we look at the situation from every angle."

For the first time that morning a trace of a smile appeared on the Director's face.

"Assuming I haven't misread you, Director."

The Director's smile broadened slightly; W.W. neither

missed nor misread anything, and was so formal that he didn't address the Director even in private as Halt. W.W. continued, his eyebrows moving up and down like the Dow-Jones in an election year.

"You asked me to assume that the President would be leaving the White House at X hundred hours and traveling to the Capitol. That would take him six minutes. I'm assuming his car is bullet-proof and well covered by the Secret Service. Under these conditions would it be possible to assassinate him? The answer is, it's possible but very difficult, Director. Nevertheless, following the hypothesis through to its logical conclusion, the assassination team would use three methods: (a) explosives; (b) a handgun at close range; (c) a rifle."

W.W. always sounded like a textbook. "The bomb can be thrown at any point on the route, but it is never used by professionals, because professionals are paid for results, not attempts. If you study bombs as a method of removing a President, you will find there hasn't been a successful one yet, despite the fact that we have had four Presidents assassinated in office. Bombs inevitably end up killing innocent people and quite often the perpetrator of the crime as well. For that reason, since you have implied that the people involved would be professionals, I feel they must rely on the handgun or the rifle. Now the short-range gun, Director, is not a possible weapon on the route itself because it is unlikely that a pro would approach the President and shoot him at close range, thereby risking his own life. It would take an elephant gun or an antitank gun to pierce the President's limousine, and you can't carry those around in the middle of Washington without a permit."

With W.W., the Director could never be sure if it was meant to be a joke or just another fact. The eyebrows were still moving up and down, a sure signal not to inter‍rupt him with foolish questions.

"When the President arrives at the steps of the Capito‍ the crowd is too far away from him for a handgun to (a‍ be accurate and (b) give the assassin any hope of escap‍ So we must assume that it's the best-tested and mo‍ successful method of assassination of a head of state—th‍ rifle with telescopic sights for long range. Therefore, th‍ only hope the assassin would have must be at the Capit‍ itself. The assassin can't see into the White House, and‍ any case the glass in the windows is four inches thick, ‍ he must wait until the President actually leaves the limo‍ sine at the steps of the Capitol. This morning we timed‍ walk up the Capitol steps and it takes around fifty secon‍ There are very few vantage points from which to ma‍ an assassination attempt, but we have studied the a‍ carefully and you will find them all listed in my repo‍ Also the conspirators must be convinced that we kn‍ nothing about the plot, because they know we can co‍ every possible shooting site. We think an assassinat‍ here in the heart of Washington unlikely, but neverthe‍ possible by a man or team daring and skillful enough."

"Thank you, W.W. I'm sure you're right."

"A pleasure, sir. I do hope it's only hypothetical."

"Yes, W.W."

W.W. smiled like the only schoolboy in the class ‍ can answer the teacher's questions. The Brain left ‍ room to return to other problems. The Director pa‍ and called for his other Assistant Director.

Matthew Rogers knocked and entered the room, ‍ ing to be asked to take a seat. He understood autho‍ Like W.W., he would never become the Director, bu‍ one who did would want to be without him.

250

"Well, Matt?" said the Director, pointing to the leather chair.

"I read Andrews' latest report last night, Director, and really think the time has come for us to brief the Secret Service."

"I will be doing so in about an hour," said the Director. "Don't worry. Have you decided how you'll deploy your men?"

"It depends where the maximum risk is, sir."

"All right, Matt, let's assume that the point of maximum risk is the Capitol, at six minutes past ten, on the steps—what then?"

"First, I would surround the area for about a quarter of a mile in every direction. I'd close down the Metro, stop all traffic, public and private, pull aside for interrogation anyone who has a past record of making threats, anyone who's on the Security Index. I'd get assistance from the PD to provide perimeter security. We'd want as many eyes and ears in the area as possible. We could get three to four helicopters from Andrews Air Force Base for close scanning. In the immediate vicinity of the President, use the full Secret Service Presidential detail in tight security."

"Very good, Matt. How many men do you need for such an operation, and how long would it take them to be ready if I declared an emergency procedure now?"

The Assistant Director looked at his watch—just after nine. He considered the matter for a moment. "I need three hundred special agents briefed and fully operational in two hours."

"Right, go ahead," said the Director crisply. "Report to us soon as they're ready but leave the final briefing to the last possible moment, and, Matt, I want no helicopters until one minute past ten. I don't want there to be

251

a chance of a leak of any sort; it's our one hope of catc
ing the assassin."

"Why don't you simply cancel the President's trip, si
We're in deep water, and it's not entirely your responsib
ity."

"If we pull out now, we have to start all over ag
tomorrow," said the Director, "and I may never
another chance like this."

"Yes, sir."

"Don't let me down, because I am going to leave
ground operations entirely in your hands."

"Thank you, sir."

Rogers left the room. The Director knew his job wo
be done as competently as it could be by any professio
law-enforcement officer in America.

"Mrs. McGregor."

"Yes, sir?"

"Get me the head of the Secret Service at the W
House."

"Yes, sir."

The Director glanced at his watch: 7:10. Andrews
due at 8:15. The phone rang.

"Mr. Knight on the line, sir."

"Stuart, can you call me on my private line and be
you're not overheard?"

H. Stuart Knight knew Halt well enough to realize
he meant what he said. He called back immediatel
his special scrambler.

"Stuart, I'd like to see you immediately, usual p
take about thirty minutes, no more. Top priority."

Damned inconvenient, thought Knight, but Halt
made this request two or three times a year, and he
that other matters must be put to one side for the mo

nly the President and the Attorney General took priority
er Halt.

The Director of the FBI and the head of the Secret
rvice met at a line of cabs in front of Union Station ten
nutes later. They didn't take the first cab in the line, but
e seventh. They climbed in the back without speaking
acknowledging each other. Elliott drove the Max's
llow Cab off to circle the Capitol. The Director talked
d the head of the Secret Service listened.

Marc's alarm woke him at 7:15. He showered and
ved and thought about those transcripts he had left in
Senate, trying to convince himself that they would
e thrown no light on whether it was Dexter or Duncan.
silently thanked Senator Stevenson for indirectly dis-
ing of Senators Byrd, Bayh, and Thornton. He would
nk anybody who could dispose of Senator Dexter. He
beginning to agree with the Director's reasoning—it all
ted to Dexter. His motive was particularly compelling,
. . . Marc looked at his watch; he was a little early.
sat on the edge of his bed; he scratched his leg which
itching; something must have bitten him during the
t. He continued trying to figure out if there was any-
g he had missed.

he Chairman got out of bed at 7:20 and lit his first
rette. He couldn't remember exactly when he had
en. At 6:10 he had phoned Tony, who was already
nd waiting for his call. They weren't to meet that
unless the Chairman needed the car in an emergency.
next time they would speak to each other would be on
lot of 9:30 for a check-in to confirm they were all in
ion.

When he had completed the call, the Chairman dialed room service and ordered a large breakfast. What he was about to do that morning was not the sort of work to be tackling on an empty stomach. Matson was due to ring him anytime after 7:30. Perhaps he was still sleeping. After that effort last night, Matson deserved some rest. The Chairman smiled to himself. He went into the bathroom and turned on the shower; a feeble trickle of cold water emerged. Goddamn hotels. Sixty dollars a night and no hot water. He splashed around ineffectively and began to think about the next five hours, going over the plan again carefully to be sure he had not overlooked even the smallest detail. Tonight, Kennedy would be dead and he would have $500,000 in the Union Bank of Switzerland, Zurich, account number AZL-376921-B, a small reward from his grateful friends in the gun trade. And to top it, Uncle Sam wouldn't even get the tax.

The phone rang. Damn. He dripped across the floor; his heartbeat quickened. It was Matson.

Matson and the Chairman had driven back from Matson's apartment at 2:35 that morning, their task completed. Matson overslept by half an hour. The damned hotel had forgotten his wake-up call; you couldn't trust anyone nowadays. As soon as he had woken, he phoned the Chairman and reported in.

Xan was safely in the top of the crane and ready, probably the only one of them who was still asleep.

The Chairman, although dripping, was pleased. He put the phone down and returned to the shower. Damn, still cold.

Matson masturbated. He always did when he was nervous and had time to kill.

Edward Kennedy did not wake until 7:35. He rose

ver, trying to recall the dream he had just had, but none
 it would come back to him, so he let his mind wander.
oday, he would be going to the Capitol to plead his case
r the Gun-Control Bill before a special session of the
nate and then to have lunch with all the key supporters
d opponents of the bill. Since the bill had been ap-
oved in committee, as he had been confident it would be,
 had concentrated on his strategy for the final day of
or battle; at least the odds were now with him. He
iled at Joan, although she had her back to him. It had
en a busy session, and he was looking forward to going
 Camp David and having more time with his family.
tter get moving, more than half of America is already
 he thought, and I am still lying in bed. . . . Still,
t waking half of America had not had to dine the
vious evening with the four-hundred-pound King of
nga, who wasn't going to leave the White House until
 was virtually thrown out; the President wasn't ab-
tely certain he could pinpoint Tonga on the map. He
 sure it was in the Pacific, but that was still a large
an. He had left his Secretary of State, Abe Chayes, to
he talking; he at least knew exactly where Tonga was,
 Kennedy had eventually crawled into bed at about
 A.M.
e stopped thinking about it and put his feet on the
—or to be more exact, on the Presidential Seal. The
ned thing was on everything except the toilet paper.
knew that when he appeared for breakfast in the
g room across the hall, he would find the third
n of *The New York Times,* the third edition of *The
ington Post,* the first editions of the *Los Angeles
s* and the *Boston Globe,* all ready for him to read,
 the pieces mentioning his name marked in red, plus
pared digest of yesterday's news. How did they get it

all completed before he was even dressed? he wondere
He went to his bathroom and turned on the shower; t
water pressure was just right. He began to consider wl
he could say finally to convince the waverers in
Senate that the Gun-Control Bill must become law.
train of thought was interrupted by his efforts to rea
the middle of his back with the soap. Presidents still ha
to do that for themselves, he thought.

Marc was due to be with the Director in twe
minutes. He checked his mail—just an envelope fr
American Express, which he left on the kitchen ta
unopened.

A yawning O'Malley was sitting in the Ford seda
hundred yards away. He was relieved to be able to re|
that Marc had left the apartment building and was tall
to the black garage attendant. Neither O'Malley
Thompson had told anybody that they had lost Marc
several hours the previous evening.

Marc walked around the side of the building and
appeared from the view of the man in the blue For
didn't worry him. O'Malley had checked the locatio
the Mercedes an hour earlier; there was only one way

Marc noticed a red Fiat as he came around the corn
the building. Looks like Elizabeth's, he thought to
self, except for the damage to a bumper. He looked
carefully and in fact it was Elizabeth's, with Elizabe
it, and she was sitting there staring at him. He opene
door. If he was Ragani and she was Mata Hari, he was
caring. He climbed in beside her. Neither of them s
until they both spoke at once and laughed nervously
tried again. Marc sat in silence.

"I've come to say I'm sorry about being so touch
night. I should have given you a chance. I really

vant you to sleep with any other senator's daughter," she
aid, trying to force a smile.

"I'm the one who should be sorry, Liz. Trust me.
Vhatever happens, let's meet this evening and then I'll
ry to explain everything. Don't ask me anything until
hen and promise that whatever happens you will see me
onight. If after that you still want me out of your life, I
romise I'll leave quietly."

Elizabeth nodded her agreement. "But not as abruptly
s you left once before, I hope."

Marc put his arm around her and kissed her quickly.
No more nasty cracks about that night. I'm looking for-
ard to a second chance."

They both laughed. He started to get out.

"Why don't I drive you to work, Marc? It's on my way
the hospital and we won't have to bother with two cars
is evening."

Marc hesitated. "Why not? Nice idea."

He wondered if this was the final setup.

As she drove around the corner, Simon waved them
wn. "Apartment Seven's car will be back late this morn-
, Marc. I'll have to park it on the street but don't
rry, I'll keep an eye on it."

Marc handed him the keys. Simon looked at Elizabeth
l grinned. "You won't be needing my sister after all,
n."

Elizabeth pulled out and joined the traffic on 6th Street.
undred yards away, O'Malley was chewing gum.

'Where shall we have dinner tonight?"

'Let's go back to that French restaurant and try the
le evening again. This time we'll do the final act of the
."

hope it begins. "This was the noblest Roman of them
All the conspirators, save only he . . ." Marc thought.

"This time I'll treat," said Elizabeth.

Marc accepted, remembering his unopened bill from American Express. The lights turned red at the corner of G Street. They stopped and waited. Marc started scratching his leg again, it really felt quite painful.

The cab was still circling the Capitol and Halt was coming to the end of his briefing for H. Stuart Knight.

"We believe that the attempt will be made when the President gets out of his car at the Capitol. We'll take care of matters at the Capitol itself if you manage to get him into the building safely. I'll have my men cover the buildings and roofs of buildings and elevated vantage points from which it would be possible to shoot."

"It would make our job a lot easier if the President didn't insist on walking up the steps. Ever since Carter took his little stroll up Pennsylvania Avenue in seventy seven . . ." His voice trailed off in exasperation. "By the way, Halt, why didn't you tell me about this earlier?"

"There's a strange quirk to it, Stuart. I still can't give you all the details, but don't worry, they're not relevant the task of protecting the President."

"Okay. I accept that. Are you sure my men can't help at your end?"

"No, I'm happy as long as I know you're keeping close watch on the President. It will give me more freedom to catch the bastards red-handed. They mustn't get suspicious. I want to catch the killer in place, with weapon."

"Shall I tell the President?" asked Knight.

"No, just inform him it's a new security measure are going to put into practice from time to time."

"He's had so many of those he's bound to believe said Knight.

"Stick to the same route and timetable and I'll leave the finer points to you, Stuart. I don't want any leaks. I'll see you after the President's lunch. We can bring each other up-to-date then. By the way, what's today's code name for the President?"

"Julius."

"Good God, I don't believe it."

"You are telling me everything I need to know, aren't you, Halt?"

"No, of course, I'm not, Stuart. You know me, Machiavelli's younger brother."

The Director tapped Elliott on the shoulder and the cab nipped back into the seventh place in line. The two passengers got out and walked in opposite directions, Knight to catch the Metro to the White House, the Director a cab to the Bureau. Neither looked back.

Lucky Stuart Knight, thought the Director, he's gone through the last seven days without the information I have. Now the meeting was over, the Director's confidence in his own stratagem was renewed, and he was resolved that only he and Andrews would ever know the whole story—unless they had conclusive proof on which to secure the Senator's conviction. He had to catch the conspirators alive, get them to testify against the Senator. The Director checked his watch with the clock on the Old Post Office Tower over the Washington Field Office. It was 8:00. Andrews would be due in fifteen minutes. He was saluted as he went through the revolving doors of the Bureau. Mrs. McGregor was standing outside his office, looking agitated.

"It's Channel Four, sir, asking for you urgently."

"Put them through," said the Director. He moved quickly into his office and picked up the extension.

"It's Special Agent O'Malley from the patrol car, sir."

"Yes, O'Malley?"

"Andrews has been killed, sir, and there must have been another person in the car."

The Director couldn't speak.

"Are you there, Director?" O'Malley waited. "I repeat, are you there, Director?"

Finally the Director said, "Come in immediately." He put the phone down, and his great hands gripped the Queen Anne desk. The fingers curled and clenched slowly into the palms of his hands until they made massive fists, the nails digging into the skin. Blood trickled slowly down onto the leather work on the desk, leaving a dark stain. Thus he sat alone for some minutes. Then he told Mrs McGregor to get the President at the White House. He was going to cancel the whole damned thing; he'd gone too far. He sat silently waiting. The bastards had beaten him. They must know everything.

It took Special Agent O'Malley ten minutes to reach the Bureau, where he was ushered straight in to the Director.

My God, he looks eighty, thought O'Malley.

The Director stared at him. "How did it happen?" he asked quietly.

"He was blown up in a car; we think someone else was with him."

"Why? How?"

"Must have been a bomb attached to the ignition. It blew up right there in front of me. Made an unholy mess."

"I don't give a fuck for the mess," began the Director on a slowly rising note, when the door opened.

Marc Andrews walked in. "Good morning, sir. I hope I'm not interrupting you. I thought you said eight-fifteen."

Both men stared at him.

"You're dead."

"Excuse me, sir?"

"Well, who the hell," said Special Agent O'Malley, "was driving your Mercedes?"

Marc stared at him uncomprehending.

"My Mercedes?" he said quickly. "What are you talking about?"

"Your Mercedes has just been blown to smithereens. I saw it with my own eyes. My colleague down there is trying to put the pieces together; he's already reported finding the hand of a black man."

Marc steadied himself against the wall. "The bastards have killed Simon," he cried in anger. "There will be no need to call Grant Nanna to screw their balls off. I'll do it myself."

"Please explain yourself," said the Director.

Marc steadied himself again, turned around and faced them both. "I came in with Elizabeth Dexter this morning; she came by to see me. I came in with her," he repeated, not yet coherent.

"Simon moved my car because it was occupying a reserved daytime parking space. The bastards have killed him."

"Sit down, Andrews. You too, O'Malley."

The telephone rang. "The President's Chief of Staff, The President will be with you in about two minutes."

"Cancel it and apologize, and tell Mr. Martin it was nothing important, just wanted to wish the President luck the Gun-Control Bill today."

"Yes, sir."

"So they think you're dead, Andrews, and they have played their last card. So we must play ours. You're going to remain dead—for a little while longer."

Marc and O'Malley looked at each other, both puzzled.

"O'Malley, you return to your car. You say nothing

even to your partner. You have not seen Andrews alive
do you understand?"

"Yes, sir."

"Get going."

"Mrs. McGregor, get me the head of External Affairs

"Yes, sir."

The Director looked at Marc. "I was beginning to mi
you."

"Thank you, sir."

"Don't thank me, I'm just about to kill you again."

A knock on the door, and Bill Gunn came in. He w
the epitome of the public-relations man, better dress
than anyone else in the building, with the biggest sm
and a mop of fair hair that he washed every two da:
His face as he entered was unusually grim.

"Have you heard about the death of one of our you
agents, sir?"

"Yes, Bill. Put out a statement immediately that
unnamed special agent was killed this morning and t
you will brief the press fully at eleven o'clock."

"They'll be hounding me long before then, sir."

"Let them hound you," said the Director sharply.

"Yes, sir."

"At eleven, you will put out another statement say
the agent is alive . . ."

Bill Gunn's face registered surprise.

". . . and that a mistake has been made, and the r
who died was a young garage attendant who had
connection with the FBI."

"But, sir, our agent?"

"No doubt you would like to meet the agent wh
supposed to be dead. Bill Gunn—this is Special A_
Andrews. Now not a word, Bill. This man is dead for

262

ext three hours and if I find a leak, you can find a new
ob."

Bill Gunn looked convincingly anxious. "Yes, sir."

"When you've written the press statement, call me and
ead it to me."

"Yes, sir."

Bill Gunn left, dazed. He was a gentle easygoing man
nd this was way above his head, but he trusted the
irector.

The Director was becoming very aware just how many
en did trust him and how much he was carrying on his
wn shoulders. He looked at Marc, who had not recovered
om the realization that Simon had died instead of him
the second man to do so in eight days.

"Right, Marc, we have under two hours left, so we will
ourn the dead later. Have you anything to add to
sterday's report?"

"Yes, sir. It's good to be alive."

"If you get past eleven o'clock, young man, I think you
ve a good chance for a long and healthy life, but we still
n't know if it's Dexter or Duncan. You know I think
 Dexter." The Director looked at his watch again:
0—ninety-six minutes left. "Any new ideas?"

"Well, sir, Elizabeth certainly can't be involved, she
ed my life by coming by this morning. If she wanted
 dead, that was a funny way of going about it."

 I'll accept that," said the Director, "but it doesn't clear
 father."

 Surely he wouldn't kill a man he thought might marry
 daughter," said Marc.

 You're sentimental, Andrews. A man who plans to
 ssinate a president doesn't worry about his daughter's
 friends."

The phone rang. It was Bill Gunn from Public Relations.

"Right, read it over." The Director listened carefully
"Good. Issue it immediately to radio, television, and th
papers, and release the second statement at eleven o'cloc
no earlier. Thank you, Bill." The Director put the phor
down.

"Congratulations, Marc, you're the only dead man ali
and, like Mark Twain, you will be able to read your ov
obituary. Now, to bring you quickly up-to-date. I ha
three hundred field agents out covering the Capitol a
the area immediately surrounding it. The whole place w
be sealed off the moment the presidential car arrives."

"You're letting him go to the Capitol?" Marc w
astounded.

"Listen carefully, Marc. I'll have a minute-by-min
briefing on where the two senators are from ni
o'clock on and six men are following both of them.
nine-fifteen, we're going into the street ourselves. Whe
happens, we're going to be there. If I'm going to carry
responsibility, I may as well carry it in person."

"Yes, sir."

The intercom buzzed.

"It's Mr. Sommerton. He wants to see you urgen
sir." The Director looked at his watch: 8:45. On
minute, as promised.

Daniel Sommerton rushed in, looking rather plea
with himself. He came straight to the point. "One of
prints has come up on the criminal file, it's a thumb,
name is Matson—Ralph Matson."

Sommerton produced a photograph of Matson, an I
tikit picture, and an enlarged thumbprint.

"And here's the part you're not going to like, sir.
an ex-FBI agent." He passed Matson's card over fo

Director to study. Marc looked at the photo. It was the Greek Orthodox priest, big nose, heavy chin.

"Something professional about him," said the Director and Marc simultaneously.

"Well done, Sommerton, make three hundred copies of the picture immediately and get them to the Assistant Director in charge of the Investigation Division—and that means immediately."

"Yes, sir." The fingerprint expert scurried away, pleased with himself. They wanted his thumb.

"Mrs. McGregor, get me Mr. Rogers."

The Assistant Director was on the line; the Director briefed him.

"Shall I arrest him on sight?"

"No, Matt. Once you've spotted him, watch him and keep your boys well out of sight. He can still call everything off if he get suspicious. Keep me briefed all the time. Move in on him at six minutes past ten. I'll let you know anything changes."

"Yes, sir. Have you briefed the Secret Service?"

"Yes, I have." He slammed the phone down.

The Director looked at his watch: 9:05. He pressed a button and Elliott came in. "Where are the two senators?"

"Duncan's still in his Alexandria town house, Dexter as left Kensington and is heading toward the Capitol, ."

"You stay here in this office, Elliott, and keep in radio ntact with me and the Assistant Director on the street. ever leave this room. Understood?"

"Yes, sir."

"I'll be using my walkie-talkie on Channel Four. Let's , Andrews." They left the anonymous man.

"If anybody calls me, Mrs. McGregor, put them through

to Special Agent Elliott in my office. He will know where to contact me."

"Yes, sir."

A few moments later, the Director and Marc were on the street walking up Pennsylvania Avenue toward the Capitol. Marc put on his dark glasses and pulled his collar up. They passed several agents on the way. None of them acknowledged the Director. On the corner of Pennsylvania Avenue and 9th Street, they passed the Chairman, who was lighting a cigarette and checking his watch: 9:30. He moved to the edge of the sidewalk, leaving a pile of cigarette butts behind him. The Director glanced at the cigarette butts: litter bug, ought to be fined a hundred dollars. They hurried on.

"Come in, Tony. Come in, Tony."

"Tony, boss. The Buick's ready. I've just heard it announced on the car radio that pretty boy Andrew bought it."

The Chairman smiled.

"Come in, Xan."

"Ready, await your signal."

"Come in, Matson."

"Everything's set, boss. There's a hell of a lot of agents around."

"Don't sweat, there's always a lot of Secret Service men around when the President is traveling. Don't call again unless there's a real problem. All three keep your lines open. When I next call, I will only activate the vibrator on the side of your watches. Then you have three minutes forty-five seconds, because Kennedy will be passing me. Understood?"

"Yes."

"Yes."

"Yes."

The Chairman broke the circuit and lit another cigarette: 9:40.

The Director spotted Matthew Rogers in a special squad car and went quickly over to him. "Everything under control, Matt?"

"Yes, sir. If anybody tries anything, no one will be able to move for half a mile."

"Good; what time do you have?"

"Nine-forty-five."

"Right, you control it from here. I'm going to the Capitol."

Halt and Marc left the Assistant Director and walked on.

"Elliott calling the Director."

"Come in, Elliott."

"They have spotted Matson at the junction of Maryland Avenue and First Street, near the Garfield statue, southwest corner of the Capitol grounds, near the west front renovation site."

"Good. Observe and post fifty men around the area, don't move in yet, brief Mr. Rogers and tell him to keep his men out of Matson's field of vision."

"Yes, sir."

"What the hell is he doing on that side of the Capitol?" said Marc softly. "You couldn't shoot anyone on the Capitol steps from the northwest side unless you were in a chopper."

"I agree, it's strange," said the Director.

They reached the police cordon surrounding the Capitol. The Director showed his credentials to get himself and Andrews through. The young Capitol policeman double-checked them; he couldn't believe it; he was looking at the real live object. Yes, it was the Director of the FBI. H. A. L. Tyson himself.

"Sorry, sir. Please come through."

"Elliott to the Director."

"Yes, Elliott?"

"Head of the Secret Service for you, sir."

"Stuart."

"The advance car is leaving the front gate now. Julius will leave in five minutes."

"Thank you, Stuart. Keep your end up and surprise me."

"Don't worry, Halt. We will."

Five minutes later, the presidential car left the South Entrance and turned left onto E Street. The advance car passed the Chairman on the corner of Pennsylvania Avenue and 9th. He smiled, lit another cigarette and waited. Five minutes later, a large Lincoln, flags flying on both front fenders, the Presidential Seal on the door passed by the Chairman. Through the misty gray windows, he could see three figures in the back. limousine known as the "gun car" and occupied by Secret Service agents and the President's personal physician followed the President's car. The Chairman pressed a button on his watch. The vibrator began to tickle his wrist. After ten seconds, he stopped it, walked one block north and hailed a taxi.

"National Airport," he said to the cab driver, fingering the ticket in his inside pocket.

The vibrator on Matson's watch was touching his skin. After ten seconds, it stopped. Matson walked to the side of the construction site, bent down and tied his shoelace.

Xan started to remove the tape. He was glad to

moving; he had been bent double all night. He screwed
the barrel into the sight finder.

"Assistant Director to Director. Matson is approaching
the construction site. Now he has stopped to tie his shoe.
No one on the construction site but I'm asking a helicopter to check it out. There's a huge crane here which
looks deserted."

"Good. Hold it until the last minute. I'll give you the
warning the moment the President's car arrives. You must
catch them red-handed. Alert the agents on the roof of
the Capitol."

The Director turned to Marc, more relaxed. "I think
is going to be all right."

Marc's eyes were on the steps of the Capitol. "Have
you noticed, sir, both Senator Dexter and Senator Duncan
are in the welcoming party for the President?"

"Yes," said the Director. "The car is due in two minutes; we'll catch the others even if we can't figure out
which Senator it is. We'll make them talk in due course.
Wait a minute—that's odd."

The Director extracted a couple of closely typed sheets
from his pocket and scanned them quickly.

"Yes, that's what I thought. The President's detailed
schedule shows that Dexter will be there for the special
address but isn't attending the luncheon with the President. Very strange: I'm sure all the key leaders of the
opposition were invited to lunch. Why won't Dexter be
there?"

"Nothing strange in that, sir. He always has lunch with
his daughter on Thursdays. Good God! 'I always have
lunch with my father on Thursdays.' "

"Yes, Marc, I heard you the first time."

"No, sir, 'I always have lunch with my father on Thursdays.' "

"Marc, the car will be here in one minute."

"It's Duncan, sir. It's Duncan. I'm a fool—Thursday February twenty-fourth, in Georgetown. I always though of it as February twenty-fourth, not as Thursday. Dexte was having lunch with Elizabeth. 'I always have lunc with my father on Thursday.' That's why he was seen Georgetown that day, must be. They never miss it."

"Are you sure? Can you be certain? There's a hell of lot riding on it."

"It's Duncan, sir. It can't be Dexter. I should ha seen it on the first day. Christ, I'm stupid."

"Right, Marc. Up there quickly, watch his every mo and be prepared to arrest him whatever the consequence

"Yes, sir."

"Rogers."

The Assistant Director came in. "Sir?"

"The car is pulling up. Arrest Matson immediate check the roof of the Capitol." The Director stared into the sky. "Oh my God, it's not a helicopter, it's t damn crane. It has to be the crane!"

Xan nestled the butt of the yellow rifle into his shoul and watched the President's car. He had attached a fea to a piece of thread on the end of the gun barrel, a t he had picked up from the Americans in Vietnam— wind. The hours of waiting were coming to an end. S ator Duncan was standing there on the Capitol st Through the thirty-power Redfield scope he could see beads of sweat standing out on the man's forehead.

The President's car drew up on the north side of Capitol. All was going according to plan. Xan lev the telescopic sight on the car door and waited for nedy. Two Secret Service men climbed out, scanned crowd, and waited for the third. Nothing happened.

270

ut the sight on the Senator, who looked anxious and
emused. Back on the car, still no Kennedy. Where the
ell was he, what was going on? He checked the feather;
ill no wind. He moved his sight back on the President's
ar. Good God, the crane was moving and Kennedy wasn't
. the car. Matson had been right all along, they knew
verything. Xan went to Emergency Plan; only one man
uld ditch them and he was certain to do it. He moved
s sight up the Capitol steps. One and one-half inches
bove the forehead. He squeezed the trigger once . . .
rice, but the second time he didn't have a clear shot, and
 fraction of a second later he could no longer see the
apitol steps. He looked down from the moving crane.
e was surrounded by fifty men in dark suits, fifty guns
inting up at him.

Marc was about a yard away from Senator Duncan
en he heard him cry out and fall. Marc jumped on top
 him and the second bullet grazed his shoulder. There
s a panic among the senators and officials on the top
ps. The welcoming party scurried inside. Thirty FBI
n moved in quickly. The Director was the only man
 the Capitol steps, steady and motionless, staring at
 crane. They hadn't nicknamed him Halt by mistake.

"May I ask where I'm going, Stuart?"

"Yes, Mr. President. To the Capitol."

"But this isn't the normal route to the Capitol."

"No, sir. We're going down Constitution Avenue to the
sell Building. We hear there has been a little trouble
he Capitol. A demonstration of some kind. The Na-
al Rifle Association."

"So I'm avoiding it, am I? Like a coward, Stuart."

"No, sir, I'm slipping you through the basement. Just
 safety measure and for your own convenience."

"That means I'll have to go on that damned subway. Even when I was a senator, I preferred to walk outside."

"We've cleared a way for you, sir. You'll still be there on time."

The President grumbled and looked out of the window as an ambulance raced in the opposite direction.

Senator Duncan died before he reached the hospital and Marc had his wound patched up. Marc looked at his watch and laughed. It was 11:04—he was going to live.

"Phone for you, Mr. Andrews."

"Marc?"

"Sir."

"I hear you're fine. Good. I am sorry to say the Senate went into recess out of respect for Senator Duncan. The President is shocked but feels this is precisely the moment to discuss gun control, so we're all now going into lunch early. Sorry you can't join us. And we caught three of them—Matson, a Vietnamese sharpshooter, and a petty crook called Tony Loraido. There may be more, I'll let you know later. Thank you, Marc."

The telephone clicked before Marc could reply.

7:00 PM

Marc arrived in Georgetown at seven that evening. He had gone to Simon's wake and paid his respects to the bewildered parents that afternoon. They had five other children, but that never helped. Their grief made Marc long for the warmth of the living.

Elizabeth was wearing the red silk shirt and the

skirt in which he had first seen her. She greeted him with a cascade of words.

"I don't understand what's been going on. My father called earlier and told me you tried to save Senator Duncan's life. What were you doing there anyway? My father is very upset about the shooting. Why have you been following him around? Was he in any danger?"

Marc looked at her squarely. "No, he wasn't involved in any way so let's try and start again."

She still didn't understand.

When they arrived at the Rive Gauche, the maître d' welcomed them with open arms.

"Good evening, Mr. Andrews, how nice to see you again. I don't remember your booking a table."

"No, it's in my name. Dr. Dexter," said Elizabeth.

"Oh, yes, Doctor, of course. Will you come this way?"

They had baked clams, and, at last, a steak with no fancy trimmings and two bottles of wine.

Marc sang most of the way home. When they arrived, he took her firmly by the hand and led her into the darkened living room.

"I'm going to seduce you. No coffee, no brandy, no music, just straightforward seduction."

They fell on the couch.

"You're too drunk."

"Wait and see." He kissed her fully on the lips for a long time and started to unbutton her shirt.

"Are you sure you wouldn't like some coffee?" she said teasingly.

"Yes, quite sure." He pulled the shirt slowly free from her skirt and felt her back, his other hand moving onto her leg.

"What about some music?" she said lightly. "Something special." Elizabeth touched the start button on the hi-fi. It was Sinatra again, but this time it was the right song:

> Is it an earthquake or simply a shock
> Is it the real turtle soup or merely the mock,
> Is it a cocktail, this feeling of joy,
> Or is what I feel—the real—McCoy?

> Is it for all time or simply a lark,
> Is it Granada I see or only Asbury Park,
> Is it a fancy not worth thinking of,
> Or is it at . . . long . . . last . . . love?

She settled back into Marc's arms.

He unzipped her skirt. Her legs were slender and beautiful in the dim light. He caressed her gently.

"Are you going to tell me the truth about today, Marc?"

"Afterward, darling."

"When you've had your way with me," she said.

He slipped his shirt off. Elizabeth stared at the bandage on his shoulder.

"Is that where you were wounded in the line of duty?"

"No, that's where my last lover bit me."

"I hope she had more time than I did."

They moved closer together.

He took the phone off the hook—not tonight, Julius.

"I can't get anything, sir," Elliott said, "just a busy signal."

"Try again, try again. I'm sure he's there."

"Shall I go through the operator?"

"Yes, yes," said the Director impatiently.

The Director waited, tapping his fingers on the Queen Anne desk, staring at the red stain and wondering how it had got there.

"The operator says the phone is off the hook, sir. Shall I ask her to beep; that'll certainly get his attention."

"No, Elliott, just leave it and go home. I'll call him in the morning."

"Yes, sir. Good night, sir."

He'll have to go—back to Ohio or somewhere, thought the Director, as he switched off the lights and went home.

11

7:00 AM

Marc woke first; perhaps it was being in a strange be‹
He turned over and looked at Elizabeth. She never wo:
make-up and was just as beautiful in the morning as
any other time. Her dark hair curled in toward the na;
of her neck and he stroked the soft strands gently. S!
stirred, rolled over, and kissed him.

"Go and brush your teeth."

"What a romantic way to start the day," he said.

"I'll be awake by the time you get back." She groan
a little and stretched.

Marc picked up the Pepsodent—that was one thi
that would have to change, he preferred Macleans—a
tried to figure out which part of the bathroom he ‹
going to be able to fit his things into. When he return‹
he noticed the phone was still off the hook. He looked
his watch: 7:05. He climbed back into bed. Elizab
slipped out.

"Only be a minute," she said.

It was never like this in the movies, thought Marc.

She returned and lay down beside him. After a mom
she said, "Your chin is hurting my face. You're no!
clean-shaven as you were the first time."

276

"I shaved very carefully that first evening," said Marc. "Funny, I was never so sure of anything. Didn't happen quite the way I intended."

"What did you intend?"

He said it out loud. "It was never like this in the movies. Do you know what the Frenchman said when accused of raping a dead woman?"

"No."

"I didn't realize she was dead; I thought she was English."

"Don't worry, Marc. I'm a full-blooded American."

"I believe you."

Later she asked Marc what he would like for breakfast.

"Gee, you get your Wheaties at this hotel too?"

"And bacon and eggs," she said. "Wait till you see the bill but you can't use American Express in this establishment."

Marc turned on the shower, getting the temperature right.

"Disappointing, I thought we would take a bath together," said Elizabeth.

"I never bathe with the domestic staff. Just give me a yell when breakfast is ready," Marc replied from under the shower and started to sing "At Long Last Love" in several different keys.

A slim arm appeared through the falling water and turned off the hot-water faucet. The singing stopped. Elizabeth was nowhere to be seen.

Marc dressed quickly and put the phone back on the hook. It rang almost immediately. Elizabeth appeared in a brief slip.

Marc wanted to go back to bed.

She picked up the phone. "Good morning. Yes, he's here. It's for you. A jealous lover, I think."

She put on a dress and returned to the kitchen.

"Marc Andrews."

"Good morning, Marc."

"Oh, good morning, sir."

"I've been trying to get you since eight o'clock la
night."

"Oh, really, sir. I thought I was on vacation. If y
look in the official book in the WFO, I think you'll fi
I've signed out."

"Yes, Marc, but you are going to have to interr
your vacation because the President wants to see you.'

"The President, sir?"

"Of the United States."

"Why would he want to see me, sir?"

"Yesterday I killed you, but today I've made yo
hero and he wants to congratulate you personally on
ing to save Senator Duncan's life."

"What?"

"You better read the morning papers. Say nothing
now; I'll explain my actions later."

"Where do I go, what time, sir?"

"You'll be told." The line clicked.

Marc replaced the phone and thought about the
versation. He was just about to call Elizabeth to a
the morning paper had come when the phone rang a;

"Answer it will you, Marc darling. Now that
lovers know you're here, it's bound to be for you."

Marc picked it up.

"Mr. Andrews?"

"Speaking."

"Hold the line one moment please. The Presiden
speak to you now."

"Good morning. Ted Kennedy. I wanted to kn

u would have time to drop into the White House this
orning at about ten o'clock. I'd like to meet you and
ve a chat."

"I'd be honored, sir."

"I'll look forward to it, Mr. Andrews, and the chance
meet you and congratulate you personally. If you come
he West Entrance, Mr. Roth will be there."

"Thank you, sir."

The legendary phone calls that the press so often wrote
ut. The Director had only been checking where he
. Had the President been trying to reach him since
t last night?

Who was it, darling?"

The President of the United States."

Tell him you'll call back; he's always on the line,
lly calls collect."

No, I'm serious."

Yes, sweetie."

He wants to see me."

Yes, darling, your place or his?"

arc went into the kitchen and attacked the Wheaties.
beth came in brandishing the *Post*.

ook," she said. "It's official. You're not a villain,
e a hero."

he headline read: SENATOR DUNCAN KILLED
STEPS OF CAPITOL.

was the President, wasn't it?" she said.

es, my sweet."

hy didn't you tell me?"

did, but you didn't listen."

m sorry," said Elizabeth.

love you."

love you too, but let's not go through this every
"

279

She continued to read the paper. Marc munched [his] Wheaties.

"Why would someone want to kill Senator Dunca[n], Marc?"

"I don't know. What does the *Post* say?"

"They haven't figured out a reason yet; they say [he] was known to have many enemies both here and abroa[d]." She began to read from the paper:

"Senator Robert Duncan (D—South Carolina) was s[hot] by an assassin on the steps of the Capitol yesterday morn[ing] at 10:06.

"The assassination took place only moments before Pr[esi]dent Kennedy was due to arrive for a last-minute effort [on] behalf of the Gun-Control Bill, scheduled for a vote in [the] Senate yesterday. Apparently expecting a demonstratio[n on] the steps of the Capitol, the Secret Service diverted the P[resi]dent's car to the Russell Senate Office Building.

"The bullet lodged in Senator Duncan's brain and he [was] pronounced dead on arrival at Woodrow Wilson Me[morial] Center. A second bullet grazed the shoulder of FBI A[gent] Marc Andrews, 28, who threw himself on the Senator i[n an] effort to save his life. Andrews was treated and later rele[ased].

"There was no immediate explanation of the fact th[at a] second presidential motorcade did arrive at the Capitol [ten] minutes before the assassination, without the President.

"Vice President Bumpers ordered an immediate rece[ss of] the Senate in respect to Senator Duncan. The House [also] voted unanimously to call a recess for seven days.

The President, who arrived at the Capitol via the con[gres]sional subway from the Russell Building, first heard the [news] of Duncan's assassination when he reached the Senate. [Visi]bly shaken, he announced that the luncheon to discus[s gun] control would continue as planned but asked the asse[mbled] Senators to observe a minute of silence in honor of their [dead] colleague.

"The President went on to say, 'I know we are all sh[ocked] and saddened by the tragic and horrifying event whic[h just occurred. This senseless killing of a good and decent man must strengthen our determination to work together in making our country safe from the easy access of arms.'

"The President plans to address the nation at nine o'clock tonight."

"So now you know everything, Liz."

"I know nothing," she said.

"I didn't know very much of that myself," Marc admitted.

"Living with you is going to be difficult."

"Who said I was going to live with you?"

"I've taken it for granted the way you're eating my eggs."

At the Fontainebleau Hotel a man was sitting by the side of the swimming pool reading the *Miami Herald* and drinking coffee. At least Senator Duncan was dead, that made him feel safer. Xan had kept his part of the bargain.

He sipped the coffee, a little hot, it didn't matter, he was in no hurry. He had already given new orders; he couldn't afford any risks. Xan would be dead by the evening; that had been arranged. Matson and Tony would be freed for lack of evidence, so his lawyer, who had never let him down yet, had assured him, and he would not be visiting Washington for a while. He relaxed and settled back in his beach chair to let the Miami sun warm him. He lit another cigarette.

At 9:45, the Director was met at the White House by Dudley Roth, the President's press secretary. They waited and chatted. The Director briefed the press secretary on Special Agent Andrews. Roth made careful notes.

Marc arrived just before 10:00. He had only just managed to get home and change into a new suit.

"Good morning, Director," he said nonchalantly.

"Good morning, Marc. Glad you could make it." Slightly quizzical but not disapproving. "This is the President's Press Secretary, Mr. Hadley Roth."

"Good morning, sir," said Marc.

Roth took over. "Will you be kind enough to com through to my office, where we can wait. The Presider will be videotaping his address to the nation for thi evening's television broadcast so that he can fly to Cam David at eleven-fifteen. I imagine you and the Directo will have about fifteen minutes with him."

Hadley Roth took them to his office, a large room the West Wing with a fine view of the Rose Garde through a bow window. A picture of John, Robert, an Edward Kennedy dominated the wall behind the desk.

"I'll get us some coffee," Roth said.

"That'll be a change," murmured Marc.

"I'm sorry?" said Roth.

"Nothing."

The Director and Marc settled down in comforta chairs where they could watch a large liquid-crystal mo tor screen on one of the walls, already alive with comi and goings in the Oval Office.

The President's nose was being powdered in prepa tion for his speech and the cameramen were wheel around him. Roth was on the phone.

"CBS and NBC can roll, Hadley, but ABC is still fix things up with their O.B. unit," said an agitated fem voice.

Roth got the producer of ABC on the other line.

"Get a move on, Harry, the President doesn't have day."

"Hadley."

Kennedy was on the middle of the screen.

He looked up. "Yes, Mr. President?"

"Where's ABC?"

"I'm just chasing them, Mr. President."

"Chasing them? They had four hours' warning. They ouldn't get a camera to the Second Coming."

"No, sir. They're on their way now."

Harry Nathan, ABC's producer, appeared on the screen. We're all set now, sir. Ready to record in five minutes."

"Fine," said Kennedy and looked at his watch. It was):11. The digits changed—and were replaced by the te of his heartbeat—72; normal, he thought. They dis-peared again, to be replaced by his blood pressure, 0/90; a little high; he'd get it checked by his doctor this eekend. The digits were replaced by the Dow-Jones dex, showing an early fall of 1.5 to 1209. This dis-peared and the watch showed 10:12. The President earsed the opening line of his speech for the last time. 'd gone over the final draft in bed that morning, and was pleased with it.

"Marc."

"Sir?"

'I want you to report back to Grant Nanna at the 'O this afternoon."

"Yes, sir."

'Then I want you to take a vacation. I mean a real ation, some time in May. Mr. Elliott is leaving me at end of May to take up the post of Special Agent in rge of the Columbus Field Office. I'm going to offer his job, and enlarge it to your being my personal stant."

Marc was stunned. "Thank you very much, sir." Bang goes the five-year plan.

"You said something, Marc?"

"No, sir."

"In private, Marc, you must stop calling me 'sir,' we're going to work together; it's more than I can stand. You can call me Halt or Horatio—I don't mind which."

Marc couldn't help laughing.

"You find my name amusing, Marc?"

"No, sir. But I just made $3516."

"Testing: one, two, three. Loud and clear. Could you give us a voice test, Mr. President?" asked the floor producer, now less agitated.

"Mary had a little lamb," said the President resonantly.

"Thank you, sir. That's fine. Let's go."

All the cameras were focused on the President, who sat behind his desk, somber and serious.

"When you're ready, Mr. President."

The President looked into the lens of Camera One.

"My fellow Americans, I speak to you tonight from the Oval Office in the wake of the bloody assassination of Senator Duncan on the steps of the Capitol. Robert Everard Duncan was my friend and colleague, and I know we will all feel his loss greatly. Our sympathy goes out to his family in their distress. This evil deed only strengthens my determination to press for legislation early in the new session strictly limiting the sale and unauthorized ownership of guns. I will do this in memory of Senator Robert Duncan, so that we may feel he did not die in vain."

The Director looked at Marc; neither of them spoke. The President continued, describing the importance

n control and why the measure deserved the support
the American people.

"And so I leave you, my fellow citizens, thanking God
at America can still produce men who are willing to
k their own lives to be public servants. Thank you and
od night."

The camera panned to the Presidential Seal. Then the
tside Broadcast units took over and switched to a
ture of the White House with the flag at half-mast.

'It's a wrap, Harry," said the female floor producer.
'Let's do a rerun and see what it looks like."

The President in the Oval Office, and the Director and
rc in Hadley Roth's office watched the rerun. It was
y good. The Gun-Control Bill is going to sail through
Kennedy is re-elected, thought Marc.

he chief usher arrived at Hadley Roth's door. He
ressed the Director. "The President wonders if you
Mr. Andrews would be kind enough to join him in
Oval Office."

hey rose and followed in silence down the long marble
idor of the West Wing, passing pictures of former
idents, intermingled with portraits of their wives, and
res commemorating famous incidents in American
ry. They passed the bronze bust of Lincoln. When
reached the East Wing, they stopped at the massive
semicircular doors of the Oval Office, dominated
e great Presidential Seal. A Secret Service man was
g behind a desk in the hall. He looked up at the
usher, neither spoke. Marc watched the Secret Ser-
agent's hand go under the desk, and he heard a
The Seal split as the doors opened. The usher re-
d at the entrance.

meone was unclipping a tiny microphone from un-
e President's tie, and the last remnants of powder

were being removed by an attentive young woman. T
television cameras were already gone. The usher a
nounced, "The Director of the Federal Bureau of Inve
tigation, Mr. H. A. L. Tyson, and Special Agent Ma
Andrews, Mr. President."

The President rose from his seat at the far end of t
room and waited to greet them. They walked toward h
slowly.

"Marc," said the Director under his breath.

"Yes, sir?"

"Shall we tell the President?"